Pippa Kelly writes extensively in the national press about dementia, with which her mother lived for over a decade. She blogs for the Huffington Post and mariashriver.com, and has her own award-winning website, pippakelly.co.uk. She lives in Wandsworth with her husband and dog, Bert.

To Mum, whose dementia stole her from me yet also revealed the incredible woman she really was.

Pippa Kelly

INVISIBLE INK

AUSTIN MACAULEY
PUBLISHERS LTD.

A CIP catalogue record for this title is available from the British Library.

ISBN 9781786124234 (Paperback)
ISBN 9781786124241 (Hardback)
ISBN 9781786124258 (E-Book)

www.austinmacauley.com

First Published (2016)
Austin Macauley Publishers Ltd.
25 Canada Square
Canary Wharf
London
E14 5LQ

Acknowledgments

This book wouldn't have been written without the advice and support of many people, including Henrietta Soames who set me on my way, Maggie Hamand and Evie Wyld who made invaluable comments and suggestions, and Jane Conway-Gordon who gave me the confidence to believe that *Invisible Ink* was worthy of publishing. My husband Charles and daughter Emily have also seen me through the long and sometimes not very pretty process of writing a novel. Thank you all.

Chapter One

Mum's said that I'm not allowed out for two hours. *Two whole hours.* And it's sunny outside. I can see it through my bedroom window. The sun's shining on the great big pile of crackling leaves underneath the trapeze tree. I want to run out of the house and push my shoes through those golden leaves and kick them high up into the air and watch them fluttering down, but I can't.

I'm sitting on my bed with a very, very old book that used to be Mum's; she's only just started to let me bring it into our bedroom – *provided you take good care of it Maxi.* It has a faded blue cardboard cover that's stretched out over my knees. I can't read its name because it's disappeared. The only bits of it left are the dirty marks where the letters were. Mum told me that it's called A Children's Encyclopaedia. She said it very slowly. En-cy-clo-pae-di-a. I counted the syllables on my fingers. Six! She said it was hers when she was little and that it has all the answers to our questions. I suppose it does somewhere but they must be hidden. They're not in long lists like at school. The old blue book has all sorts of strange and wonderful things in it. Inside the front, on the hard cardboard cover, Mum's written: *This book belongs to Kate Mary Summers.* Her writing's very neat – much neater than mine – and it slants forward as though it's running. I lower my face into the pile of dirty yellow pages and breathe in its smell. It's a dusty, papery smell that makes me want to sneeze. I squeeze my lips together and hold my breath and just about manage to stop myself.

There are hardly any colours in the en-cy-clo-pae-di-a, but every now and then there's a whole page of them. I turn the pages carefully until I find my painted butterflies. Here they are. All different colours, with amazing wings full of spots and dashes and markings that look like tiger's eyes. These shiny pages are like jewels in a pile of black and white paper. There's another one that's black and white and red. At the top it says, *Little Verses for Very Little People* and then *As I was going to St Ives, I met a man with seven wives*. There are seven fat ladies underneath with red and white striped dresses on and funny, curly white things on their heads. Underneath them it says, *Every wife had seven sacks*. And there's a row of seven black sacks. What I want to know is who chooses which pages are going to be coloured in and why there aren't more of them. Though I can sort of see why it's good not to have too many. It makes them more special.

I turn over the page, holding the corner of the paper carefully between my finger and thumb so as not to tear it. *The Boy Who Would Not Grow Up* it says at the top of the pictures – no, not pictures, photographs – of a family. This is my favourite page of all, even though it hasn't got any colours. It's black and white. There's a mum in a long dress, a dad giving someone a piggy-back, a boy in his pyjamas and a girl in a long white nightie. And there's a dog who looks really friendly. The writing says, *The Darling family at home, showing Michael on his father's back*. The next photograph is the best. It's Peter Pan coming in through the window to look for his shadow. An actual photograph of Peter Pan – and I can see that he's flying! I bend closer until my eyes are almost touching the paper and I can see the hundreds and hundreds of tiny black dots that make Peter Pan's jacket so black, but I still can't see any strings coming from his shoulders. No – he's definitely flying.

And that was what I'd wanted to do with Peter – my Peter. I look up, out of the window, to where the trapeze hangs from the knobbly branch. Dad made it for me in his shed out of a bit of wood and some rope. Trapeze. What a word! Trap-ee-ee-eeze. I like the knots in it – the clever way they hold the wooden bar in place. Dad told me that ladies in tight spangly costumes could swoop right across the sky on their trapezes. I can almost see Dad – not really of course, but in my head – hovering behind the ropes. Like a sort of shadow. The leaves flutter and the trapeze moves ever so slightly in the breeze. A trapeze breeze – I like the sound of that. And when the trapeze swings, its shadow swings with it over the grass and I can almost imagine that Dad's still here, watching me.

It's an easy tree to climb. A breezy-easy-trapezey tree. You wedge your shoe into the split at the bottom of the trunk and pull yourself up until you can hoik your other foot onto the spindly bit sticking out on the right. Once you've got that out of the way, you're off. It's like climbing a ladder. The branches are in just the right places. We'd got right to the top. Peter was ahead of me, just like I used to go ahead of Dad. *In case you fall lad, you see, then I can catch you.* Well that's what I was doing. Climbing behind him in case he fell. He was good though and after the first tricky bit, he raced up. One minute his brown sandal, his white sock and his freckly skin were just above my head, the next minute they'd gone.

He climbed right up to the top and shook the branches so hard that I could feel the whole thing swaying – my feet moving out from under me, my arms reaching forward where I was holding on. Through the dancing yellow leaves, I could see flashes of muddy grass down below – so far away they made my head spin. It was me who told him to stop it, to come straight down before we fell off and broke our necks. He didn't want to come. He was showing off, shouting and laughing, so I told him that the tree was fitted with a launch

13

pad. That had got him interested. He didn't even know what a launch pad was.

"It's for rockets – for when they jet away into space with their supersonic thrust."

He looked down at me, his fringe falling into his eyes. "Are we going to jet away?" The yellow ridged soles of his sandals were just above my face.

"Yep – we're going to jump off the tree."

"From here?" His eyes opened very wide.

"No silly – I'll show you."

I dangled my left leg until I felt the branch beneath my shoe, shifted my right hand along a bit, and then slid my right foot down the tree. I could hear Peter's short, panting breaths as he followed me down. Good – I'd had enough of his shaking.

"This is it," I said. We were much closer to the ground now. I could see each blade of grass sticking up and the dark, furry green moss that Dad always used to moan about. I edged along the branch to give Peter room and he dropped down next to me. He made it look so easy. "Now –" I said, "Copy what I do." I made sure that I had a firm grip of the higher branch and pushed away with my feet, swinging up and off and landing on the grass with a thud that made my ankles hurt. I sprang up and looked around. "There you are," I said. "Easy-peasy."

Peter had one hand on the tree trunk. With the other he was trying to reach the second branch, but it was too high. I could see the white tips of his teeth as he bit his bottom lip and waved his arm in front of him.

"It's too far away," I said. "You'll just have to climb down the way we got up."

I started to walk back towards the tree, pushing my feet through the crispy leaves, watching them shower up in front of me and twirl back down again. I hadn't known he

14

wouldn't be able to reach the other branch, I really hadn't, and that made it better somehow, because I hadn't planned it. Then, just as I kicked my leg again, out of the corner of my eye, I saw a dark flash. I heard a shout and a thump – a heavy, dull thud – and then silence. I looked up. Peter was lying on his front on the grass, his arms and legs sticking out like a starfish. He must have jumped!

I could hardly breathe. All the air seemed to have been sucked out of me and my feet were stuck in the grass beneath the leaves. Why wasn't he moving? After a moment, one of his legs twitched, and then his knee bent. He wriggled and pushed himself up with one of his arms and shook his head. Bits of dried mud fell out of his hair onto the grass. One of them got stuck in his jumper. And then – just as I was thinking that everything was going to be okay – he started to wail. So loudly that the sound seemed to echo inside my head. I covered my ears with the palms of my hands and, before I could think what to do next, Mum ran out of the back door. I'd never seen her go so fast. She raced towards Peter. She bent over him and said something that I couldn't hear and he knelt up. That was when I knew that he really was all right, and all the breath that I'd been holding in came out in a great big whoosh.

"It wasn't my fault Mum!" I shouted it out and chased over.

Mum didn't answer. She sank down onto the grass – even though she had her dress on – and pulled Peter onto her lap and kept kissing his head. I stood there, twisting my hands behind my back.

"I'll deal with you later." She said it so quickly it made me jump.

"But it wasn't my fault Mum."

She still didn't reply, just kept on kissing his hair until his crying turned to hiccups.

Norah's downstairs with them now. Mum asked her to come over when she took Peter to hospital on the bus. She said she was pretty certain that he'd broken his finger. She hadn't looked at me when she'd said it but I knew what she was thinking. It was as if I could read the words behind her eyes. Or under the skin of her face. When she and Peter finally came home, it turned out she'd been right. He had broken his finger. The little finger of his left hand.

Chapter Two

He turned his key in the lock, pushed open the door and clicked on the light. Colours and shapes as familiar as the features of his own face jumped out at him: the faded wallpaper, the upturned umbrella in its fake Grecian urn, the repro of Constable's Haywain, so dark now that the image was almost lost. Her 'Cornish pasties' were sitting on the carpet. She refused to buy new shoes, just as she refused to change the threadbare old carpet or the outdated, garish yellow front door. *It's my splash of hope Maxi!* The phrase ricocheted about in his head. When had *our* splash of hope turned into *hers*?

"Mum –?"

No response. But he knew where she'd be and found her in the kitchen, stooped over the sink, tight, white curls running across the back of her head in rigid rows. She must have been to the hairdresser's on the village green. He wondered if Norah had taken her and felt the familiar tug of guilt. The red Formica table was covered in a lacy cloth and laid out for tea in her best wedding china. *Thin enough to see your fingers through it Maxi.*

He took a deep breath. "Hello Mum."

She cranked herself round, glasses flashing under the overhead light.

"Maxi – at last." Frothing suds dropped off the spoon in her hand, onto the lino.

"Careful."

"What for?"

"Your spoon's dripping."

"Well, you're late!" Her words flipped back at him like a rubber band.

"I'm not late. I said I'd be here by four and it's ten to."

"Not by my watch." She turned to the sink, shoved the wooden spoon in among the dishes and yanked at the tap. Water sprayed off a bowl onto the floor. "Whoopsi –!" She fiddled with the tap and the fountain stopped.

"Come and sit down Mum." There was little to be gained from pointing out that she wasn't wearing a watch – hadn't, as far as he could remember, for years now.

She shuffled over without replying, seemingly oblivious to her sodden apron, and lowered herself gingerly into a chair. She pushed her glasses up her nose. In the half-light her face was made up of shadowy planes that transformed her into a stranger to whom Max couldn't think what to say.

Finally, to break the thin, ticking silence, he said, "So – what have you been up to then?"

"What's it to you? You never come and see me now. Not now you've got your hands on my purse strings –"

"Oh Mum –"

"On the levers of power or the power of levers or whatever it's called."

"Don't be ridiculous Mum." She was talking about the Power of Attorney he'd got her to sign a few months ago. Even though it was merely a precaution, he'd still baulked at making her do it. Now his conscience whined as the hand on the kitchen clock clicked around, counting out the seconds – the minutes and hours, weeks and months since he'd last been down. Mum sat, staring ahead, her hands clasped together on her best lacy cloth, reprimanding him with her silence. He turned towards the cupboard.

"What you doing Maxi?"

18

"Just getting the bread out Mum."

"There's a good boy." The tone, the inflection, the love in her voice, curled around him like an arm.

He took half a stale-looking bloomer out of the enamel bin and pulled a bread board from its cubby hole beneath the counter. A shower of crumbs sprinkled the floor. *Clean house, clean mind.* Max could hear her saying it. He thought of her dusty mind, slowly falling into disrepair and something like panic washed over him. How much longer could she carry on living here? How long before he had to use the Power of Attorney his shaking hand hadn't wanted to sign and 'do something about her' (he never let himself dwell too long on what exactly that meant)? Long enough surely, he thought, resting the knife on the cliff edge of the loaf, for him to become a partner at Baker Warnes – and then he'd give Mum his full attention. God knows he owed it to her. And he thought again of her splash of hope, and when it had ceased to be theirs.

It was Mum of course who'd taught him to slice bread. He'd stood on the kitchen stool, with her behind him, her hand resting on top of his. He could still feel the weight of her fingers on his schoolboy skin as he began to saw down through the loaf.

"How's Helena?"

Her voice made him jump. "What's that Mum?"

"How's that girl of yours – Helena isn't it?"

"Eleanor."

"Who?"

"She's called Eleanor Mum – my girlfriend – not Helena." He thought of Eleanor writing up a travel piece in her flat. Tucking her blond hair behind her ear as she conjured up the perfect phrase.

"Might remember if you ever brought her down here."

"Don't start that again Mum."

19

"Well – why don't you? Not ashamed of me are you?"

"Of course not."

"Well, when are you going to bring her then?"

Max didn't answer. What could he say? How could he explain that bringing Eleanor into this house would be like watching two worlds colliding. Eleanor had a bijoux Notting Hill apartment with various 'meeja' types for neighbours. She belonged to his London world, in his three-bed, one-and-a-half million pound Holland Park pad, with its large, open-plan spaces and self-closing drawers – in the place he could hardly believe was his – not in a pebble-dashed semi in the deathly grey suburbs.

"What flavour are we going to have?" Mum's voice, tetchy and impatient.

"What?"

"Don't say 'what' Maxi. Say 'excuse me' or 'sorry'."

"Sorry – what were you saying?"

What was he saying? He felt caught between tectonic plates and could feel the ground shifting beneath his feet.

"What flavour sandwiches are we going to have?" She was gazing up at him.

He put the bread knife down. "Well – what have you got Mum?"

"Peanut butter!" She grinned. A sudden flash of her old self.

"Peanut butter it is then."

Max opened the larder. Tins of baked beans and sardines were crammed in beside jars of strawberry jam and pickled onions. He picked up a tin of Carnation milk. High days and holidays she'd turned the milk into caramel by boiling the can for hours and hours in a saucepan of water.

How d'you do it Mum?

It's magic Maxi!

And it had been. Just like the curlers that transformed her hair, the miasma of perfume that followed her out of a room. The unknown stuff of grown-ups. He turned the can in his hand, saw the sell-by date on its lid, realised the milk was over 10 years old.

"You need to have a good clear out," he said, without looking around. They were meaningless words. She couldn't do it on her own and who was going to help her? Not him. Not now. Not yet, he corrected himself. Not till he'd made it to partner; he didn't have time. He pushed aside a tin of tomatoes and saw, right at the back of the cupboard, a half-used jar of peanut butter. He reached in and lifted it out. Behind him wood scraped on lino.

"Stay there Mum – I'll get it."

He tried twisting the lid but it wouldn't budge; he held it closer to his chest and applied more force. From behind him came a loud crash and then a thump.

His head whipped around. "Mum!"

She was lying on the floor in a sea of shattered china, her eyes shut, her arms sticking out at right angles like those of a broken doll. He crunched over the china and knelt down beside her, breathing in the tang of cold cream.

"Mum!" It was a whisper now and when her eyes didn't open he repeated the word as if the very sound of it might revive her. Her eyelids remained firmly shut.

He took a deep breath to steady himself and saw a flicker of pulse at her temple. *It'll be all right Maxi love.* He could almost hear her voice in his ear. He stroked her cheek with the back of his hand. How long was it since he'd been so close to her, touched her, felt her warmth? It must have been years. And even as he thought, it he was eight again, scared and unsure what to do, a frightened voice squealing in his head. *Don't go Mum – not yet!* But with a rustle of her skirt she'd turned and walked out of his bedroom, shutting the door, leaving him alone when he wanted her to stay.

21

Her eyelids fluttered open, just for a second, then closed, and then reopened. He pulled away slightly.

"Mum?" It was the high, questioning staccato of a schoolboy. Max released a long, slow breath and watched his mum's cloudy old eyes gradually beginning to focus.

"Maxi?" Her voice was barely audible.

"I'm here – it's me, Maxi …" He nudged her glasses up her nose and she shifted a fraction and winced. "Don't move!" It came out too sharply. Her eyes, magnified behind thick lenses, latched onto his. "Sorry Mum but you mustn't move."

He put a hand on her shoulder. When had it got so thin? He fumbled in his pocket with his other hand, yanked out his mobile and dialled 999, conscious the whole time that her gaze had never left him.

It seemed to take forever for the ambulance to arrive. He covered her with his coat and sat down, curling his legs under him and cradling her head in his lap. It was surprisingly heavy, and up close he could see how thin her hair had become, how the perm disguised its paucity. Her scalp was clearly visible, pink between each small white curl, each hair springing from its own pinprick follicle. He kept stroking her face with fingers that trembled and told her off for giving him such a scare. He felt like an actor in the wrong role; he didn't know the script, or what to say. But then he hadn't for a long time, had he – not really – not if he was being honest with himself? Which was why he'd been coming down less and less, relegating Mum and Hillside Close to the bottom of his list of priorities. Now fate had dropped her in his lap, quite literally. As he sat on the cracked, worn lino his legs grew stiff under her weight and, shifting slightly, careful not to disturb her now that she'd finally drifted off, he leant back against the table leg and shut his eyes. The house seemed to wrap itself around him. The smells, the creaks, the very texture of the air, all seemed to be pulling him back, reclaiming him, and an image, a scene as clear as crystal, came into his mind.

The three of them are standing in the kitchen. Mum's trying to brush Peter's hair. It's all mussed up from where he's been playing in the sandpit. She's pushing his thick fringe out of his eyes but he's squirming away.

"Stand still!"

Peter's arm shoots out and shoves her in the tummy. Max knows that she'd kill him if he did that. Kill him! But instead all she does is scowl and pull Peter closer. Max watches out of the corner of his eye as he kneels to pack his satchel. The sight of the dog-eared covers of his books soothes him. Nothing – nothing – can get to him today because it's the last day of term. His very last day at St Joseph's. In September he's off to the Grammar on the other side of town. Where the big boys go – the clever ones that is.

Mum's yanked Peter back so she can finish fiddling with his hair. "You're not to go up on the fields love because the grass will set off your coughing and we don't want that." He chews on his bottom lip and doesn't answer. Max knows that Peter will disobey Mum and like always he'll get the blame. As if she's reading his mind, Mum says, "You'll make sure that he doesn't go up there won't you Maxi?" He stands up and flings his satchel over his shoulder. "Maxi?" She's let go of Peter and is staring at Max, her eyebrows dipping into a V as she frowns.

"Yes, yes."

"Because he's not been well Maxi."

Doesn't he know it? Peter's kept him awake with his coughing.

"Maxi!" She repeats it loudly.

"Okay Mum. I get the message."

"So long as you do." She turns to Peter, who's standing there like an idiot. His tie's skew-whiff and a green trail of snot is beginning to slime out of his nostril. It makes Max feel sick. Mum pulls a handkerchief from nowhere and wipes it away. "Have you got your tissues Peter?"

"They're in his pocket."

She turns to Max. "And have you got his medicine?" He nods. "You've got to give it to Miss Sally, Max." He nods again. It's about the tenth time this morning that she's told him that. "Okay then." She marches out into the hall and whips the two blazers off their pegs.

"Oh Mum, we don't have to wear those do we? It's so hot."

She looks around and for a moment he thinks that she's going to insist, but she says, "No Maxi, you're right. It's far too hot, and it's the last day of term. I don't think they'll mind." She opens the front door. "Off you go then you two." He feels her hand on his back as she herds them out. "Bye-bye little man." He pictures her bending down to Peter and kissing his forehead like she always does. He knows she's standing on the doorstep in her flowery apron, watching him as he opens the gate. He doesn't turn around. He's far too old to wave back at her. He can hear the rattle of all that disgusting stuff in Peter's nose as he follows through behind him, the clang as the gate bangs shut. It's his last day at St Joseph's. Hooray! His. Very. Last. Day.

When he got home Eleanor was sitting on the sofa, wrapped in a towelling robe. She looked up from her book and the sight of her face – the symmetry of its features, the way the lamplight caught her eyes and glanced off her cheekbones – touched something in him. Each time he saw her it was as if it was the first time, provoking the same sharp intake of breath, that same sweet jolt of disbelief. She was so bloody gorgeous.

She uncurled herself and came quickly towards him, her bare feet squeaking on the wooden floor. Wordlessly, he pulled her close and buried his face in her hair as the hospital's disinfectant smells and its stained rubber floors melted away. He could feel the sharpness of her shoulder blades under his touch, the rise and fall of her breath – and then, too soon, she eased away. She studied his face, her blue-grey eyes flicking over his features, and stroked his cheek with the palm of her hand. "My poor darling – you look like you need a drink."

He did. My God he did. He suddenly realised how bone dead tired he was and flopped down into the sofa. Eleanor moved about his open-plan kitchen as fluidly as if it were her own – releasing a blast of cooking smells as she checked something in the oven and then reaching into one of the cupboards, her robe riding up to reveal the soft white skin at the back of her knees. She glugged whisky into a glass, walked back over and handed it to him before dropping down beside him on the sofa.

"Now – tell me all about it. How's your mum? What are they saying?" He groaned inwardly: too many questions. All he wanted to do was to sit with her, drink his whisky, forget it all, but Eleanor was leaning forward, her eyes full of concern, so as he drank, he told her what had happened. He said that Mum had been very lucky, that though shocked and bruised, she hadn't broken anything and, all being well, according to her consultant, she'd be out within a week.

He didn't say how he'd stood outside Mum's bedroom, too scared to enter, listening to the clanging and banging of doors being opened and shut as the paramedics manoeuvred her stretcher into the ambulance. Or what it had cost him, finally, to nudge open her bedroom door only to be ambushed by the floral scent of her talc. Or that as he'd pulled Mum's battered old case from under her bed – a bed that had once long ago seemed big enough to sail away in –

a cloud of moths had fluttered out, their dusty wings heavy with long-forgotten memories and shades of hide-and-seek and treasure trails played out in that forbidden room. Max didn't tell Eleanor any of that.

For her part, Eleanor said how lucky it was that he'd been there when his mum fell. She regaled him with all the things that he ought to do, including sorting out Mum's house, finding a neighbour to come in and help, maybe thinking about the future. The future. The two words, the concept, in the context of Mum were simply beyond him. He couldn't contemplate her future. He knew – of course he knew, without Eleanor having to tell him – that he should. But he couldn't. So he nodded at all the appropriate moments as Eleanor's words washed over him.

When she'd finally had her say, she elegantly unfolded herself and stood up to see to their supper. Max stretched his arms across the back of the sofa and felt the whisky beginning to relax him. Actually, there *was* time enough to deal with Mum; for the moment her future *was* secure. She was safe in hospital. Eleanor was bound to see it differently; things were always so straightforward with her. She inhabited a crisp, clean, black and white world of clear demarcation lines: this is what's happened, this is what you need to do, now move on. Hopefully, now she'd told him what to do, she'd leave Mum to him. Max wondered, not for the first time, how much Eleanor's magazine column had influenced her modus operandi. Had it turned her into the single-minded woman she was or had it been the strength of her beliefs, her sense of right and wrong, that had landed her the job in the first place? Bit of both, probably.

"I thought you might need some comfort food." Eleanor's voice interrupted his thoughts. She set down a steaming dish of shepherd's pie. It was just what he needed. The lamb was succulent, the aromatic flavours of garlic and rosemary piqued his taste buds. "So – which of her neighbours do you think you can ask?"

Of course she wasn't prepared to leave his mum to him; she hadn't received all her answers yet. He put down his knife and fork, picked up the glass of Merlot she'd just poured him and gently swilled its contents, watching the wine's meniscus trace.

Eventually he said, "There's someone called Norah." *Salt of the earth that one.* He could hear Mum saying it. And as if it were yesterday he saw Norah dunking her finger of Kit-Kat into her tea, lifting it to her mouth and winking at him. "Anyway El, could we talk about something else. I'm done in now – I'll think about it all tomorrow."

As if to underline his point, he took a slug of wine. Eleanor watched him silently as he ate. He heard her bangles tinkle as she reached for her glass and knew she was thinking, weighing things up. He willed her to let it go.

"I think you'd better take this as a wake-up call. Your mum may be okay now, but she can't go on living in that house forever."

"She's fine."

"She's palpably not fine." Palpably. A ripe, plump word derived from *palpabilis*, to be touched. But right now all he could hear was Eleanor's irritating smugness. He set down his cutlery and looked up. Her wide-set eyes were fixed on him. "You know I'm right Max; I don't know why you won't admit it."

Because I can't! Because to admit it would be to open up the floodgates, to get swept away, to lose myself and all that I've become and everything I've strived for.

Max drained his glass, refilled it from the bottle she'd left standing on the table and finally said, "You may be right Eleanor – you probably are – you almost always are – but let me do this my way. I'll phone Norah tomorrow. She can look after Mum when she comes out of hospital. For the moment she's absolutely fine."

"But –"

"Don't!" His voice snapped at her, harsher than he intended, and he saw her flinch, then take a sip of wine to steady herself. Fine tendrils of hair formed a golden rime around her head.

Eleanor put down her glass, lowered her eyes, and said in a tight voice, "Okay Max – if that's what you want." She picked up her knife and fork and continued to eat, one birdlike mouthful at a time.

As they ate in silence he thought how much his mum would love Eleanor. She'd admire her looks and her figure of course, but most of all she'd respect her drive and determination in the face of what life had dealt her. Because Eleanor's seemingly perfect life wasn't perfect at all. Orphaned at 16, she'd somehow managed to put it behind her and forge a seamlessly successful career. She'd done what Mum had always exhorted him to do. *To just keep going Maxi. Never look back.* And he knew that Mum, always a bit of a snob behind her net curtains, would have basked in the reflected glory of Eleanor's wealthy roots – and marvelled at a woman who thought nothing of eating her supper in a towelling robe.

But he didn't want to talk about Mum and Norah and Hillside Close. So he drank his way steadily through the bottle of Merlot, and by the time he'd drained the last drop, his mind was hazy and his muscles relaxed. He noticed that Eleanor's robe had fallen open to reveal a hint of her breasts. He pushed his chair back and walked around to stand behind her, placing his hands on her shoulders and bending to kiss her neck.

"Sorry El – I'm not very good company tonight. Can we go to bed?"

His lips brushed the tattoo behind her left ear. Though small, it was a detailed and very beautiful depiction in muted blues and greys of a swallow in flight. It was so discreet, such a surprise, that when Max had first discovered it inked in Eleanor's skin he'd been reminded of antique marks on porcelain. When he didn't receive an answer he wondered if she was still riled with him, but then she nudged her chair back and rose to her feet.

"Why not?" She sighed, extending her hand. "You're obviously not in the mood to talk. Come on."

As she led him into his bedroom Max imagined how the curve of her hip bones would press against his flesh.

Their lovemaking was strangely muted and yet for Max it was very intense; he held back, prolonging each heightened moment for as long as he could until he ached with desire, and finally letting go in a rush of elation. Afterwards he held her in his arms as she slept, feeling the rise and fall of her breaths, the warmth of her skin against his, as his mind, high on post-coital endorphins, let go of the whirlwind of emotions stirred up by the events of the day and he fell into a dreamless sleep. It wasn't until he woke in the cool early hours to find Eleanor curled away from him, her head buried in the duvet, that the memories pushed their way back.

He's looking up, more frightened than he's ever been, into the eyes of a very tall man with a bristly moustache. Max knows he's a policeman. Behind him sits Audrey and over in the corner is Mrs Maishman – they're all in her room and it's later that day. That very last day.

"There's a book son," the policeman's saying. His voice isn't much more than a whisper and Max can see Mrs Maishman leaning forward, trying to hear. "There's a book in which is written all our lives. And nothing – *nothing* –" he repeats the word so loudly that Max almost jumps out of his skin – "that we say or do can change the final outcome. You just remember that."

And Max had. He'd always remembered those words. But even back then, all those years ago, and young as he was, he'd known that they weren't really meant for people like him.

***

I'm sitting on the front step, arms clasped around my legs, chin on my knees, breathing in the warm biscuit smell of my skin. Beside the toe of my sandal I see a stone. Round and smooth as a sweet – as one of the orange sweets Mum makes me suck in the car. I don't like them. They're boring and too hard to bite. I pick up the stone. It fills my hand so that I have to curl and stretch my fingers at the same time. I remember that this sort of stone – all round and smooth – is called a pebble. The Ps and Bs pop against my lips as I say it out loud. When I look up, the sun's in my eyes, making me blink, and all I can see is red and gold. I tip my head down again and wait until the colours fade behind my eyelids and I can see the ground by my feet. And there, moving quickly along it is a small black shape. I lean forward until my face is very close, and watch as an ant carries a piece of soil even bigger than itself towards a crack in the path. I put the pebble down and the ant turns and marches over it with its thin legs. That's amazing! How do its feet stick to the smoothness even when it's upside down? How come it doesn't drop the soil? I hold out my finger to wobble the pebble, but the ant's already off it and marching on, so instead I pick up the pebble and put it in its way. When it's just started its climb I gently nudge the stone. The ant drops off onto its back. Its legs waggle helplessly. I push it with my fingernail, trying to turn it back the right way up, but all I do is edge it along towards the pebble. Without meaning to, I wedge it underneath and then – again without really meaning to – I move the pebble ever so slightly and push it down. When I roll it away there's hardly more than a dark squidge on the grey path, with a trace of orange-red. That's all there is. A squidge. No movement. No squirms. Nothing. And I realise the game's over and I suddenly feel empty. I think about picking up the pebble but decide not to, not with that stuff squashed on it. It's no longer clean and smooth and pebbly and I don't want it. I stand up and wonder what to do next.

Before I know it I've pushed at the gate. It squeaks as it opens and then clangs shut. I stop in case Mum's heard it. An aeroplane booms above me and I look up into blueness with a white mark in it that's growing as I watch. The white mark's called a "vapour trail". Dad told me that the other day. I like the sound of it. Vapour trail. It's important. Like 'revved up', 'engine throttle' and 'the speed of light'. Other things that Dad's told me about. When I think of them, I think of his dark, scratchy suit brushing against me and the smell of the white sticks that he sets fire to and puts in his mouth, that Mum doesn't like, and his loud voice. The aeroplane's vapour trail seems to have cut the sky in half. It's made of hundreds of thousands of water droplets, Dad said. My neck aches from looking up and I drop it back down, certain now that Mum's not coming. That it's safe for me to go.

I know exactly where I'm going. The sun's hot on my knees and my cheeks and my nose. My sandals make no sound on the pavement and, luckily, no one's around. I trail my hand along the wall as I walk. It goes up and down over the bricks. There's a word for the way the top of the wall goes up and down. We learnt it at school. It has to do with castles. It's long and difficult and begins with 'c'; I can't think what it is. The bricks are rough under my fingers and I remember the smoothness of the pebble, the small squirt of orange that came out of the ant, and suddenly my tummy rumbles. It'll be teatime soon and Mum'll be out to fetch me. I hurry past the first drive. No gates on that one, just two old wooden posts. Up down, up down, the roughness of the wall under my fingers feels good. The two yellow gates at number 5 shine bright and my fingers slick along them and make me think of ice cream. The banana ice cream we had when we went to the seaside. Yum! I can almost taste it. The way it magicked away on my tongue. Mum had one too, and she smiled at Dad over the top of it as she bit some off. I sucked mine to make it last. Grown-ups are funny like that. The way they eat some things so quickly and then spend hours and hours chewing liver and cabbage. And now here I am at Norah's.

Her house looks asleep. The front curtains are shut. She's out. Good. I hitch my foot up onto the dip in the bricks in the wall. Crenellations! That's what they're called. The up and down bits around the top of castles. I'm pleased I've remembered. I wedge my sandal in the gap and pull my other leg up. I uncurl myself like we do in PE until I'm standing up, wait for a moment or two, then step onto the upright bits of the cren-e-lla-tions and balance my feet on the bricks. I'm tall now. As tall as Dad. And far down below me, shining in the sun, looking as if it's been waiting for me all afternoon, is Norah's fish pond.

Most of it's covered in flat green leaves. Some have white flowers in the middle. They're like green plates with white stars. Insects buzz over them. There – over to the right, just about to settle on the biggest star of all, is a huge fly with an extra-long body. Its wings shimmer with different colours. Shimmer. That's another good word. Miss Dodson read us a story on the last day of term about a man with a coat that shimmered and clanked as he walked. He was a soldier. A knight, she told us, and she showed us a picture of him with his uniform made of metal. That must be heavy, I'd said, and she'd nodded and said, "Yes Max, clever boy, the knight's uniform was called a suit of armour and it was very heavy indeed, but it kept him safe when he fought battles." The monster fly is sitting quite still on the white star. Only the tip of his tail seems to move at all, and then it's hardly a movement, more of a breath, or a shiver. Like the movement of the leaves themselves, or the brownie-black water. Almost a shimmer really. There are other, smaller, greenie-brown leaves and two giant spikes with black velvet tips. I want to run my fingers over those tips. I wish I could, but know I can't. They're out of reach, even when I'm standing in Norah's garden, holding onto her hand as she pulls me back. "Careful Maxi – not too close."

There, now, just below one of the green plate leaves, I see the orange shape of my first fish. It's George, the big one. He's like a submarine patrolling under the sea. And then, in the way that it always happens, I quickly see another fish. Smaller this time, swimming across George's path and disappearing into the shadows. And then another. That's three. Norah's told me there are six of them in there, but I've only ever seen five. I want to see all six. Sometimes I wonder if there really are six. Perhaps George has eaten one. "Would he do that?" I ask Norah. "Well now –" She stirs her Kit-Kat into her tea – "I really don't know but I suppose he might." I tell her I'll ask Dad – he's bound to know. He knows everything. "You do that Maxi. See what he says." And I've been meaning to, but there's always so much to ask Dad, and he's always in such a rush. "Don't disturb your father Maxi." It's all Mum says when he's around.

"Maxi – teatime!"

My heart jumps into my mouth. My legs wobble. I take a deep breath, get down off the wall and run as fast as I can towards our gate.

"Coming Mum –" I'm back in the garden before she comes around the corner of the house.

"There you are – come on in now, your tea's ready."

My heart's still thumping and out of the corner of my eye I can see the gate swinging. Will she notice? She's already turned. It's okay. "Come along quickly now – I've got something exciting to tell you –" Her words drift over her shoulder.

"Are we going to the seaside?" I hurry to catch up with her, but she's so quick. Her shoes scrape on the concrete path as she strides off. "Are we though Mum?"

My tea's laid out on the table. Two sausages, mashed potato and beans from the garden on a blue and white plate.

"Sit down Maxi." She pulls up a chair and sits down next to me, pushing my beaker of orange squash towards me. "And take a drink – you look boiling."

There's another flutter in my chest when I think she's going to ask me why I'm out of breath. I pick up the beaker and take a long drink, hiding behind the glass. I'm thirsty and it goes down quickly.

"Now –" Mum's looking at me in a strange way. I stab a sausage with my fork and bite into it. "Maxi – use your knife please." She tut-tuts. Something's still not right about her. What is it? She licks her lips and then pushes her hair behind her ear. I've never seen her do that before.

"I've got some very important news for you."

I pile mash into my fork and pat it down with my knife. "Can I have some ketchup?"

"What? Oh – yes." She stands up, pulls the bottle down from the cupboard, gives it a shake, takes the top off and sets it on the table. I turn it upside down and hit its bottom with my hand until it all rushes out and turns my white potato all bloody and red. I glance up, ready for her cross words. "As I was saying Maxi –" She sits back down, draws her chair in towards the table, fiddles with her hair again. "I've got something to tell you." She stretches her arm across the table and puts her hand over mine, where it's holding my fork loaded with potato. Her hand is warm and a bit wet. Damp, I think. It's never normally damp.

"I'm going to have a baby," she says.

I want my potato. I want Mum to move her hand so that I can dip my fork in the ketchup and eat my potato, but she keeps holding it there, and my tongue seems stuck to the roof of my mouth. I can taste the piece of sausage I've just eaten. My tongue moves over my teeth and finds a bit of it, wedged in like plasticine.

"You're going to have a little brother – or sister – isn't that wonderful?" Mum's licking her lips again now, and beside her eye, under the skin, I can see something like a heartbeat, ticking fast. "What d'you think Maxi –isn't that great?"

I nod slowly. My tongue travels back over the tooth with the bit of mashed sausage wedged into it. "When's it coming?" My voice sounds faint and thin; I don't know why.

Mum sits back and takes her hand away from mine. I shove the potato quickly into my mouth without bothering to dip it in the ketchup. "In about five months' time Maxi. In the autumn. In November. It'll be an early Christmas present."

I nearly choke on my potato. "But what about my football boots? You promised that I'd get them!" I bang my knife handle on the table. "You promised!"

"And you will Maxi – of course you will." Mum's surprised. I can see that. Her hand's gone up to her hair again. "The baby isn't *instead* of a Christmas present – it's a wonderful extra present. For us all."

"An extra present?"

"Yes."

"For Dad as well then?"

"Of course for Dad." Mum laughs, but she's frowning too. As if something's not quite right again. And she's watching me too closely again. I don't like this. I don't like the idea of a baby. I put my knife and fork down.

"So how will it come?"

"What d'you mean love?"

"How will the baby arrive in our house?"

35

"Ah well …" Mum settles her hands in her lap. She looks more normal. "Do you remember Mrs Varley?"

"Mrs Varley at school?"

"That's right. Do you remember how big her tummy grew – before Miss Dodson came to take her place?"

"Yes." I nod. "What does Mrs Varley have to do with Mum's baby?"

"Well, growing inside her tummy was her baby."

"It came out last week."

"Did it?" Mum's eyebrows shoot up. "How do you know that?"

"Miss Lovell told us. She said it's a little girl."

"Well there you are then Maxi – you know how it happens. The baby will come out of my tummy in November and then you'll have a little sister – or a brother."

"It won't be a brother," I say firmly.

"We don't know that Maxi." Mum's eyes have crinkled up again, in that strange way, as if she's not quite sure.

"Yes we do. Miss Lovell said that Mrs Varley's family was perfect now. A boy and a girl."

"But –" Mum leans over the table. "What about Tom? He's got a brother hasn't he, not a sister?"

"Yes … but …" How to tell Mum that Tom's different – that I don't like him and he's not me?

"And then there's Neil and Ian –"

"Ian hates Neil."

"Max!"

"Well he does. He told me."

"Well he should never have said such a thing." Mum's cheeks have gone pink.

"It doesn't matter anyway because you'll have a girl."

"Would you like that Maxi?"

I think about it for a moment and then nod my head because I think that's what Mum wants me to do.

"Well perhaps you'll be proved right – we'll just have to see. Oh!" Mum's hand flies to her belly. "The baby's moving – feel!" And before I know what she's doing, she's caught my hand and placed it on her tummy. There's a sudden movement under my skin. I snatch my hand away and my body shakes really quickly just like it did when that big hairy spider ran out from under the bath. "Don't be frightened Maxi – it's the baby kicking."

"I'm not frightened Mum!" I stare at the flowers on her apron, the way it's pulled tight. I hadn't noticed that before. I know she's watching my face. I don't want to touch the material. My hands are clenched by my sides. I keep expecting the flowers to jump or jiggle. I take a step back.

"It's my fault – I shouldn't have surprised you with it like that."

"It's okay Mum." But it's not okay. My eyes are fixed on her apron. The sausage and potato seems to have got stuck in my throat. The taste of it makes me feel sick. I want to run to Mum. I want to throw my arms around her like I always do, turn my head and rub my cheek against the flowers. I know exactly how warm and soft her apron feels, I know how it rises and falls as she breathes, and how it smells. But now I know I might feel that sudden spooky movement. I push my chair back. Its legs scrape on the floor.

"Is that all you want love?"

I nod and wait for her to tell me to finish my plate.

"Are you sure?"

"Yes."

She's tilted her head to one side. "That's okay then love."

Why's she letting me off?

"Are you sure you're okay?" She's frowning again, so I nod quickly.

"Would you like an apple – or a yoghurt?"

"No thanks."

"Off you go then love."

I stand up. She's still sitting, watching me. But I can tell she's not going to tell me off. She smiles. I love it when she smiles at me like that and suddenly I feel hot tears coming. I turn quickly so that she can't see me crying. I don't want her to think I'm a baby and I don't know why I've started to cry. I walk back around the side of the house to the step. The edge of it stands out red where she polished it earlier. I smell the wax and remember how I watched her yellow duster going around and around, back when everything was all right. I sit down and prop my chin in my hands. I sniff once or twice and the tears stop as suddenly as they started. I notice the pebble and beside it the small, black mark where I squashed the ant. I kick the stone away and think about walking back to Norah's to count the fish. Perhaps if I go along now I'll see all six. Perhaps that's what I'll do.

***

In a picturesque village close to the edge of the New Forest, a well-built man, his upright bearing belying his age, made his way along the narrow path dissecting the green. Every now and then he stopped to admire the first of the bulbs pricking the soil of front gardens like sharp green pencils. It was chilly today, the sky heavy with bruised clouds, and the pain in his knee that had recently started to bother him was hindering his progress. Still, he knew that Mr Patel would have saved his newspaper so it hardly mattered how long he took. Nevertheless, he couldn't help glancing up at the church clock – it was half past nine. My God, the day was slipping away. It was no fun getting old but, as Dora used to say, there was no point moaning either. Trick was to get on with it.

The way that woman had coped with her illness had been a revelation to him. He was the one who was supposed to be inured to the uglier aspects of life and yet he'd turned to jelly at the first mention of the C word. His little Dora, on the other hand, had showed resilience and courage that he – and many of his former mates in the force – would have been hard-pressed to summon up. And now she was gone. Two years gone. Hardly seemed possible. The soupy, drugged-up days in the hospital, when her shrunken face was barely recognisable, save for the tiny flicker of spirit in her eyes, were some of the worst in his life. God knows, he'd seen enough deaths, but this one, the quiet extinguishing of the woman who'd been his soul mate for almost half a decade, came close to breaking him.

Routines had saved him, providing a framework to cling to. Eight o'clock alarm call (positively luxurious after his years of 6am starts), shower, breakfast of porridge and thick brown sugar in the winter, Special K once the mornings grew lighter, bit of fruit 'to get things moving', stroll down the garden to check on the borders, make sure next door's dog or a scavenging fox hadn't made it through the fence in the night, a quick once-over whatever he had in the greenhouse, tip the food waste in the compost bin, give it a stir, and then, after his one coffee of the day, he'd head off down the green to pick up his paper. The bell tinkled reassuringly as he pushed open the newsagent's door.

By ten o'clock he was sitting on the bench beside the duck pond, feeling thankful for his scarf and his thick coat. Unless it was raining – and even then drizzle wasn't enough to deter him, it had to be proper, drenching rain – or so cold he couldn't hold his pen, latterly more of a problem, he always sat here to do the crossword. The air helped him think, just as it had back in the day when he'd had real, solid problems to solve. He watched the wind ripple across the surface of the water and thought about *Find record above (8)*. What was another word for record? LP? Forty-five? And what about 'above'? 'Over' was the obvious answer. Ah – he'd got it. Easy – surprisingly easy for a Tuesday, which was normally one of the Telegraph's more difficult days. A record was a disc. Above was over. Find was disc-over. With stiff fingers, he crudely penned in the letters and turned his attention to six down.

Dick hadn't started to do crosswords until he retired. He'd had neither the time nor the inclination. His once physical job had become increasingly desk bound the higher he rose and his preferred hobbies had been various means to let off steam. Early in his career he'd played a bit of footie for the station team; when an Achilles injury put an end to that, he'd turned to cricket; and when, at Dora's behest, he'd started to help her with the heavier jobs around the garden (historically her domain) he'd found, much to his surprise, that he thoroughly enjoyed it. "Comes to us all," Dora had said, hitching up her eyebrows in that way she'd had. "Religion or gardening. They're both balm to the soul." And certainly, for Dick, Dora's words, as so often over the years, had proved true. As time went by, he found himself repeating her phrases to himself more and more; it seemed to bring her closer.

Half an hour later, crossword complete, paper folded into his pocket, he was on his way home. His task for that morning was to dig over the small bed next to the greenhouse. It was no more than four foot by five, but he had to pace his digging now or risk doing in his back. He could take his time over it and, provided his back wasn't giving him gyp, plant that bag of bulbs he'd discovered behind the tower of pots. They looked right enough and it would be a shame to waste them. Once that was done he'd reward himself with a brew-up and a couple of rounds of cheese on toast. There was some chutney in the cupboard and a few tomatoes kicking about the fridge.

After lunch – then, and only then – he'd allow himself to indulge in his latest passion. One which he knew Dora would never have approved of. She hadn't liked the Internet at the best of times. "Time waster," she'd called it. Truth be told she just couldn't get the hang of it, it seemed to frighten her with the sheer volume of its knowledge and reach. Elizabeth had tried to show her how it all worked, but Dora had shown unusual impatience, insisting the library was good enough for her. Before she died, Dick had restricted his computer use to the evenings she was out at her bridge. Now, though he didn't like to admit it, he was fast becoming addicted. It wasn't just the breadth of facts at his fingertips that he found so exhilarating, but the ability of the Net, as he'd learnt to call it, to make hitherto unexplored links between seemingly disconnected events. It was, of course, what he'd done throughout his professional life, for the majority of his career without the aid of broadband, search engines or high-speed connections. The paper evidence of his work had consisted of meticulously checked records organised in bulging colour-coded files lined up on groaning floor-to-ceiling shelves.

For the most part Dick's innate intelligence, his memory, his love of order, discipline and problem solving had served him well. He'd risen swiftly, his career taking him and his young wife Dora from "Beastly Eastleigh", to nearby Southampton, followed by a short, wet spell in Truro, then Surrey, Suffolk and finally, the wheel turning full circle, to his last stint as Chief Super in Hampshire.

When the time came, he'd been ready to retire – ready, as he'd thought, to spend more time with Dora. They'd had too little of it. A couple of trips, first to Canada where she had some family, and then to Africa; that last a magical time where the wide plains and huge skies had seemed to bring them closer. He wasn't a romantic sort, but it was as if he and Dora had reconnected after so many years of being pulled apart by the demands of his job. Spending a stretch of time together, free from the ceaseless interruptions of his work, he'd remembered – not that he'd ever completely forgotten, it was more a question of creeping complacency – what it was about her that had first smitten him. And then, just as he'd rediscovered her, her wry humour, her soft skin and her pithy observations about the human race, she was snatched away.

He wasn't sure whether it was the gaping hole that her passing had produced in his life, but in the months that followed he found himself dwelling more and more in the past. Elizabeth told him off for looking backwards when life had "so much more to offer". But did it? Did it really offer much more than a shuffle down the green and the odd bit of gardening when he was up to it? He knew he'd never live with anyone else. Dora had – and it had taken her passing to show him this – been the love of his life.

Anyway, whatever the rights and wrongs of it, at just before two, replete with his lunch and with neither wife nor daughter to answer to, he carried his mug of instant coffee into his den, sat down at his desk, switched on his computer and slipped his glasses onto his nose. In his long career – 55 years to be precise, and Dick was precise – a handful of cases had remained open. Such was the way of detective work, and he'd learnt to let them go. Or so he'd thought. The busyness of his work and then, for the few years of his retirement when Dora was still here, filling the bungalow with her chat and the clatter and smells of her kitchen or the companionable silence of her sewing, he'd simply got on with life. There wasn't time, or perhaps he hadn't the inclination, to start looking back. But now, with empty hours on his hands and the worldwide web at his disposal, he found himself returning, like a dog, to a long-buried bone. It wasn't just the unresolved nature of the case – over the years he'd encountered instances of similar, unfinished business. No, it was more than that; there was something about that little boy that had never really left him. And with the slackening of his life, the memories had crept back in.

**

The glass lift rose silently through different coloured zones – from his orange 'corporate' division on the second floor, to the silver of 'employment', the green of 'litigation' and the muddy brown of 'commercial' to the top floor. Max didn't like orange as a colour. Who did? But if garish deals with global energy giants accelerated his partnership chances, so be it. The door slid silently open and he strode across the marble floor. Up here, in the rarefied atmosphere of Sir William Stockley's world on the sixth floor, all was tastefully muted grey and cream.

Max never walked into Bill's office without a pang of envy and this morning was no exception. He coveted Bill's job and he coveted his Room with a View. Within a decade, sooner if Max got his way, Bill's room – or its equivalent in another of London's top law firms – would be his.

Bill was facing away from him, hands in his pockets. The skyline opened up in front of his tall silhouette, centuries' old stone jostling with soaring metal and glass that loomed darkly against a dirty sky.

"How's it going Max?" He turned to face the younger man. His voice took strangers by surprise. With his thick head of white hair and his bespoke suits, Bill looked too suave for the northern vowels he'd never lost. Sly old fox probably cultivated them for their novelty value.

"Well, thank you Bill. I've got a conference call with the associates in about –" Max glanced at his watch – "twenty minutes. Lucy and Nick are going over the guarantees."

"Good, good – won't keep you long. I can't emphasise strongly enough how important NDD is to us."

"Sure – I know." Max tried to keep the impatience out of his voice. He had more papers to read before the conference call at midday, and then he wanted to give the hospital a ring.

"I wanted to talk to you about Britannic Oil."

Max's antennae bristled. This was interesting. Britannic Oil had been a major Baker Warnes' client for 10 years, bringing in regular fees of over £3million a year. And he knew that recently the Kremlin had been pressing Britannic to reduce its 75 per cent stake in Russoil, a Russian oil and gas exploration form and give a Russian company a share of the action.

"Mike's handling it isn't he?"

Bill sat down behind his desk and motioned for Max to sit opposite. "He is, but – and this is why I wanted to speak to you Max – his wife's just been diagnosed with lung cancer."

"God, that's terrible." Max kept his gaze fixed on Bill as he tried to assimilate what this meant for him. "How bad is it?"

"Pretty bad – it's spread to the kidney and liver they think."

Max thought of Mike. Only a few years older than himself, lean as a whippet, he had a brain like a steel trap. Max remembered how envious he'd been when Mike had been given the Britannic account. He kept his expression passive as his breathing quickened.

"To be honest Max," Bill continued, "it's not looking good and I want you to shoulder some of Mike's load. I've told him to take time off – much as he likes. Now that you've completed the NDD deal you're an obvious choice to take up the slack. How long would it take you to get up to speed?"

"I'm pretty much there." Max tried to keep his voice even. "I've been taking an interest even though I'm not involved – the fallout from it has affected the NDD business."

"I thought as much. I want Mike to be able to concentrate one hundred per cent on Diane. And I want you to take over from him. He's been drawing up the new shareholders' agreement between Britannic and Gazprov; he's already done most of the donkey work. Should be straightforward enough for someone of your experience – you just need to close it."

Just need to close it. How simple. How sweet. This was the big one. Bill knew exactly what he was doing and his eyes – sharp as flint at 60 – showed it. This was a huge piece of work and Bill couldn't risk Mike making a mistake because he was distracted. Max knew his partnership was all but in the bag as long as he didn't screw this up. His Room with a View one very large step closer.

"Speak to Mike as soon as you can. You'll be dealing with Sergei mainly – he's heading up Gazprov's legal team." Bill said the Russian name with a theatrical flourish. "Watch him – he's clever. Doesn't worry about the niceties."

"No need to tell me Bill. For Sergei, energy is political power first, fuel second. I'll speak to Mike ASAP."

"Good." Bill stood up, signalling the meeting was over. Max was already at the door when he heard the Yorkshire voice again. "How's Eleanor by the way, I haven't seen her byline for a while."

"She's well – very well," Max said, turning his head.

"Good." Bill had picked up a sheet of paper and now he looked up over his reading glasses. "I'm very fond of my niece."

Eleanor, being as shrewd as her uncle, hadn't told Max about her connection to his boss until he made the link and confronted her with it several weeks into their relationship, by which time it was all too late. Max was in it up to his neck, and she knew it.

He'd first met her at a dinner in Mayfair hosted by one of Baker Warnes' clients, the evening of the day Max exchanged on his flat. When he'd slid into his seat he was basking in the golden glow of his purchase. As he scanned the table, nodding at the faces he knew, he'd registered the blonde straightaway. He'd taken in that she was slim, good looking in an understated, well-groomed sort of way, about his age and well above his league. When she turned, her eyes caught his; they were thoughtful, blue-grey and clear as water, wide-set above an aquiline nose. She'd regarded him coolly.

"Eleanor." It was all she said; just the one word to introduce herself. He repeated it silently inside his head and, somewhat awkwardly given their close proximity, shook her hand. A dusting of tawny freckles ran across the tops of her cheeks. He held her gaze for just a fraction longer than necessary and then released her hand.

During the course of their conversation, he told her about his good news and at the end of the evening he asked her if she'd like to join him for a glass of champagne to celebrate and she said yes.

They made love two weeks later. She'd invited him to the theatre to see *Who's Afraid of Virginia Woolf* and he'd been caught off guard by the savageness of the ugly, human emotions being laid bare in front of him. It was like watching the bloody autopsy of a relationship. When he turned to Eleanor as the lights went up she looked unmoved; she placed her finger on her lips. "Don't say anything yet, we need a drink." She led him to a restaurant she'd booked, where the maître d' obviously knew her. Over Dover sole and filet mignon, it quickly became clear that she was familiar with the play, and Max realised that he was in the company of a woman who liked to be in the driving seat and left little to chance. She suggested they go back to hers. It was said quite matter-of-factly after he'd insisted on picking up the tab for the meal, but they'd both understood the significance. He remembered thinking that, like an animal, she wanted to be on her own territory.

As she led him through to her bedroom he registered the cream minimalism of her flat, and its neat, uncluttered feminism. When she kicked off her shoes and peeled her dress over her head, the ladder of her ribcage was just visible in the light filtering through the window. She sat on her bed and watched him watching her for a second, then extended her hand.

"Come on."

***

Mum's promised me shepherd's pie tonight. I'm thinking of it as I stuff my football boots into my PE bag. I have to stand on tiptoe to hang up my bag, shaping the string into a loop and then pulling it down. Next to my peg is a window with my name written in it. I wrote it. MAX RIVERS it says, in red and blue felt-tip. I thought about doing it in red and white Man U colours, but Miss Dodson said the white wouldn't show up on the paper. Mrs Varley would have let me. She'd have thought of a way around it like she always does.

Mum's shepherd's pie is magic. Sometimes she lets me mash the potatoes. White worms wriggle through the holes when I push the masher down. She starts it off. She scrapes butter into a pan with the potatoes and then she pours in milk from the bottle. She pushes the silver bottle top with her thumb and pulls it off. It looks easy but when I tried it my hand slipped and the bottle tipped up. My heart jumped into my mouth. Milk spilled all over the table – a great big white lake that spread over the red top and ran over the edge onto the black and white lino. My legs were trembly. I couldn't believe there was so much milk in the bottle. Gallons and gallons of it. Mum rushed over to the sink. "Stand up! Stand up!" She was shouting at me at the top of her voice. When I stood up she shouted again, "Not there – not in the milk you silly boy!" I didn't know what to do. I looked at my sandals standing in the white milk. I felt very hot. Mum pushed me to one side. "Now look!" I looked down at where she was pointing. There were white milk marks where my feet had been. "Take your shoes off!" I bent down, but when I tried to undo the buckles, my fingers got all knotted. It took me forever. At last the buckles came undone and I stepped out of my sandals – a great big step so that my socks weren't in the milk. "Good boy – that's better." Her voice had changed and I knew it was all right now.

Underneath the mashed potato is mince with carrots and things. I can almost taste it as we all walk down the corridor and out into the playground. It's sunny and I shield my eyes with my hand as I scan the faces in the playground for mums. I see Ian and Stephen's mums and then I see Norah. She's waving at me and calling "Max!"

"Where's Mum?"

"She's in the hospital pet. The baby's decided to come very early, cheeky little thing."

"Oh." I feel a flutter in my tummy and remember the way the flowers on Mum's apron suddenly moved.

"Don't you worry," Norah says, "I'm going to look after you for a day or two."

She's bending down so that her face is close. Her eyes seem to be searching mine for something. I look down and see a fleck on her shoulder. It's white against the dark of her jumper. A piece of cotton twisted into the shape of an M. M for Max. M for mum. M for mashed potato.

"Are we going to have shepherd's pie?"

"What's that love?"

I watch Norah's mouth as it moves. There are hairs over her top lip.

"Are we going to have shepherd's pie?"

"Ah well, I don't know about that Max. I thought we might have fish fingers."

Norah's face disappears. I'm looking at the buckle of her belt, the bulge of her tummy pushing out above it.

"But she promised me."

"Sorry love, it's just one of those things. But I tell you what I have got –"

"What?" Ian and Stephen have gone and there aren't many people left in the playground. The concrete looks white in the sun.

"Chocolate Instant Whip. How's that?"

I love Instant Whip. But I don't say anything. I'm watching the white concrete. When Norah holds her hand out and tells me to come along, I put mine in it without looking up. This isn't how the afternoon was meant to be.

Norah's house is just like ours. But different. The doors are in the same place, but the rooms look darker and they smell strange. They smell of something sweet. Not flowers or sweets. More like the small plastic thing that dangles from the mirror in the car.

When you come into our house you walk up the swirly green carpet to the kitchen. There's a window on one side of the door and a row of hooks on the other side, where we hang our coats. When you come into Norah's house the kitchen's in the same place but everything else is the other way around. You can't see the window because there's a cupboard there, and it's very dark. There's a mat inside her door that says, *WELCOME HOME*. But what if it's not your home?

"Take your shoes off Maxi."

I crouch down and unbuckle my sandals. Norah's got a new carpet. Down here, close to it, it smells like nothing I've ever smelt before. A new, furry smell. I don't know where to put my shoes so I line them up beside the Welcome Home mat.

Norah's kitchen doesn't smell sweet like the rest of her house; it smells like the school dinner hall. The cupboards are dark green and she always keeps the blind low down in the window. To stop anyone looking in, she says. Who? I ask. Oh, I don't know, she says. Strangers perhaps. I've never seen anyone looking in Norah's window. It's because she lives on her own, Mum says. The blind has pictures painted on it of old-fashioned ladies in skirts like bells and men in baggy trousers that stop at their knees. There are white pom-poms running across the top of the blind. Three in from the end, one's missing. I look for it now – and there it is. The gap.

"Now then – let's get these fish fingers on." Norah's just about to open the small white door at the top of her fridge when the telephone on the counter rings. Drrrring-drring, drrring-drring. I know it's going to be about Mum. I don't know how but I do. I stare at the yellow telephone. Norah picks up the handle.

"Ashbury 4571"

I watch her face.

"Oh hello – yes – oh –" Her eyes are wide and she's smiling at me but she's talking to someone else, down the phone, that I can't see. "Well that's wonderful John –"

It's Dad. I step forward. My chest's all jittery.

"– Four and a half pounds, well that's not bad –"

Norah's still looking at me, but only with her eyes, not her brain. She's not really seeing me.

"And how's Kathleen? Good – good – well that's a blessing."

I step forward.

"I've got a little man here who'd like to speak to you …" And now she's looking at me properly and holding out the

50

handle bit of the phone. It's big in my hand but surprisingly light.

"Hello Max." I hear Dad's voice in my ear.

"Hello Dad."

"You've got a little brother Max!"

I feel as if all the stuffing's been knocked out of my chest.

"Max? Are you there?"

I want to speak but I can't.

"Max?"

"Say something love." Norah's face is down at my level. Her twinkly eyes are looking at me.

I force myself to speak. "Hello Dad." It comes out squeaky.

"Well – what do you think son?"

All the words I know have run away. I try to run after them and catch them up, but I can't.

And then I say, "Are you sure?"

The question just leaps out of my mouth.

"Sure? What d'you mean, sure?"

"Are you sure it's a boy?" I'm looking into Norah's eyes.

"Of course I'm sure!" Dad gives one of his great big laughs. I imagine him, down the telephone, roaring with laughter. I'm relieved that he's not angry with me. But I'm also confused.

I wait until he's finished and then I say, "But it's meant to be a girl."

"A girl? Whatever gave you that idea?"

I think about telling him about the perfect family. The mum and the dad and the boy and the girl. Norah's eyes have stopped being twinkly. She's looking at me strangely.

"It's what Mum wanted."

51

"No, no, she's happy as Larry son, believe me."

Who's Larry?

"But she told me," I say.

"Well, she's over the moon Max – and so should you be. You'll have someone to play football with."

It's Dad's voice in my ear but I'm looking at Norah. She's sort of frowning.

"Shall I have a word pet?"

I hand over the telephone. I already have someone to play football with. I have Ian and, even better, I sometimes have Dad. Doesn't he want to play with me anymore?

"Hello John." Norah says it firmly. "Yes – yes – don't you worry. We're absolutely fine here." She's nodding her head, not looking at me now, but turned away so that she's facing the sink. The curls on the back of her head bob about. "It'll be fine. No – no – okay then John – yes – give her our love – give them *both* our love." She's talking about *him*. *Him*. He exists. My chest seems to tighten. "Oh – yes – I almost forgot – what have you decided on? Oh lovely!" Norah's curls jump about again. "No – no – I think it's better to wait – yes – yes – okay then John – okay – okay – bye-bye then – bye-bye." She puts the phone down and turns to me.

"So Maximillian Christopher Rivers – you've got a lovely new baby brother."

She's standing there, her hands on her hips, looking down at me. No one ever calls me Maximillian. No one. I feel the tightness in my chest building up until it feels as if it might explode and before I know it I've rushed out of the kitchen into the hall and out of the door, straight past the fish pond. It's only as I push through the gate that I realise I haven't got my shoes on.

***

Max had to steel himself against the hospital's smells and sounds when he went to visit Mum; he'd armed himself with scented roses from Moyses Stevens, which she'd peered at suspiciously.

"We're not allowed those in here."

"You're in a private room, Mum – you can have what you want."

"I don't know why you wasted your money Max. I'll be out before you know it."

But her eyes had followed the young nurse as she decanted the flowers into a vase, and Max knew she was chuffed with them. She'd looked insubstantial in her bed, her head propped up on a pile of pillows, the bruise on her forehead now a sickly shade of green. She was wearing one of the nighties that he'd shoved in her case. It exposed the crepey skin at the top of her concave chest and made him uncomfortable. It was as if she was revealing things she shouldn't. As if the glue that had been keeping her together had come unstuck and the joins were showing. She hadn't lost her spirit though. All she was concerned about was when she could leave.

"When they say you're ready to Mum."

"When will that be?"

"I'm not sure, but they'll let you know."

"When?"

"When you're ready."

"I'm fine now."

"I don't think so Mum."

They'd gone around and around, getting nowhere. Part of him wanted her to stay in there forever. He'd phoned Norah and asked her if she'd go in and check on Mum once she was discharged. He'd found it strange and disorientating to hear Norah's voice again after so long. She'd sounded older of course; he realised that she must be in her 70s now, but the faint Geordie accent was still there and so was the no-nonsense woman he remembered. She immediately offered to help. *Nothing much else to keep me busy now pet – and to be honest it'll give me something to do.* Even so he knew that he'd have to keep in touch and take control – that Mum, and Hillside Close and all that it stood for, were about to assume a much greater role in his life. Seeing Mum lying on her pillows, looking as though all the stuffing had been knocked out of her, was too much for him. After ten minutes or so he made his excuses and left for the gym, sidling out of her room and striding quickly down the corridor as if he could escape his feelings of guilt. As if.

The pool was waiting for him, calm and serene. It was empty and it surface was coolly inviting. Standing on the side, his toes curled around the edge of the tiles, he watched the lights glancing off the water. He enjoyed every aspect of swimming: the flight through the air when it was too late to turn back, the cold, shocking force as he plunged in, the weightless suspension, the rhythmical power, the solitariness. He'd found a space that existed outside of time. It was his space, his place, where no one else intruded as he swam between the different coloured tiles of the floor several feet below him and the chlorine-smelling warmth of the air above. He adjusted his goggles and dived in.

Eleanor had her own gym, her classes and weights, her Pilates and yoga, her fixation with carbs and the speed with which she could burn them off. Max had his swimming. He'd found this club a couple of years ago. It was perfect. Five minutes' walk from the office, it opened at six and closed at midnight, and its pool was often empty. It hummed with money and class. Its grey towels even fluffier than the ones that Eleanor stored in the open shelves of her all-white bathroom in her Notting Hill flat. It cost an arm and a leg of course, but he could afford it. Max didn't constantly weigh himself like some of the pricks in the changing rooms, or look at himself in the mirror, or attend any of the gay-boys' buttock-clenching classes. He swam. Twice a week, without fail. Length after length. A hundred at a time. Two hundred a week. His breaths bubbling out in regular streams as the lines on the bed of the pool slid silently beneath him and the detritus of his mind was sluiced away.

Only as he towelled himself dry in the pale, echoing changing room did his thoughts return. Mum was sorted – for now – though her fall was only the beginning. He knew that. She was getting old and she needed more help; Norah was merely a stopgap. He wouldn't dwell on that. The fact was, Mum was dealt with for now, which allowed him to concentrate on his work. Gazprov provided him with his ticket to a partnership in Baker Warnes. The scale of the project was vast and Britannic's old woman of a finance director was taking his time coming to terms with the implications of the company's holding being watered down to 50 per cent. The project would need some careful handling.

And then – and now he felt himself beginning to relax – there was Eleanor. She was coming around tonight. He imagined her letting herself in, tilting her head as she arranged flowers with her elegant fingers, trying to give his flat a more 'lived-in' feel. What she really wanted – Max knew it, Eleanor knew it and (though he wasn't 100 per cent certain of this) he was pretty sure she knew he knew it – was to move in with him. For the past few weeks they'd been performing an elaborate verbal dance around the subject. One large chunk of him wanted it too. The trouble was, he wasn't quite ready yet. Soon – when he'd made it to partner – the time would be right. He'd know then that his professional success was more than what Mum would call a flash in the pan. For now, his flat was the concrete symbol of how far he'd come – the solid, bricks and mortar evidence of what he'd achieved. He loved it. He loved the light, the space, the open-plan, brushed stainless steel kitchen – but most of all he loved the fact that the name on the title deeds was his, and his alone.

As Max walked into his apartment he could smell chicken roasting and a hint of garlic. There was no sign of Eleanor, but it augured well that she was cooking more comfort food and a frisson of anticipation ran through him. He dropped his coat over the back of the sofa, took a beer from the fridge and headed towards his bedroom.

The bed, with its smooth expanse of grey linen, dominated the room. Facing it, mounted on the wall, was a 60' flat-screen plasma TV. Eleanor loathed it. Luckily, the choice wasn't hers. She'd made her mark though. Pillows were banked up on the bed. Max was forever throwing them off. They got in the way and he couldn't see the point of them. "Aesthetics, Max." She'd raised a perfectly plucked eyebrow. Several cashmere blankets were folded over the duvet. Why so many? "Layering, Max." Layering? It sounded like something to do with dry stone walls. Candles were another of her obsessions. Scented; the more expensive the better. One of them, he'd discovered on closer inspection, was called 'tobacco'. A substance that Eleanor had persuaded him, against his better judgement, to give up. She didn't seem to see the irony. He had to admit that he felt better for it, less puffed from his swimming and finally rid of his morning cough. But from time to time – preparing for a difficult client meeting, or coming up against a too-tight deadline, or that recent dash to the hospital in the wake of Mum's ambulance – the strength of his nicotine cravings still knocked him sideways. And now, damn it, even the thought of that drive – eyes on the flashing blue light, the noise of the siren blaring into his head – was enough to make him want to light up. He took a deep breath and inhaled the reassuring scent of expensive bath oils coming from beyond a half-closed door at the far side of his bedroom.

In the mirrored confines of his elegant bathroom, Eleanor was lying in a sea of foam, her head leaning on the curved back of the bath, her hair piled loosely on top of her head, her eyes shut. Max leant on the lintel and watched her for a moment or two, taking in the sweep of her neck, the supercilious tilt of her nose. He tiptoed across and bent until their faces were so close he could feel her warm breath on his face. She opened her eyes and stared straight into his. Two inches away. Pale irises fractured with shards of grey and green.

"Fancy a fuck?"

She rarely swore; hardly ever talked dirty. When she did it was as if she'd touched him in the sweetest spot. His clothes were off in seconds, water slopping over the sides of the bath as he stepped in and she knelt up to make way for him, her breasts squashed against his knees, her mouth laughing, exposing the white tips of her teeth. And then she lowered her head and in the exquisite moments before he closed his eyes he saw, caught in the light, the downy hairs on the nape of her neck and the two perfect arcs of the swallow's wings.

An hour or so later, as they ate what they could salvage of the charred chicken and the empty bathroom dripped and glistened, she told him that she was going to have to work through the coming weekend. He feigned insouciance and muttered something about having lots to do on the new Gazprov account, but in truth, watching her sitting in his shirt, picking up a bone in her fingers, biting into it, licking her lips, he was bitterly disappointed. In fact, he contemplated taking the leap and asking her to move in, so that no matter how long their days apart, they'd always end up together in his bed. But as soon as she'd finished eating she started to question how he planned to look after his mum "*in the long term*" now that she "*so obviously*" needed more help. She stressed certain phrases as if to ram home what an irresponsible son he was being. He topped up his wine and told himself not to rise to the bait.

"It's only when something's taken away from you that you realise how important it is Max."

He pushed the remains of his food away. "I take your point."

"Do you?" She frowned at him as she rose and leaned over to collect his plate.

"Of course I do. I know you lost your parents."

She froze, a plate in each hand. "This isn't about me Max, or my parents."

"Sorry Eleanor, perhaps I shouldn't have said that."

"No you shouldn't ..." She paused, frowning, as if weighing up whether to continue. And then she sighed, her face slackening. "Do you realise that I've never even met your mum?"

He stared at her, taken aback.

"We meet, we go out together, we make love," Eleanor continued. "In fact we've been going out now for almost two years but I still haven't met any of your family."

"There's only me and Mum."

"Yes ... yes ... I know." She sounded almost contrite and Max thought he might have silenced her. Then she said, "But still, don't you think that's odd?"

"No."

"Come off it Max. In some ways it's almost odder because it's just you and your mum. Why on earth can't I meet her? What's wrong with me? Not ashamed of me, are you?"

"Course not!" Eleanor's echo of his mum's words touched a nerve and he paused for a moment and then said more gently, "Leave it will you El. Please."

She stood watching him, her face inscrutable, before walking over to put the plates on the draining board. She remained there for a moment, her head lowered, her back to him, and then swung around.

"Okay – I will leave it for now Max. But you need to know that I'm not prepared to go on forever with you withholding so much from me."

He nodded. One small part of him had always known that it would come to this; to her demanding more than he was prepared to give. It always did. Sooner or later his girlfriends always gave him an ultimatum he couldn't meet.

The two of them tidied away the supper things in uneasy silence. Max knew that the following morning she'd be off to work and he wouldn't see her again until Monday or Tuesday, when he'd almost certainly have to fly out to Moscow. He knew he should say something but he couldn't find the words. What exactly would he say? When she announced she was off to bed he told her he'd have one more glass of wine before joining her. They both knew that this amounted to a brush-off. He heard the loo flushing, the tap running as she cleaned her teeth. He imagined her slipping off her robe and climbing into his bed and thought of her sweet-smelling skin between his sheets. He sipped his wine. One day – when he'd made it to partner, when he'd nothing left to prove and nothing to lose, and when Mum was 'sorted' (he could see the quotation marks around that meaningless word) – he'd be ready for Eleanor to move in.

The office was deserted when he arrived late on Saturday morning, and eerily quiet. His heels clicked on the marble floor as he walked across the empty lobby, past the vast bronze Solomon Diez sculpture. The lift glided silently up to the second floor and he emerged into the tasteless orange and grey confines of his division. Not for the first time Max wondered why the otherwise unimpeachable taste of Baker

Warne's interior designer had got the colours for this floor –
and this floor alone – so spectacularly wrong.

Janis's desk, separated from his office by a glass wall,
was empty except for her PC and the telephone console. She
was the only PA he'd had who was neater than him. Each
evening, without fail, she cleared her desk. And he knew,
because he'd looked one night, that inside the drawers
everything was as tidy and ordered as her appearance.
Walking past her spotless desk into his office rarely failed to
calm him. He'd replaced the swivel chair that he'd inherited
with a chrome and black leather Charles Eames. And the
chunky, hardwood desk had been cast out in favour of a sleek
walnut table, a black laminated filing cabinet and a floor-to-
ceiling bookcase that covered the entire back wall.

Since Max had been given the Gazprov project, the third
shelf of the bookcase was devoted to it. He hung his coat on
the hat stand, pulled out three of the fat black files from the
shelf and started to read. It was luxury knowing that, this
being Saturday, he could lose himself in the flow of words,
disentangle the complexities of meaning, uninterrupted.

When he was young he used to sit and watch Mum
ironing in the kitchen. There'd be two piles. The precariously
balanced jumble in the basket and the compact pile of folded
clothes. On and on she went, whole afternoons would be
taken up with it. He didn't understand what she was doing
but he liked the way she transformed the messy pile of
clothes into the neat tower and he liked the soothing,
satisfying hiss of the iron as it glided backwards and
forwards. Working through contracts was just the same. He
pushed into pleats and corners of detail, his eyes scanning
the lines, left to right, left to right, left to right. He made
sense of purposely abstruse language, flattening out its kinks
and creases, folding clauses and sub-clauses away in his
mind for later use. It was just that he charged more for his
ironing.

After an hour or so he discovered, buried away in the small print of the shareholders' agreement, an unacceptable condition that would give Gazprov the right to veto every board appointment, plus the ludicrous requirement for at least half the board to have a Russian passport. Even if a Brit was able to get a Russian passport he would be just as likely to have it taken away from him at Domodedovo airport and never returned. Good. Max rubbed his temples. This was what he was paid for. Spotting landmines. Why Bill had put him on the case. And what he was known for. Max Rivers, the detail merchant.

He worked for another few hours, until the light was starting to fade, then pushed his chair back and walked over to the window overlooking the square. Ever since Eleanor had challenged him about their future her words had been rolling around his head like pebbles in a shoe; and no matter how many times he reflected on them they always settled in the same painful pattern, digging into the soft skin of his conscience.

From the very first moments, as she'd spoken her name at that client dinner, he'd known that Eleanor was different. Her self-possessed confidence, her air of independence, had set her apart from other women he'd known, and in the buzz of it all, with the realisation that she felt the same as him, he hadn't let himself consider the future. The two of them were busy at work and initially the fact that her parents were both dead seemed to make things simpler. She couldn't take him home to meet her folks; why should he take her to meet his dippy old mum? Because, said that persistent little voice in his head, she still existed. She was there. She was his mum and she was, however much he tried to pretend otherwise – and he wouldn't have it any other way – a part of his life.

He stood, trying to unravel the different trains of thought competing for his attention and trying – and failing – to make sense of them. Thin threads of rain shone in the lamplight outside the window, falling silently, mesmerising him, drawing him back, leading him onto a dancefloor.

He's shuffling awkwardly under a revolving glitter ball with a girl whose head comes up to his chin, her freshly washed hair smells of green apples. She's Julie Bellicardi. Small, French and not even pretty, she's somehow alluring. Petite, that's what she is, with a certain *je ne sais quoi*.

When Julie first joined the Grammar in the upper sixth, the rumour mill went into overdrive. It was such an odd time to be changing school; ergo her dad must be a diplomat on a last-minute posting, or a foreign correspondent, or an actor on the West End stage. Max had had visions of Brigitte Bardot in her polka dot bikini. In the event, Julie was short, with horn-rimmed glasses and long dark hair. But there was *something* about her. They did history together with Mr Galbraith and while the old man wrote dates on the white board and informed them all of the origins of the Second World War, Max watched the way Julie rubbed her finger absent-mindedly backwards and forwards under her chin. He noticed how, unlike the other girls with their thick black tights and clumpy shoes, Julie wore ankle socks and sneakers. She didn't seem to mix much, keeping herself to herself, spending hours in the art room at the top of the school. Sometimes he saw spots of paint on the back of her hands and the cuffs of her jumpers and whenever he heard her speak, her accent added to her patchouli-scented mystery.

He was amazed to see her at the leavers' disco; he'd assumed she'd returned to France. But towards the end of the evening, when he was thinking about going home, he saw her sitting on her own at the side of the gym, the glitterball fleckling her with silver and pink. She'd taken off her glasses and pinned her hair up to reveal the curve of her neck. He watched her surreptitiously for several minutes and when Mr Shaw announced George Michael's "Careless Whisper" as the last song, he took a deep breath, walked over and asked her if she wanted to dance.

She glanced up and he was taken aback by her almond-shaped eyes; he suddenly wanted, more than anything else, for her to say yes. He wanted the closeness, the physical contact. He wanted to know how her body in that thin little dress would feel against his. She paused for what seemed like forever, her eyes – those marvellous hidden surprises – fixed on his, and then, very quietly, said yes. He could barely hear her, hardly believe her. But she'd dipped her head a fraction and now she was standing up. His feet felt like size 18s as the two of them walked towards the other kids mooching about, and his heart pumped. He wasn't sure what to do with his hands – where to put them, how to touch her. He clasped them around the base of her back; he could feel her buttock muscles moving under them; it was so, so sensual – it made him feel suddenly grown up and ready for this. Her head tilted to one side. Was she about to kiss his neck? Her breath tickled as he heard her say, "I'm so sorry about Peter."

Everything stopped. The crackling music. The turning bodies. His pounding heart. He felt her tense and pulled away from her as if she was toxic. Her eyes stared back at him through the dark but he couldn't speak; he couldn't explain what was happening. He wanted the floor to open up and swallow him. Blood rushed into his head and he turned and ran, shoving blindly past shuffling shapes, searching for the pale oblong of the exit and rushing through it into the welcome coolness of the night. He inhaled great lungfuls of air and then carried on, running up the school drive, through the gates and onto the road. After a while he stopped and hung, panting, over his feet; his breath coming in painful gasps, his thighs aching. When at last his breathing slowed he began to walk – past the first off-licence towards the cheaper one further up the hill where he knew they'd sell him some cans of Newcastle Brown. And then he drank and drank until the world started to turn again.

It was the first time that he'd got pissed. He liked how it made everything spin away out of his head. He got drunk again a few nights later, taking his cans up to the patch of scrubby common land at the end of the road and sinking them quickly. He always made sure he was home by eleven because he knew that Mum would be lying in bed, waiting to hear the turn of his key in the lock, his footsteps on the stairs. The summer term finished the night of the disco. School was out, forever, and he never saw Julie again.

Standing by the window in his office, as the worsening rain began to batter the glass, the memory of that dance – of the unknown sensation of holding a girl in his arms, of feeling her weight against him, of allowing his emotions to open up like the petals of a sea anemone, only to be clamped shut into a glossy, inviolable ball at the mention of a name – came flooding back so fast he had to steady himself against the wooden sill.

***

It was Dad who taught me how to write in invisible ink. I must have been about six at the time because it was just before he left us – though of course back then I didn't know that he was about to disappear out of my life. To vamoosh in a puff of smoke – *juzlikethat!*

We'd been out in the garden. It was cold and getting dark, towards the end of the afternoon, with a hint of Christmas in the air that should have been enough to sprinkle everything that I touched and saw with a shimmer of excitement. Dad had been pruning the apple tree and I'd been helping him, gathering armfuls of twigs and tipping them into the wheelbarrow. I'd been using his secateurs. Sec-a-teurs. I remember thinking that it was a dad sort of word, a strong, snip-snappy word. When we'd almost finished, I bent down to rake through the grass with my hand for one last time and my fingers curled around a feather. Picking it up, studying the weightless blade of oily black in the falling light, I could see at once how perfect it was. When I held it out to Dad he agreed and, turning it carefully in his muddy hands, he suggested that we use it as a quill.

"A quill?" I breathed the word through my lips, savouring the sound of it. "What's that Dad?"

"It's a pen made out of a feather Max, they used to use them in olden times."

Olden times. The phrase uncurled itself in my mind, leading me along a narrow, twisting lane with green bushes either side. I could see slivers of light, leading me on, towards the sun. It was the faded picture on the front of the *Olden Times Nursery Rhymes* book that Mum and I sometimes looked at.

Back inside the house, as we breathed in the smells of cooking, Dad showed me what to do. I took Mum's plastic Jiffy lemon from the larder – the one we used on our pancakes on Pancake Day – and squirted juice into a blue and white ringed saucer.

"Now, fetch me a piece of paper son."

I looked over at the dresser. A pile of offcuts from Dad's office sat ready and waiting – for shopping lists and notes, and scribbles and drawings and sometimes, provided Mum drew the lines for me, one of my stories. A clean sheet flapped between my fingers as I handed it over.

He sat at the table and smoothed down the paper, picked up the feather between forefinger and thumb and dipped its end in the saucer of juice as if it were a nib. I watched him move it from left to right, his hand tracing loops and curls as it left a glistening, transparent trail, like a snail's trail, over the white surface.

I was just about to ask him what he was writing when he said, "The acid in the lemon juice weakens the paper."

"Acid?" The word tasted sharp and sour on my tongue.

"You'll learn about it at school son. All you need to know for now is that it affects the paper it's written on."

"What have you written Dad?"

"Ah –" He picked up the sheet and gave it a shake. "When it's dry I'll show you how to make the words appear so that you can read them."

"Really?" I could scarcely believe what we were doing. It was so grown-up, so magical and mystical. The stuff of dreams and olden times and fairy tales – and Dad seemed more like he'd used to be. Upstairs I could hear Mum moving about as she got the baby up from his nap. I knew that all too soon she'd be bringing him down and the spell between Dad and me would be broken.

Dad blew on the paper and on his breath I smelt the cigarette that he'd smoked out in the garden, where Mum couldn't see him. It was a burnt, cindery sort of smell. Dad's smell.

"Now you have a go."

"Me? What, writing you mean?"

"Yes." His eyes were laughing and he was holding out the feather. "Go on. Dip it in the lemon juice and write something – anything."

I took the feather from his outstretched hand. It was like holding air. I dipped it into the juice and held it, dripping over the bowl, as I thought about what to write. After a moment or two, because I couldn't think of anything else, I decided on MAX. But when I looked down at the paper I saw that the wet trails of Dad's words had completely disappeared so I couldn't see where he'd written them. I looked up.

"Go on lad – anything you like."

I rested the nib on a spot in the middle of the paper and wrote my name. It scratched and squeaked and it was hard not being able to see exactly what I was doing; so before the trace of the letters completely disappeared, I wrote underneath them, DAD, and underneath that, MUM. And finally, almost as an afterthought, PETER.

And then Mum came bustling into the kitchen. I hadn't even heard the stairs creaking or her footsteps in the hall. She was just there, in the doorway, with the baby in her arms, looking about him with his big blue eyes.

"Come on now you two – supper's ready – can't you smell it?" She frowned and held out the baby. "Take him would you John."

Dad scraped back his chair, Mum handed the baby over and, before I could stop her, swept the piece of paper off the table and replaced it on the pile.

"But that's got our secret writing on it!" I jumped up.

"Well I don't know about that. It looks clean to me." Mum was opening the oven door and bending down. Her backside stuck out.

"Never mind Max – I'll get it. Here we go." Dad swung around. And the baby's foot, with his sock hanging off it, clipped the paper on the dresser and pushed it over. A waterfall of pages cascaded onto the lino.

"For God's sake!" Mum tutted as she straightened up.

I ran over and crouched down, plucking at the fan of pristine sheets, but each was indistinguishable from the next.

I looked up at Dad. "What are we going to do?"

"Nothing for now Max; I'll take a look later."

I knew he wouldn't. *Later … In a minute …* They were words that Mum and Dad didn't use properly. When they said them, *later* and *in a minute* meant *never*.

"Clear those up now love, there's a good boy."

"But I want to find the one with the writing on." Identical white rectangles slipped and slithered underneath my fingers.

"Do as your mum says lad."

I could hear Dad opening the cutlery drawer and the clink as he took out the knives and forks. He gathered the sheets into his arms and put them on the dresser.

"Will we be able to find it Dad?"

"Course we will."

"Go and wash your hands now Maxi." Mum, lifting the lid off the stew, said it without looking around.

My feet thumped on the carpet as I plodded upstairs. Holding my fingers under the water, I thought about the lost, invisible words. And as we were having supper, Mum holding the baby in the crook of her arm and feeding herself with one hand, I told her about what Dad and I had done.

"Well that's very exciting love." She looked down at the baby's face as she said it.

"But what if we can never find the one with our writing?"

"We will Max," Dad said in his gravelly voice. Yet even then, as his eyes slid over to the pile of paper, I had my doubts. Over the next few days I kept on at him to tell him what he'd written but he just laughed, and after a while he said he'd forgotten. I half believed him because it was just the sort of thing that a grown-up would do.

Within a few weeks he was gone. The stack remained on the corner of the dresser, an ever-decreasing reminder of the times we'd had together. I made my way through it until there was none left, but I never found a trace of our writing, so I never knew what it was that he'd put. When I mentioned it to Mum, she simply shook her head and said I must have written over it without even knowing.

Years later, I realised that what Dad and I had accidentally created was a ghostly palimpsest.

Palimp-sest. Now there was a word to conjure with. At the time, standing in our kitchen at Hillside Close, all I could think of were Dad's invisible words, lost among the blank, white pages.

***

The restaurant buzzed with conversation, the clink of glasses and metal on china, and ripples of laughter that echoed in the high-ceilinged space. Max picked a warm roll from its silver basket, broke a piece off, dipped it in a saucer of olive oil and placed it in his mouth. On the table beside him, a bald banker was ordering a bottle of Crystal to impress his girlfriend. On the other side of the plate glass window a black cab pulled up alongside the kerb, its wheels splashing through a gutter brimming with the rain that was finally easing off. Max watched as Eleanor uncurled herself from it and stepped carefully onto the pavement. She was wearing a belted mac that showed off her waist, and very high heels. Her hair was caught back in a ponytail.

Max watched as a waiter took her coat. He watched the other man's gaze following her as she walked towards him across the shiny floor in an immaculately tailored dress. There was something about the way her high heels made her walk, an air of manufactured vulnerability about her. It was as though she was subtly whispering to everyone around her: look at me. And everyone did. He could see them now, their eyes darting towards her and lingering a fraction of a second longer than they should. He took a sip of Marquez de Riscal.

Tomorrow, in an attempt to close the first stage of the Gazprov negotiations, he was flying out to see Sergei face to face. And tonight he'd secured – or rather Janis had secured for him – a coveted table in one of London's most sought after restaurants. This was the first time that he and Eleanor had met since he'd woken on Friday morning, stretched out his arm and discovered she'd gone. She'd phoned and asked if they could meet and he'd suggested L'Artignol. The timing was hardly perfect; he still had more reading to do before his meeting with Sergei and although he knew that he could work on the plane, he regarded it as his option of last resort. But something in Eleanor's tone had told Max that he should see her.

She slid into her seat and pulled the starched napkin onto her lap, unfolding it slowly, her eyes lowered, seemingly unwilling to look at him. He leant across and poured her some wine.

"Just a little." Her hand brushed his and he glanced up. Their eyes caught and in that heartbeat they both said each other's names in unison and laughed awkwardly.

"After you," he said, quite expecting her to shake her head.

But instead she nodded. Her grey eyes flickered, her face, normally so composed and confident, suddenly that of an unsure young girl. "The thing is Max …" She paused.

"Go on."

"Well …"

He didn't want her to say what he suddenly knew she was about to utter. As he opened his mouth to interrupt, his mobile buzzed in his pocket. "Shit!"

Eleanor froze for an instant and then reached for her wine. Nearby diners glanced around. He pulled out his phone and was about to switch it off when he saw that the screen said, '*Mum calling*' which meant that she was at home. She should be in hospital. The time, displayed in the corner of the screen, was 21.16.

"Sorry Eleanor – one second I promise." He pressed the green button.

"Max, is that you?" Mum's voice whined in his ear. "I've been trying to get you all night. Where are you?"

"I'm in a restaurant in Mayfair. Where are you?"

"Your dad had an auntie who lived in Maidstone."

"Not Maidstone, Mayfair." He couldn't believe he'd just said that. He glanced at Eleanor, who was watching him closely.

"She was one of his favourite aunts."

"Mum," he said firmly.

The bald banker shot him a pitying look.

"Mum, I can't talk now. Are you at home?"

"Yes. A young man came to see me; he was nice enough, wanted me to stay in hospital. I told him – I need to get home. He didn't want me to go but you know me Maxi, no stopping me when I've got the bit between my teeth."

"God – what did you do?"

"I walked out of course."

"Didn't anyone try to stop you?"

"Nope."

He tried to imagine it. Mum, barefoot, in her hospital gown, shuffling along the white-tiled corridor, through the heavy swing doors.

"Anyway Max – just as well I came home."

"How the hell did you get there?"

"Never mind that."

He mouthed 'sorry' at Eleanor, who shook her head and held up the palm of her hand to signal that she was fine.

"Are you still there Maxi?"

"Still here."

"You'll never believe it – it's a horrible, horrible shock." Mum paused for effect.

71

"What? What is it Mum?"

"I've been burgled Maxi. Burgled."

The taxi purred away up the road and he was left outside Mum's front door, its colour lost in the thick shadow thrown by its porch. He scanned the front of the house which was partially revealed by light filtering through the hedge from a street lamp. Everything was in order, just as he'd known that it would be, and in that moment he cursed Mum and her raddled old mind.

He thought back to his hurried departure from the restaurant, Eleanor's wide, disbelieving eyes.

But Max, why don't I come with you?

No! He'd seen the hurt cut across her face as he said it too sharply, registered other diners turning their heads, and realised at once that she hadn't, after all, been about to end it with him. He should have let her come. Of course he should. What was she supposed to do? She'd asked the very same question.

I'll get you a cab El.

She'd looked at him with an expression in her eyes that he'd never seen before. It took him a moment to realise what it was. Disappointment. Tinged with anger, yes, because he'd made her look a fool. But her overwhelming emotion was a sort of confused shame for him – the look that Mum used to give him when he'd done something wrong. He took all this in as he paid off the waiter and followed Eleanor across the gleaming floor, threading between white-clothed tables and upturned faces, out through the wide glass door. She'd turned and walked quickly away, pulling her coat around her, lowering her head against the wind. He'd thought about running after her, but he had to get to Mum. A taxi's yellow light loomed out of the traffic; he stuck his arm out to hail it; Eleanor had got there before him and it pulled up beside her. Before he could stop her, she'd climbed in and banged the door shut; he watched it rumble off with her inside it, her eyes fixed ahead.

His hand fumbled with the key and he heard a tinkling sound as it dropped onto the front step. He scrabbled for it blindly, scraping his knuckles. There was a rattle as someone a few doors up put out their empties. The key found the lock, turned, the front door opened and double-clunked shut and he was enclosed in whispering darkness. His arm brushed against something soft – Mum's anorak hanging on its hook? – as he felt for the light, and then the colours sprang out at him. The yellowing walls, the chipped white woodwork and there, sitting on the carpet, her beaten up shoes. Her Cornish pasties. All just the same. The house felt cold though, far too cold. He shivered at the realisation that intruders could have broken in through the back and began to walk quickly, breaking into a run as he reached the end of the hall and barging through the kitchen door.

Mum was curled on a chair, staring at the floor, swamped in a large brown coat he'd never seen before, surrounded by a sea of broken china. He exhaled with relief, brushing aside the thought that he should have been back to clear up the china. When she raised her head her face shocked him. Her cheeks were hollowed out, her normally rigid hair flattened onto her scalp like a lopsided cap, the bruise on her forehead now a purple smudge.

"What took you so long? I thought you were never coming." Her voice was Mum's alright: sharp and complaining. "Look –" She nodded at the china. "I told you, I've been burgled!"

She stared at him in triumph with rheumy eyes too big for her shrunken face. He didn't know whether to laugh or cry; to shout at her for giving him such a shock or to throw his arms around her because she was okay. He let out a long sigh.

"You haven't been burgled Mum." The chair scraped on the lino as he pulled it over and sat down beside her. "You fell down, remember."

"Fell down?" Her eyes flickered with confusion.

"It was a few days ago ... it doesn't matter. The main thing is, you're okay." He hesitated for a second, then slipped his hand over hers, felt the skin and bone of it, remembered how comforting it used to be. Coldness emanated from her in waves.

"I put my teeth in first mind."

"What?"

"I put my teeth in before I came home – they made me take them out."

He almost laughed, but then she pulled her fingers from under his and began kneading her hands, turning them over and over with a strange, obsessive compulsion.

"How did you get home Mum – did you take a cab?"

"Course not – far too expensive!" She frowned at him and stopped her kneading. "I took the 319 – bit draughty but still."

He thought of her waiting at the bus stop. She must have shuffled out of the hospital in someone else's coat. Didn't the hospital have any sort of security? How could they have allowed her to wander off? Her hands had started up again, and were turning over and over.

"Stop it Mum!" He gripped her arm and felt her shrinking back inside her freezing, tissue-paper skin. "Sorry, I didn't mean to make you jump." She was staring straight ahead like a frightened rabbit. He took a deep breath. "Come on – up we go." He stood up.

"Up the wooden hill to Bedfordshire."

His heart missed a beat. She hadn't said that for years. Not for years. Now she was gripping his wrist and hauling herself to her feet. He put his hands on her oversized woollen shoulders and turned her round. He could feel her boniness through the strange brown coat. Whose was it? Where had she got it? He pushed aside the questions and guided her up the stairs. It seemed to take forever. One soft, slow, sheepskin footstep after another. She must have worn her slippers on the bus. Why the hell hadn't someone stopped her? Because they'd all turned away or looked down at their newspapers, just as he'd have done. They reached the ink stain on the landing. Quink ink. Half a pot of it. In the shape of Africa. Mum came to a standstill.

"Keep going Mum; we're nearly there." He couldn't keep the quiver out of his voice, and when they passed the door to his old bedroom, he took a deep breath and fixed his eyes on the faded carpet. Mum inched forward. The moment she crossed the threshold to her bedroom, something seemed to click inside her.

"Off you go now Maxi." She said it over her shoulder. "Of you go – there's a good boy."

There's a good boy. The phrase stole around him and things were almost back in place again.

"If you're sure Mum."

"Course I'm sure dear. Off you go."

He paused at the door and watched for a minute or two as she sat on the side of her bed, laboriously kicking off her slippers, and then he turned away, unable, literally, to face anymore. When she was within it, her bedroom was sacrosanct and to watch her any longer would be an intrusion. He stood on the landing listening to the creaks and shuffles, his gaze concentrated on the border of brown dots running along the edge of the carpet. Above him, he knew without looking, was the oblong trap door to the loft with all its whispering secrets. When the noises coming from Mum's room finally stopped, he poked his head in. The small mound under the pink covers was dwarfed by the bed. Hidden. Safe. He trod softly along the landing and down the stairs.

He spent the night on the sofa in the living room, strange broken images flickering through his half-waking dreams. Eleanor's walking towards him across a crowded restaurant humming with chatter and laughter, money and success; she's smiling as she approaches and he reaches out his arms to her, but then she walks on by and he realises she's not smiling at him at all. She's meeting someone else who's standing just behind him.

He woke with a start and eased himself up, his back stiff as a board. Through the open curtains, it was still dark. He walked through to the kitchen, swept up the broken glass and made himself a cup of tea. He noticed that the counters were spotted with stains, the tap was loose and the stainless steel sink was dull with dirt, its plughole a nasty brown. He wondered how he'd missed it all before. In the same way he'd missed how thin Mum had become, how much she'd changed, how old she was. Hadn't noticed or didn't want to see? He sipped the scalding liquid. *There's nothing that a good cuppa won't make better.* He realised it was months, years, since he'd heard her say that.

He steeled himself to go back upstairs, stepping carefully over the ink stain, and then stood in her doorway for a moment, watching the rise and fall of the covers. Without meaning to let them, his eyes slid over to the kidney-shaped dressing table sitting under the window. It was where he'd used to hide when they played hide-and-seek. He'd kneel beneath its pleated pink skirt and listen to the soft, muffled footsteps coming towards him across the carpet. He'd hear quick, shallow breaths a few inches away and his own heart beating in big, fat thumps. He'd be crouching, still as a statue, his knees pulled up to his chin. The velvet trembles. The curtain whips back. *Gotcha!* Navy blue eyes stare straight into his.

His head span as he made his way back downstairs. Until Mum's fall he'd hardly ever ventured upstairs. Occasionally, on one of his visits, she might ask him to fetch something from her room and then the hushed atmosphere, the scent of her face cream hanging in the air, would sweep him back and he'd search hurriedly for whatever it was and rush back out as if he was a burglar who'd been disturbed.

He'd overheard Mum once, long ago, talking to Norah. *I've got to be strong Norah – for Maxi – I've just got to keep going.* And she had. But now she was faltering. He stood at the foot of the stairs, his hand on the banister, staring out of the window at the still-dark street. He wasn't sure he could do this; not sure he could take on the responsibility of looking after her. Not just because he was in London, an hour or so away. Not just because of his work load. Those were just his readymade excuses. He couldn't do it because he wasn't as strong as her. He'd run away to university as soon as he could. Great big coward that he was. *Cowardy, cowardy custard!* Leaving her on her own.

A couple of years ago he'd called in on Mum unannounced. He'd been in Sussex for an off-site client meeting. He rarely had to leave London for work and on a whim – and because it was a beautiful summer's day and he'd just celebrated a pay rise by buying a Porsche – he'd decided to drive. His route had taken him close to the bypass and it struck him that if his meeting finished early enough, he could call in on Mum on his way home. He hadn't phoned because he hadn't been sure, right up till the moment he'd indicated to turn left, that he'd do it.

Standing on the doorstep, having rung the bell three times, he'd realised that she wasn't in. He'd been surprised at the strength of his disappointment – she was always there waiting for him when he called and he wanted to show her his new car. As he turned away, his eye was caught by a movement inside the house. Through the window beside the front door he could see into the hall and beyond the open living room door to where Mum was letting herself in through the French windows.

He was about to ring the bell again when he paused, hand in mid-air. He wasn't sure what he was expecting to see, or why he waited before pressing the button again. But in the gap of those moments it was as if he was seeing – understanding – for the first time how alone Mum was. Not lonely: he didn't think Mum was lonely; she'd repeatedly made it clear that she didn't crave company. He'd always known – even as a young boy, innately sensed – that this was partly due to Dad leaving them so suddenly. Once betrayed, she was never prepared to let anyone else into her life. When it became just the two of them they seemed to function as a unit. It was him and Mum against the world. Now, looking through the window, watching her fiddling with the catch on the French doors, it struck him how alone she was. And he'd vowed then, as he pressed his finger on the bell, to visit her more frequently.

He remembered all this as he stood in the cramped little hall, watching the squares of light appearing in the houses across the road. She'd never doubted him; never not been there for him, even during the darkest times. Whereas he'd let her down again and again, never really been there for her. Sometimes it seemed as though all he'd ever done, his entire life, was fail Mum.

***

Dick knew of course that the trick was to keep busy. He'd seen too many of his friends reach retirement and let themselves go, both in mind and body, hence his daily walk and his daily crossword. Today's was a bugger – excuse his French – and he wondered if the Telegraph had a new setter. The first few clues had been fine. '*Fish and chips cooked with lard (9)*'. Easy: pilchards. '*Get employed right away in Surrey (6)*': Woking. His job had in fact once taken him to Woking. The lead had proved to be a false one and he couldn't remember much about the place other than that the pub next to the station had served a decent pint. But after a good start he'd encountered various clues that didn't seem to conform to any of the standard types. '*Eccentric as three-quarters of the characters in Fiji? (5)*' This obviously referred to the two *i*'s and the *j*, but what the devil was the answer? Likewise with seven across and four down. The clues made no sense. For the first time in several weeks he had to admit defeat and push the paper into his pocket with the crossword unfinished.

His mood wasn't helped by the fact that Elizabeth was coming around to take him out to lunch. She had a day off she'd said on the phone, and as it was such a beautiful day she thought she'd pop by. Very kind of her and all that, but why did she feel the need – no doubt duty – to spend it with him? He didn't like to say it but slowly but surely, poor, childless Liz was beginning to mother him. Before she'd become ill, Dora had told him that Liz was undergoing IVF. She said she hadn't been sure what the problem was – "where it lay" as she'd put it, thus hinting in an illogical, female way, at some sort of blame – because Liz had been vague. Dick didn't want to know the ins and outs, but it would have been nice to have grandchildren, particularly with Dora gone. He knew that however sad it was for him it must be much worse for Liz and Simon. So, he felt sorry for his daughter. His heart went out to her, it really did. He just wished that he wasn't becoming the outlet for her unfulfilled maternal instincts.

As he felt for his key, he thought of the plug plants he'd bought at the nursery. This morning would have been perfect for putting them out. Now he daren't start. He'd have to change his trousers not once, but twice, and everything took so much longer these days. He hung his coat on the hook and switched the kettle on, staring out at the garden as he stood by the sink. There was only one thing for it; he'd use this odd hour or so before Elizabeth turned up to finish the reading he'd started last night. He'd be breaking his self-imposed rule not to switch on his computer before lunch, but what else could he do?

And so, clutching his mug of coffee, he walked through to his den and sat down at his desk. He'd known, deep down, even as he'd saved the sites in his list of *Favourites* – a trick Elizabeth had shown him – that he'd be opening them this morning. By Googling certain details that had never been in the public domain, he'd created a list of fifteen cases with important similarities. The dates during which they occurred, the type of location, the age and sex of the child. He knew that what he was doing was as likely to produce a result as "the moon was to be made of cheese," as Dora used to say. He also knew that filed away in a 12ft by 10ft document cage were the reams of paperwork that he and his team, and successive teams, had collated. But who looked at those files now? If there were other people somewhere out there who shared his interest in unearthing the truth after all these years, did they have the time that he had, or the skills that he'd learnt in a career devoted to the service? He shook his head and clicked on the mouse to reveal a newspaper report to which he kept on returning.

He still didn't know why this case stood out from the rest. Perhaps in that young boy he'd seen the son that he and Dora never had. He was clever and sharp; you could see that immediately, by the words he used and the way he talked. Yet the lad's fear had virtually crushed him. It was more than a child's natural wariness of adults; there was guilt involved, Dick had been sure of that.

***

The driver who picked him up at Domodedovo airport told him it was minus 12. It felt it. His thick wool coat might have been a cotton sheet. But it was warm in the battered old

Volga, and it smelt of his treacly black fag and the hundreds of others that he and his fares had smoked before. He thought of the packet of untipped Belomorkanal in his pocket. He hadn't been able to resist them; everyone smoked here. It was still like bandit country. And, though he didn't want to admit it to himself, it felt good to be in this dark, battered landscape a million miles from home and Mum and Hillside Close.

Caught in the inevitable evening traffic, his cab crawled through flocks of predatory women. One of them, well over six foot in her stilettos, fag in one hand, hideous 'designer' bag in the other, caught him looking and gave him a one finger salute. She was wearing a fake fur bomber jacket and a pelmet of a skirt displaying thick, dimpled thighs. He wound down the window and replied in Russian. He knew she'd hate the fact that he could speak her language. She tossed her head, with its big red helmet of hair, and linked arms with one of her mates, guiding them all away from the cab, tossing an insult over her shoulder that he didn't catch.

Max had learnt his Russian at Moscow's imposing university. A Gothic skyscraper of a building set on Sparrow Hills. When he was on his trainee stint with Deveres-Colne, three times a week, after work, he'd travel south on the teeming metro, jostling for a place with state workers in grey overalls and tall, heavily made up women reeking of cheap perfume. His teacher looked like someone out of the Addams family: she had long black hair and a brutal fringe. To begin with he was out of his depth – Morticia Addams babbled too fast, striking the blackboard with a thin cane that reminded him of being at school. After two nights he was ready to quit. Salvation came in the form of Dan Singer, a middle-aged accountant with Ernst and Young. He claimed to be doing the course to improve his accent, though he already spoke virtually faultless Russian. In reality Dan was on the prowl for women. He was a balding, overweight chain-smoker, with breath like a hyena. He taught Max the basics of the

81

Russian language – and introduced him to Moscow's nightlife.

The Crazy Horses soon became Max's second home. After their lesson, at about nine-thirty, quarter to ten, he and Dan would head to the seedy looking bar on the edge of the city and down several Moscow Mules in quick succession, interspersed with cheap, unfiltered cigarettes. On a few occasions, when Dan managed to get his hands on some, they'd also score a line of coke. Dan showed him how to take the loose tile from the top of the cubicle in the gents, rest it on his knee and square off the powder using his credit card. Max made sure to keep a crisp, unused 50 ruble note in his wallet to roll into a tight tube. He'd go to the loo and emerge, recharged and coked up, ready to take on whatever the night held in store.

It was a strange, fractured time of extremes – a time that Moscow seemed made for. Commitment was unheard of, sex was something to be bought, cigarettes cost less than sweets and vodka was cheaper than water. Max played hard – frequently getting pissed and rolling home to his second-floor flat with some nameless tart – but he worked hard too. He made his mark at Deveres-Colne and by the time he left Moscow he was more fluent in Russian than Dan.

A month or so into the course someone told him about the Luzhiniki sports halls and on nights when he wasn't at the Crazy Horses he started to go swimming. It became his antidote to the wild excesses and more addictive than the lines of white powder. He started to swim in the mornings, handing in his *spravka* (his doctor's note) to the fat babushka and pounding up and down the gleaming, eight-lane pool to wash away the sins of the night before.

He returned to London a new man, with a new goal to aim for: to become a partner in one of London's leading law firms by 36. Why 36? Because he'd worked out it was the youngest he could feasibly achieve it. When he'd made this pact with himself, his deadline had seemed a long way off.

Now, staring out at a low, weak sun setting over the skyline, he felt it rushing up to him meet him.

The taxi pulled up beside the Metropol's elegant arches and Max couldn't help thinking how quickly he'd grown used to things that were once way out of his grasp. The hotel was an oasis of international style amid Moscow's tasteless excesses – a lifetime away from the Crazy Horses. He dumped his overnight bag in his pale blue room and discovered, with a slew of curses, that he'd forgotten his phone charger. He told himself that it didn't matter; he'd be out of here soon and on the first plane home. He still hadn't managed to contact Eleanor; her mobile had always gone to voicemail and she wasn't returning his texts. He very much wanted to talk to her.

Max's junior counterpart in Baker Warne's Moscow office was sitting in the high, echoing lobby, waiting for him. A few expensively fur-wrapped figures loitered on the black and white marble tiles. Nick glanced up from his Financial Times as Max approached, his flushed, public-school cheeks looking as if they'd just been scrubbed clean.

Even before Max had sat down Nick said, "'Fraid we've got a problem."

"Really?" Max crossed his legs, flicked an imaginary piece of fluff from his trousers.

"There's a poison pill at the heart of the new clauses."

"Can't be. I've been through them with a toothcomb – they're all ready to be signed off."

"It's buried in clause 143."

"Impossible." But a shiver ran through Max; he'd started to double-check the clauses on the plane and fallen asleep.

"It's the right for Gazprov to challenge 'unreasonable' management decisions in the lower court in Russia."

"Can't be right." Max uncrossed his legs, sat forward. "We'd never have missed it."

Nick didn't say a word, but Max knew what he was thinking. *We didn't miss it. You did.* Max felt for his fags in his pocket. Nick shook his head when he offered him one.

"Given up."

Of course he had. Max had to concentrate to stop his hand from shaking as he lit up. He could feel Nick watching him like a hawk. He took a slug of the Baltika beer that the waiter had just placed in front of him.

"Have you got the clause with you?"

Nick bent and fished it out of his briefcase and Max scanned the lines as the smoke curled from his cigarette. The younger man was right. There it was, buried in the dense black print at the bottom of a page. He should never have missed it. They couldn't let the clause through. Britannic management wouldn't be able to order so much as a pizza without ending up before a bent judge. Out of the corner of his eye he saw Nick set his empty glass on the table. Remnants of froth stuck to the sides and slid slowly down.

Max looked up. "I'll meet Sergei tomorrow and tell him it's off – we'll have to find another excuse for pulling out."

"Like what?"

He could see the hard pleasure behind Nick's gaze. He remembered it from the days when he'd caught out his own boss.

"I'll let you know – is Anya still in the office?"

"Think so, yes."

"Good." Max stood up.

"Why?"

He didn't bother to answer. "See you tomorrow Nick."

The leather soles of his Church's shoes squeaked as he strode over the endless marble floor towards the revolving door.

As his cab pulled away from the Metropol he longed to shout out, to make the driver stop so that he could walk away, back into the hotel, up the wide sweeping stairs into his cold blue room, where everything would be smoothed away with the gentle hiss of a steaming iron. Instead he was going to have to spend the night trying to find some other reason for the delay to mitigate the worst of this. He watched out of the window as they sped along streets bordered with scaffolding and the onion domes of the Kremlin and St Basil's cathedral blossomed out of the night sky.

He and Anya worked all night, fuelled by caffeine and copious supplies of cigarettes. He liked Anya. She was in her early 20s, a bright Russian graduate of Moscow state university on a trainee stint with Baker Warnes, driven by her career, which was her way out of the grim concrete tower block she lived in with her mother. She reminded him of himself at her age. The worst part about that fruitless night was that he knew, even as his eyes swam with words, that it was all a waste of time, that he'd blown it. That he, Max Rivers, the detail merchant – how ironic the label sounded now – had well and truly screwed up.

The two of them found nothing, not even the flimsiest of lines with which to save face, and at half past ten Max was sitting in the orange and grey reception waiting to be called into Sergei's office to tell him that they couldn't, after all, sign off the clauses – even though he'd just flown two thousand kilometres to do just that. Max had decided to play it as if he'd wanted to confront the Russian with his deal-breaking condition. As if he'd known all along and had purposely taken the other man to the brink. He didn't think Sergei would be taken in by his chutzpah, but the alternative – scuttling back to London without meeting him at all – simply wasn't an option. A headache was creeping over his skull, starting above his eyes and moving back above his ears, where it paused, throbbing. He rubbed his temples and tilted his head from side to side to ease the tightness in his neck. When his mobile trilled he fumbled in his jacket pocket and pulled it out. It said 'Private number'. He noticed that his battery had almost run out and switched it off.

The meeting was by far the most humiliating of his career to date. Sergei had seen right through his false bravado. For the second time in just a few hours Max looked into eyes that didn't attempt to hide their contempt for his professional ineptitude. They'd both smoked and by the time Max closed the door behind him, his brain was as thick and acrid as the office he'd just left, and he was sick to his stomach.

The next flight to London wasn't until late afternoon. He bought a fur hat at the hotel boutique then took the metro up to Vorobyovy Gory. Emerging into icy winds that sliced into his face, he strode out on the snaking path towards the huge, concrete ski jump looming above. His chest pumped, his breath cut his throat. At the top, he stopped and turned. Beyond the leafy, rolling waves of trees was the flat, ugly Luzhniki stadium. Over in the distance, beyond the stadium, he could see the domes of the Kremlin.

When he'd lived in Moscow, Max had come up here to get away from it all, if, as sometimes happened, the echoing, chlorine-smelling confines of the Luzhniki had seemed too claustrophobic. He'd forgotten how alien it was. How bitterly, bitterly cold. He must have been hardened to it then, or simply younger and tougher. He knew there was no point trying to light up – his fingers would freeze the moment he took his gloves off. He managed to pull his mobile from his pocket and fumbled with it, trying to switch it on. It was hopeless: his fingers were frozen sausages. It was probably dead anyway. He shoved it back inside his pocket. He felt cut off from the world. Raw and numb. His mind detached from his body, floating above it, separate from it, as he tried to sort through the events of the past few days and decide what to do, not only about Mum but Eleanor too. He couldn't. A memory kept distracting him. It was of DI

Gould. He was bending down so that his eyes were level with Max's, his moustache so close that it almost tickled Max's face, as he told him about The Book in which was written all their lives.

***

I knew that something terrible was going to happen. I could feel it coming. Like when Dad and I waited for the non-stop trains to come through Betchworth crossing. First we heard them – just a small, thin noise from a long way away, then the rails began to buzz, and then, in the distance, where the sky meets the earth, we could see a black dot. It got larger as the noise grew – louder and louder, larger and larger – and then with a roar of wind filling my ears and flattening my hair to my head – it thundered past and was gone. And all that was left was a whirring noise between my ears where my brain should be.

I'd felt it as soon as Mum brought the baby home. He slept in my old cot in Mum and Dad's room. Except he didn't sleep, not when he should have done. He kept bawling his eyes out in the middle of the night and waking us all up. One morning I found Dad asleep on the settee covered in the car rug. When he opened his eyes and realised where he was and what time it was he jumped up and knocked over the coffee table and said "Bugger! Bugger! Bugger!" He didn't even seem to see me. He ran out and up the stairs. The next thing I knew the front door was banging shut behind him. "It was only 'cos he was late for work love," Mum said later, but I wasn't sure and I could tell by the look in her eyes that she wasn't either.

Norah started picking me up from school almost every day. At first I liked it but it soon got boring. All she ever wanted to cook for me was fish fingers and chips. Once they'd seemed delicious, now I longed for her to cook me

87

something else. "Baked beans love? Spaghetti hoops? Alphabet pasta?" Baby stuff. I wanted shepherd's pie or Mum's lamb stew.

Christmas was coming. Other people in Hillside Close had put up their Christmas decorations. The house on the corner had its giant red Santa Claus sledging down the roof. Two doors down, the windows were covered in red and silver lights. Norah's big, gold tinsel star hung in the porch above her front door. We hadn't done anything. When I asked Mum about making paper chains like we always did, she promised me that we could do it after school and I thought about it all the way home as Norah and I walked past everybody else's Christmas trees glittering in their front windows. I could just about taste the glue on my tongue, but when we got home Mum was in bed. It wasn't even four o'clock!

"Why's she in bed in the afternoon?" I said to Norah.

"She's tired love – from looking after the baby."

"But she promised me we'd make paper chains."

"And I'm sure you will later." Norah put a glass of milk on the table in front of me.

"I want to make them now!"

Norah held her finger to her mouth. She was always doing that nowadays. Everyone was. Seemed that as soon as I started to speak up went the finger. Mum's finger. Dad's finger. Norah's finger. Sssh!

We never did make the paper chains. A few days later when I came home from school, there were other decorations up. Horrible silver shiny things, not at all like paper chains. When I told Mum that I didn't like them she told me off for being an ungrateful little boy.

"Your father bought them," she said.

She never called him father. I didn't like the word. It didn't suit Dad. She turned away to do the washing up then and I knew not to say any more. I saw the way her shoulders drooped as if there was nothing in her dressing gown and she didn't have anything on her feet even though the lino must have been cold. The pretty pink nail varnish on her toes was all coming off. It was black outside the kitchen window. I could see her face reflected in the glass, looking all long and strange. I snuck away up to my bedroom, pulled the shoe box out from under my bed and started looking through my football cards. Mum had helped me to make the dividers out of old cereal packets. She was good at things like that. Up in the loft, on the other side of the door in the ceiling outside my bedroom were all the Christmas decorations that we'd ever made. We'd used loo rolls and sweet wrappers, pipe cleaners and special white paper things called dollies or something that sounded like that. The decorations should have been on the tree ages ago but we hadn't bought it yet.

One night when I was in bed and Mum was downstairs watching the TV, I heard the front door open and close, heard the rustle and shake as Dad took off his coat and hung it on the peg, and the clatter and bang of pots and pans in the kitchen as he made his own supper. Why hadn't he gone in to say hello to Mum? Why didn't she make his tea anymore? I drifted off after that, listening to the drone of the telly, the opening and shutting of cupboard doors. Then I heard their voices. His deep boom and hers lighter, higher. Not a proper conversation, just bits and pieces.

Got to pull yourself together ... almost two months now ... don't know how much longer ... All very well for you John ... I've got to try and earn a living ... You don't know how it feels ... For God's sake woman ... You don't understand ... Here you go again ... Forget it ... How can I?

I lay there, my face turned to the wall, twisting the corner of the pillowcase between my fingers, trying to listen yet at the same time not really wanting to hear.

After a while I buried deep down into my duvet and made myself think about something nice. I thought back to a morning before the baby'd arrived, when Dad and I were in the garden. It was early and very cold. The grass was covered in thin, silvery cobwebs that sparkled in the sun and my sandals had turned dark around the edges. Dad was standing beside me, one huge, muddy wellington boot resting on his spade as he smoked his cigarette. He held the thin white tube between his forefinger and his thumb, just like the cowboys in the film we'd watched at school. I copied him, putting my fingertips together and holding them up to my mouth. When he tipped his head back I did the same and when he pushed out his bottom lip and blew smoke into the air in one long breath I did it too, only without the cigarette and the smoke.

"Better get on." Dad tossed his cigarette onto the soil that he'd just turned over. There was only about an inch of it left, the red end still burning, smoke curling out of it.

"Isn't that –" I started to say. Then stopped myself. It couldn't be dangerous or Dad wouldn't do it would he?

He grasped the handle of his spade and pushed his welly hard down onto the top of the metal. It cut into the soil right by the edge of the board that we were standing on, taking a thin slice of the lawn with it, like a slice of fruitcake. I bent and looked closer. There was a steep brown cliff at the side of the flower bed, with roots sticking out of it.

"Stand back a bit Max." He dug his spade into the great big chunk of earth that he'd just turned over. Chop-chop-chop. He broke it up like Mum broke up the butter and flour with her fingers when she made cheese scones. *Scones Maxi, like stones, not scons like songs.* Dad moved along, lined the metal blade right up against the board again, plonked his huge foot on it and pushed down.

"Can I try Dad?"

He stopped, his boot resting on top of the earth. He wiped his forehead with the back of his hand and looked down at me with his bright blue eyes. I prayed that he'd say yes.

"Course you can – just let me turn this one." He pushed down on the spade and swung it over. The thick, square piece of earth crashed down and he mashed it up – chop-chop-chop – and stood back, his fingers resting lightly on the handle so that it wouldn't fall over. "Here you go."

I shuffled sideways along the board towards his outstretched arm and tried to wrap my fingers around the wood but they weren't long enough, I couldn't get a proper grip. I stood on tiptoe but that made it worse and I almost fell forward onto the soil. Dad's hand suddenly appeared from behind me so that I was standing in between both of his arms, caught safe inside them, our four hands resting in a row along the wood. His – mine – mine – his. Big – small – small – big. Our knuckles were white.

"One, two three!" He pushed down and I pushed down too. The spade cut into the ground. It was just like when I cut my birthday cake with Mum's hand on top of mine, only better. "Now push." Dad stood back a bit and pressed the handle down. I bent my knees so that I could help. "That's it – over we go." My arms were almost yanked off my body and I had to let go. He chopped into the big clump of soil again. His rolled-up sleeves rubbed against my ears and made them burn until it really hurt and I had to squeeze my eyes shut. "There we go – how's that?" I opened my eyes. His arms were stretched either side of me like wings, the heavy spade dangling from one of his hands as if it were light as a feather.

Light as a feather. I turned over away from the wall, pulling the duvet with me, thinking of the glistening feather that Dad and I had found just the other day, the one we did the magic writing with. As I drifted into sleep, I remembered how the tall stack of paper on which we'd written our invisible words had tumbled off the dresser onto the floor, a bright white fan of empty sheets.

***

The plane descended into Heathrow through dense cloud that didn't seem to stop. When it touched down, rain was falling heavily, spearing off the ground. Welcome home. Max's gut tightened as he ran through the possible scenarios with Bill. "I don't need to tell you, Max, how damaging this is to our reputation … This is a disappointment Max …"

Disappointment. A ball-breaker of a word. Max could hear the older man saying it. He leant his head against the black leather seat. The smell of warm rolls emanating from the first class galley, the discreet, attentive hosties, all served to emphasise his failure, and the unaccustomed weight of it slowed his steps as he walked across the Arrivals hall.

"Max Rivers." The two words locked together in his brain. He was being summoned on the tannoy. "Could passenger Max Rivers, recently arrived from Moscow, please go to the information desk in Zone C." A trolley rammed into his heels as the message sank in.

He thought of Mum's hands kneading over and over, her shuttered eyes, her footsteps shuffling up the stairs. He started to run, weaving through the crowds towards the desk, his briefcase banging against his legs. He remembered the sharpness of Mum's shoulder blades under his fingers.

A brunette in a navy blue uniform was chatting to a colleague behind the desk. Max skidded to a halt.

"I think – you've got a message for me – I'm Max Rivers –" His words came in breathless bursts. Sweat pricked his armpits and he had a sudden craving for a fag.

The brunette passed him a handwritten note. Small, slanting letters. *Please call Lydia Waters on 07876 383 542.*

There was a glimmer of familiarity about the name. Eleanor had mentioned Lydia once or twice, she was one of her colleagues. He let out a sigh. So it wasn't Mum. His breathing slowed, his muscles began to relax, his mind calmed down. Mum was okay.

"Is everything all right?" The brunette leant forward over the desk.

"Yes, yes, I'm fine." Max turned, aware of the noise and bustle around him. A child was screeching, a woman laughed, a trolley-load of suitcases rattled past. But why should Lydia want him so urgently? He thought of yesterday's missed call, felt in his pocket for his mobile and remembered, as his fingers closed around it, that the battery was dead.

After several minutes of searching, he located a public phone in the far corner of the terminal. It had been years since he'd used one. When he lifted the old-fashioned receiver, he struggled to recall what to do and suddenly he was back at uni, in the student bar, pumping coins into a rattling slot as he talked to Mum. Whenever he heard her voice on the line he'd see her long, thin face before his eyes. Chatting to her on the phone was much easier than speaking face to face and they'd speak for quite a while. Adult to adult. Person to person. Now Max couldn't remember what to do. Did you dial first or slot in the money? He had to read the instructions. One. Two. Three. He was dizzy with tiredness, spent with failure, and his head was beginning to throb. He heard a faint ringing in his ear, a click as someone picked up.

"Hello?" The voice was wary.

"Is that Lydia Waters?"

"Yes."

"This is Max Rivers. I've got a message to call you."

"Max! Thank goodness!"

His pulse quickened. "What's the matter?"

"It's okay … Eleanor's okay … she's going to be fine …" Lydia paused and Max thought of Eleanor's hesitancy in the restaurant the night before he left – "… but they're not sure about the baby."

In front of him a family of Indians with huge silver suitcases were settling down to have their supper. A plump woman in a flame red sari was handing a sandwich to a girl in pink trainers. The girl stretched out her arm to take it; as she did so it slipped through her fingers. The plump woman swooped with surprising speed and caught it deftly in her hand.

"Excuse me." A polite voice behind him, a gentle tap on his shoulder. He turned to see an old woman's face. Soft blue eyes framed with grey hair. "Have you finished, only I need to call my son?"

Eleanor was lying in bed, covered in a faded hospital sheet that rose and fell with each breath. Her cheeks were drained and her lips slightly parted so that Max could see the shiny tips of her teeth as she slept. There was a tube coming out of her arm, snaking its way across the sheet into a machine with a flickering needle. Outside, beyond the double doors, heels clicked up and down the corridor and the place had the sharp, gut-churning tang of disinfectant. Eleanor's face was unmarked; she looked as serene as ever. There were no bruises or scratches. Her arm, in its bandage, was underneath the sheet. Apparently she'd thrown it out in an instinctive gesture to protect the baby and twisted it badly. There was nothing to show that Eleanor was in any way changed; that silently growing inside her – "right as rain" so the nurse had said – was part of Max.

He stared down at Eleanor's creamy skin, the sprinkling of freckles across her cheeks, the tracery of veins just visible at her temple, the strands of hair fanned out across the pillow, and remembered how nervous she'd been in the restaurant. *The thing is Max* ... She was pregnant. And yet she'd walked away, head down, hands in her pockets, and jumped into her taxi without a second glance. He'd known she was cool, but this was something else. She must have planned it: Eleanor wasn't one to forget to take the pill. He thought of the calculating way in which she'd embarked on their relationship, taking the upper hand, steering him into situations, even choreographing their first screw. Not revealing that Bill was her uncle until she knew it was too late for Max to back out. He shifted in his seat, sat back, felt his chest constrict as the realisation dawned. Bill. He'd be the baby's great uncle.

A fan whirred above his head, stirring Eleanor's hair. A thin finger of sunlight filtered through the louvred blind and fell across her face like a golden scar. There was a slim possibility that it was an accident. A sliver of a chance that the pill had failed, that she was the one in a million. That she wouldn't want to keep it; and at that thought he shivered despite the warmth of the room.

At the nurses' desk, a stocky man in a charcoal suit had overheard Max asking the way to Eleanor's room and asked him who he was. It was as if he'd tripped Max up. Stuck out his black-shoed foot and caught him around the ankle. Max had stared back, aware that the other man was busy, that his bleep was going off in his pocket, that he had lives to save and was waiting for an answer. An easy enough question. "Who are you?"

"I'm Max Rivers." He'd paused, aware that the man wanted something more. "I'm her partner."

It didn't have the weight of husband, but it had been enough for Mr Reeves, who had introduced himself as Eleanor's consultant. As if to pull Max into the secret, he handed him a grainy black and white photo. At first Max hadn't known what it was, but then Reeves pointed out a tadpole shape, a bulbous head, and an eye. A quite easily distinguishable black dot of an eye. He showed Max the barely perceptible arms and legs, like microscopic fins, and told him that the eyelids – the *eyelids* – were beginning to form and the two separate hemispheres of the brain were growing fast.

It was unbelievable. It was six weeks and two days old. Barely there. The merest slip of a life. A cluster of cells.

"It's a survivor," Reeves had said, patting Max on the back. And Max had known, without a scintilla of doubt, out there in the echoing corridor, that he was going to be a father.

"Max?" Eleanor's eyes opened a crack.

"I'm here." He leant forward, caught a trace of her scent.

"Max, are you there?"

"Yes, I'm here."

"Is it okay – the baby?"

"It's okay."

"Ah …" She exhaled. Her eyelids fluttered shut and she was gone again. Removed from him, with his seed inside her. He put his head in his hands and rocked gently to and fro, still unable to believe it.

Early in their relationship Eleanor had taken him away for a surprise weekend. She hadn't revealed where they were going until she'd handed over his boarding pass in the Champagne bar at Heathrow airport. It was Venice. "Because you once said that you'd never been," she'd said, her eyes glittering with excitement behind her brimming flute. "My mother took me there for my sixteenth birthday and it's the most magical place on earth."

They'd arrived on a water taxi as the sun was setting behind the Duomo. She led him by the hand through narrow cobbled streets to an apartment that later turned out to be owned by Bill. It was an old palazzo on the Grand Canal, an echoing place with a wide flight of stairs and an air of past grandeur; its dusty velvet curtains were torn in places and many of the marble tiles on its floors were chipped and stained. But it still maintained a high-ceilinged, faded beauty. Next morning she'd taken him shopping in the market – ruby red chillies and milk-white asparagus were piled in high, geometric patterns, like modern art installations. And he'd discovered – another surprise – that she was fluent in Italian. The musical words sprang from her lips and he'd known then, watching her testing the fruit and joking with the stall holders, that she was different from the other women he'd known. That evening she took him to an oboe concerto at the opera house. Max had never even heard of Tomaso Albinoni. The two of them floated back on his haunting tunes and later, in the sparsely furnished kitchen, she'd cooked him a simple risotto. He'd been bowled over. Eleanor was everything that he wasn't. He saw her as a sleek, well-bred Siamese cat. Elegant, aloof and independent. A woman born into culture and seamless success nurtured down the generations.

"Eleanor …" Max breathed her name as he watched her sleeping face. From the very first moments they'd met she'd given him a glimpse – and then a view, and a life – on the other side. A million miles from Mum's pebble-dashed terrace and her pitiful splash of hope, a place where anything was possible. Eleanor was already of that other world – of the Metropol and one-and-a-half-million pound flats in Holland Park and gleaming new Boxters. She was part of it.

It was only when they'd returned from Venice that she told him about her parents' death and how she'd gone to live with Bill and his wife for a couple of years in a white stucco mansion overlooking Regent's Park. Max discovered that the fatal car accident had occurred just a week after Eleanor and her mother had returned from her birthday trip. He'd been amazed at the revelation.

"But the place didn't seem to hold any fears for you."

"Fears?" She'd looked puzzled.

"Venice – I mean – didn't you associate it with your parents' deaths?"

"Of course not Max. Why should I? It's a beautiful place – it always will be."

She'd been so sure, so unflinching and confident of who she was. Striding out ahead of her without once, even for a moment, turning her head to glance back from where she'd come. And now she'd linked her arm through his and pulled him with her.

***

Mum's hand's lovely and cool in mine, and the baby's nowhere to be seen. I think Norah's got it.

"Come with me Maxi. I want to talk to you."

It's Saturday morning and I know that Mum's going to tell me about the Christmas tree and why we haven't got it yet. I'm waiting for her to say it. *These things happen,* she'll say. Dad's been saying it to her all the time recently. "I'm sorry," he says, "but These Things Happen." I don't know what they are – These Things – but I know that when they happen everything else goes all wonky and out of place.

Mum leads me into the living room and sits down on the settee. She pats the gold stripy cushion next to her. "Sit here Maxi."

I do as she says and the material feels cold under my thighs. I've got my football shorts on. Mum let me wear them even though it's December and that was when I knew that we wouldn't get the Christmas tree today. It goes like that. She lets me do something I'm not normally allowed to do and then she does something I don't like.

"Now, I want you to be a very grown-up boy for mummy." She stops. She's looking at me and her eyes have gone all swimmy as if they're going to overflow. I can smell that sickly sweet smell she's had since the baby arrived. "Do you think you can do that for me Maxi?"

I nod my head.

"The thing is ..." She stops again and sniffs quickly. "Well, the thing is Maxi that daddy's got a lot of work on at the moment – so much work in fact that he's got to go away for a little while." She's looking at me. Right into my eyes as if she can see deep down inside me. "Do you understand Maxi?" Her eyes are still glued to mine. How blue they are, and now they're filling up again and going all wobbly. She blinks and brushes the back of her hand against them.

"He's coming back though – right?" My voice is small and scratchy and when Mum doesn't answer straight away I feel as if my stomach's being squeezed too tight and I need the loo.

"He loves you very much Maxi."

"He *is* coming back isn't he?" I sit up straighter and pull myself an inch or so away from Mum.

A tear rolls over the edge of Mum's eye and plops onto her cheek. I watch it roll all the way down to her mouth. And in that moment I know. It feels like the whole world's stopped, like all the cars and lorries and trains and buses and planes and flies and bees and birds and cats and dogs and cows and pigs and sheep and lambs have stopped moving and breathing. But then outside in the road a car hoots and I hear someone shout. How can they? How can they shout when Dad's not coming back? I feel as if I've jumped off Norah's wall and the pavement's vanished. I'm falling and falling, racing towards the ground but it's not there.

"But what about Christmas?" I say it as I'm thinking it. The words tumbling out of my mouth.

"Christmas?" Mum's staring at me, her eyes wide open. For a moment I think she's going to laugh, and I want her to so badly. And for Dad to walk in through the door and throw back his head and laugh with her and say that it's all been a joke. A great big fantastic joke. But Mum's not laughing. She's looking down at her lap and I know that she's forgotten all about our Christmas tree and the old grey suitcase in the loft with all our Christmas decorations and making our paper chains. Beside Mum's head, through the window, I see Norah. She's on the other side of the wall, out in the street, pushing the baby. I can't see the pram. It's hidden behind the wall. Norah's holding her arms out in front of her and when I see her it all slots into place in my mind like the pieces of my Scooby Doo jigsaw puzzle. Norah's taken the baby out so that Mum can talk to me.

"It's all because of him isn't it?" I jump up. Mum's looking up at me and frowning. Her eyes are dancing about and her face is all muddled and confused. And right now I hate her and I hate him. The baby.

"What d'you mean Maxi?"

I can hear the blood pumping inside my head. It's pumping too hard for me to speak. When I feel Mum's hand on my shoulder I shrug it off.

"Maxi – darling –"

I pull away as she tries to stop me and before I know it I'm out of the door and up the green stairs, two at a time and into my room. I slam the door shut so that the poster of Gordon Hill rustles and flaps and then lies still. I've never been so angry. Never, ever, ever. Without meaning to, I burst into tears.

***

Bill was standing by the window in his office, his hands thrust into his pockets as he stared out over the murky skyline.

"You must understand that she's like a daughter to me Max."

"I know."

It was mid-morning. Hours earlier, on the plane, Max had been rehearsing this meeting with all the wrong lines. He'd come straight from the hospital, still wearing the suit he'd flown home in. His head ached and his jaw bristled with stubble. His instinct had been to see Bill as soon as he could, but now he wondered at the wisdom of it.

"When her parents died she was just sixteen, teetering on the verge of adulthood, it was a very difficult time. And when she came to live with Valerie and me – well, we just had to do the best we could. It was the most tremendous shock. Terrible, for all of us." Bill stopped abruptly and I could see that he was fighting his emotions. "But Eleanor showed us the way really; it was extraordinary the way she coped. She and Valerie became very close very quickly – I suppose you do when something like that happens. I know that Valerie liaised with the school. They were excellent. And Eleanor simply decided that she was going to give it her all, to work as hard as she could to get good results as a tribute to Stephen and Jane. I've never seen anyone apply themselves so single-mindedly to anything."

Bill turned. Under the overhead light his face looked tired, older, and there was a certain tightness to it beneath the surface, revealing his tension.

"She *is* extraordinary," Max said. And he remembered the anxious tug to Eleanor's voice as she'd stirred in her sleep and asked him about the baby.

Bill nodded, and as if reading Max's thoughts said in quite a different voice – in his professional, business voice, "And now she's having your child. You look after her Max."

Max nodded. "I will." He felt overwhelmed with exhaustion, swept up in a tide of events that was pushing him on.

"Good. Right." Bill moved behind his desk. "Now tell me about what the hell's happening with the Britannic-

Gazprov account. I've had Toby Wilson on the phone, expressing some concern at the latest developments."

It was as if the tide had turned and carried Max back onto the firm sand of the shore.

"I can explain Bill." And he did his best. However awkward the situation, it was good to be back on work territory. He sat facing his boss across three feet of maple desk and reeled off the list of excuses that he'd compiled on the flight. His mouth was sour with stale tobacco. All the while Max spoke, Bill turned his pen between his immaculately manicured fingertips, barely concealing his disappointment. They both knew that Max was papering over the cracks. When Max had completed his inadequate explanation, Bill revealed that Wilson had suggested that it might be useful for one of Britannic's in-house lawyers to sit in on further meetings.

"I'm afraid I couldn't say no under the circumstances. I'm sure you understand Max."

It was bad; worse than he'd thought. Britannic had lost confidence in him. If Bill hadn't been Max's quasi father-in-law, he'd probably have kicked him off the account there and then.

The northerner was already on his feet. "I'll be going in to see Eleanor later this afternoon if you'd like me to take her some flowers or anything."

Max was swept back out to sea again. Eleanor was having his child. He took a deep breath. "It's okay. I'm going tonight."

"Of course." Bill ushered Max out, his hand on his shoulder. "I should go home and take a shower lad – you look all in. You can always come back later."

Max collected Eleanor from the Chelsea and Westminster a few days later. While she was in hospital he hadn't asked her anything about the pregnancy – why she hadn't told him, whether she'd planned it, or any of the details. It hadn't seemed the right time.

"I've brought some of your clothes over from your flat," he said, keeping his eyes on the car in front.

"Really?"

"Yes. I thought you might want them and I don't want you ferrying backwards and forwards. The doctor said you should rest."

Eleanor remained silent beside him. He knew she'd be working out the significance of what he'd just said – that he was taking her home to his flat. As he'd pushed open the door to her apartment to collect her clothes, he'd realised that he'd hardly ever been there alone and the enormity of what was happening had hit him again: the fact of Eleanor and him – the hard, concrete reality of their relationship – was inescapable. There could be no running away now; the two of them were bound together for the rest of their lives by their child. A mixture of different emotions – humility, fear and an extraordinary sense of what he could only describe as subdued elation – had washed over him. The lingering scent of her candles had seemed to infuse the place with her presence and when he'd opened the ornately carved door of her wardrobe and seen her expensive dresses and suits hanging in front of him, he'd felt like an intruder into the exotic life of someone he hardly knew.

Propped up beside her bed had been a photo of him. His hair was plastered to his head and he was grinning inanely; it wasn't flattering, but she'd said she liked it because it captured the boy inside him. It had been taken at the top of the Empire State Building a month or so after they'd met.

They'd flown First Class and he'd booked them into the Plaza on the corner of Fifth Avenue. It had cost him a small fortune but he'd wanted to repay her (and impress her) after their Venice trip. It was early autumn and Central Park had been spectacular: crimson trees blazed under an azure sky. They'd stayed in bed long into the day, their bodies tangling among warm sheets and croissant crumbs, then wandered idly through drifts of leaves. It was just the sort of dreamy girlstuff that he'd imagined she'd want. But on their final morning she'd announced that what she'd really like to do was go up the Empire State building. He'd been astonished but he wasn't about to argue.

They bought their way to the front of the mile-long queue with fast track tickets and had their picture taken with a guy in a King Kong suit on the 65th floor. It was his idea of hell. But right then, bewitched by Eleanor's cool, classic beauty and her understated style, he was ready to do anything. And to his surprise, when they'd walked out onto the viewing platform, he'd been blown away. The air was crystal clear and the view stretched away to the far horizons, above all the other skyscrapers, out over the Hudson.

"My God El – we're on top of the world!" He'd had to shout above the roar of the wind and she'd laughed and kissed his face, and then stood back to take the photo. His head had swum. The concrete beneath his feet had seemed to rock and sway as if it hardly existed, as if they were walking on air, and he could almost feel his knees buckling.

He remembered the sensation as he inched the car forward – the feeling of being in such an extraordinary place, high above everyday normal life, buffeted so hard by the wind that he could no longer stand straight or think straight.

"So," Eleanor said, and he could sense her watching him. "Let me get this right – are you suggesting that I move in with you?"

He told her that that was exactly what he was suggesting. As soon as he'd seen the photo of her scan he'd known that it was what he wanted. The car in front of them stopped abruptly; he braked hard and they jolted to a halt. His left hand shot out.

"Sorry – bloody idiot!" His eyes flicked down to her stomach. The queue moved forward and he released the clutch. "When did you know, exactly?" He hadn't meant to ask the question, but the words were out of his mouth before he could stop them.

"I knew for sure just over a week ago."

Which meant, he thought to himself, that he'd been right: she'd known in the restaurant the night before he flew to Moscow. It had been what she'd been about to say when Mum's call had interrupted them. He remembered the determined set of her head as the taxi swept her away. The car behind them hooted; he let out the clutch and they moved slowly forward.

"Did you ever think ... about ...?" He paused, struggling to find the right words.

"About not going ahead with it?" Eleanor's voice was firm.

"Yes." He kept his eyes on the tail lights ahead. She remained silent; the air between them bristled with expectation.

"No. I never had any doubts." She paused. "No matter what."

No matter what. The phrase was unyielding. He knew exactly what Eleanor meant. It was what he'd felt as soon as the consultant had shown him the scan, the tiny limbs, the dot of an eye, the pulsing beginnings of something that was part of him, yet separate from him. The constancy – the certainty – of that heartbeat was humbling. It had taken him back to the kitchen at Hillside Close and to Mum struggling to find the words to tell his five-year-old self that he was soon to have a brother.

In many ways, in the first few days after Eleanor was discharged, Max found it hard to believe that anything had changed. The white bandage on her arm was the only visible sign of her hospital stay and if anything, she looked even slimmer than usual. She quickly returned to work and Max, in an effort to rebuild his damaged reputation, was putting in long hours at the office. He still swam at his gym, though sometimes only once a week. He'd managed – just – to keep off the fags, and he was keeping in touch with Mum through calls to her and Norah. And yet, of course, although neither of them explicitly acknowledged it, everything had irrevocably changed.

Eleanor had a glow, an aura, a sense of contentment that went far beyond her usual air of self-assured calmness. Whereas Max was wary of making love, she was anything but.

As they lay in bed she airily dismissed his nervousness. "I asked the doctor and it's quite all right."

"Are you sure?"

"Sure I'm sure."

There had been a hint of spring in the day and the curtains were open, the sash pulled down to let in the breeze.

"Well – I don't want – you know –"

"Ssssh …" She brushed her lips against his, stopping his words.

And as he moved on top of her and slid into her, as she wrapped her arms around his neck and arched her back, he felt the jut of her hips and imagined the concave dip between them that somehow, unbelievably, cradled their baby.

***

When Elizabeth was little she'd been tiny; the merest slip of a thing, with Dora's smile and enchanting dimples in her cheeks. She'd been a mummy's girl. Dick's job hadn't left much time for his young daughter, for what would today

106

(over-judgementally in his view) be called 'quality time'. Dora had given Lizzie plenty of that. She'd sacrificed her teaching career before she'd barely begun it to concentrate on motherhood. And how it had suited her: she had the patience of a saint and an enviable ability to be kind but firm, gentle but disciplined. Intolerant of adults' foibles, Dora thought children were undervalued. "We should listen to them more," she used to say. "They have such a lot to teach us." He'd nodded of course, but in all honesty he hadn't been so sure.

Lizzie was lovely – delightful – of course she was. Dora always ensured her clothes were spotless and her manners, as his wife frequently liked to tell him, were the envy of all the other mums. If he got home from work in time, he'd make a point of nipping up to read Lizzie a story. She'd be sitting in bed, the rosebud eiderdown tucked under her chubby arms, a legion of fluffy animals lined up beside her, a book – its size diminishing and its thickness expanding the older she grew – propped on her knees. He knew she'd have heard him coming up the stairs and she'd glance around as soon as he walked through her door and give him a shy smile. He'd perch on the side of her bed and she'd hand over her book for him to read it aloud. These were special moments shared between the two of them, but they were too few and far between. On those weekends when Dick wasn't working, the three of them might go to the park; Lizzie would pack as many of her animals as she could fit into her toy pushchair and wheel them along. Their progress was painfully slow and Dick, used to rushing around at work, longed to stride out and stretch his legs. It seemed that Lizzie was no sooner old enough to walk at a decent pace than she was off with her friends; he and Dora relegated to the inevitable role of the world's most embarrassing mum and dad.

Loading up the car to take her to college, Dick had marvelled at where the time had gone. One moment he'd been picking her and her mum up from the maternity ward, the next he was helping her carry her cases into the functional red-brick building that was to be her home for the next three years. He'd urged her to move into student digs in her second year so that she could get a taste of the real world, but she said she liked living in hall with her gaggle of girlfriends, all of whom seemed to Dick, though he'd never say it, a bit drippy. Dora, for her part, was only too pleased not to have to worry about her little girl living in some insalubrious flat, paying rent to a lecherous landlord.

"She should spread her wings a bit love," Dick had ventured.

"Time enough for that," Dora fired back and Dick had left it there. He'd long ago learnt not to argue where Lizzie was concerned.

For the truth was – and he'd only come to admit it (possibly even see it) once Dora passed away – he'd been no more than half-engaged with Lizzie's upbringing. The two females in the family had inhabited a fragrant, shopping-and-gossip-and-clothes-and-make-up sort of bubble into which his size 12 feet didn't fit. He hadn't minded at the time because he'd been far too busy with his work. But now that Dora was gone and Lizzie seemed intent on re-entering, not to say reordering, his life, he'd set about wondering just how well he'd ever known his daughter.

He'd also begun to think more and more about what it would have been like to have a boy. A testosteroned male to kick a ball about with and, later, to chew the fat with over a pint. Would he have been a more hands-on dad if he and Dora had produced a son? Though it pained him to say it, he believed that he would. Whenever he had such thoughts he'd hear Dora's voice in his head telling him to stop being so maudlin. "Life's life" had been another of her expressions. True, but hardly helpful.

That lunch with Lizzie the other week hadn't been helpful either. She wanted him to move, that was the long and the short of it. She'd dressed it up of course, just as she'd used to dress up her dollies in frills and nonsense, but it was obvious as soon as they sat down in the Ramblers' Return that it was why she'd asked him out to lunch. He hadn't even started on his pint of Ruddles County before she seized on the difficulty he'd had hauling himself out of her sports car to start in on him.

"There's no shame you know, Dad, in getting old." She'd sipped at her sparkling water then and opened her eyes wide – as if she was talking to a child. He'd taken a long slug of beer before responding in order to quash his desire to tell her that neither was there any shame in reaching middle age – the trick was not to make a fool of yourself with inappropriate cars.

"No." He could see that she wanted him to say more but quite frankly he had nothing more to add on that particular subject.

"Simon and I were only saying the other day that we don't know how you manage to keep on top of your garden."

"What you going to have then love?" He'd picked up the thick leather menu and looked at her over the top of it, cutting off further discussion.

She hadn't given up though. Not our Lizzie. During the course of what he had to admit was a very good lunch – he'd treated himself to steak and kidney pie followed by rhubarb crumble and custard, all home-made, and well worth provoking Lizzie's look of disapproval as she ate her quiche – she kept on chipping away at him with dogged perseverance. It was just the sort of thing that Dora would have done, he'd found himself thinking, but with so much more subtlety. Adorable Dora – how clever she'd been. So many of the things he missed about her now she was gone he'd never noticed when she was here. Lizzie, sitting opposite him with a hint of a moustache on her top lip, only seemed to accentuate her mother's absence. How could sharp little Dora have produced such a soft – and though he didn't mean to think it – silly daughter?

As Dick carved into buttery pastry and piled gobbets of meat onto his fork, he tuned Lizzie out. Draining the last of his Ruddles, he caught the waitress's eye and asked for another.

"Are you sure Dad?"

"Course I'm sure. What about you?"

"I'll stick to my water; I am driving you know."

His second pint – a rare treat – leant a hazy glow to his surroundings and warmed the cockles of his heart. No longer listening to or hearing his daughter, he let his mind float away to what he'd do when he got home. He'd now found 20 similar cases scattered around the country, six based in the south-east. He was cross-referring his Internet discoveries with the box-loads of faded newspaper cuttings piled up in the spare room. Patterns were emerging; the advent of DNA profiles in the 1970s had revolutionised investigations. Only the other month there'd been a major breakthrough in a 27-year-old case. He knew, deep down, that he was becoming fixated, that Dora would have chided him and told him to "let it go".

When Lizzie insisted on taking his arm as the two of them crossed the car park towards her car, he rather ungraciously let her; he was, he discovered much to his chagrin, a bit wobbly on his pins. She wasn't going to push him around though. He felt like telling her she was wasting her time and that she should shut up and save her breath. He'd never leave the bungalow; it had too many rooms full of too many memories far too precious to move.

***

Over there, under the apple tree, is the pram. The baby's having its nap. It's sunny today. "The first day of spring," Mum said. She smiled when she said it, but it wasn't one of Miss Dodson's buttercup smiles. I know that Mum's not *really* happy.

She's put our washing on the line. It stretches across the lawn between the fence and the hedge. The wind catches it so that the baby's small white suits, the legs of my trousers, the arms of my shirts and Mum's skirts and blouses are all being pulled away. They look as if they're trying to escape. The wind's got the apple tree too. Its branches shake and its pink and white blossoms bounce around. Some of them fall onto the grass around the pram. As I walk closer I see that one or two of them have landed on the navy blue cover that stretches tightly above the baby.

There he is. I can see him. Peter. I say the word in my head and it twangs back at me. Peter. He's not asleep at all. His eyes are wide open. His great big eyeballs stare up at the waving blossoms. He hasn't got any hair and his head is huge. It's massive. Sitting beside it is Charlie Rabbit, the knitted rabbit that Norah's given him, with its yellow jumper. Peter's legs are kicking up the pram cover and he's making squeaky noises, a bit like the ones he makes in the middle of the night, only much quieter. Sometimes when I'm sleeping he wakes me up. Mum says he wakes her up *every night*. She says that's why he's still in her room. I don't understand. I'm never allowed to sleep in her room, not even now Dad's gone and his side of the bed is flat and empty. I'm still not allowed. But Peter – Peter with his massive head! – he gets to sleep in that room every night even though he wakes her up with his crying *every night*. "He's only a baby love," Mum said when I asked her. But he's six months old now – nearly seven. How long's he going to be a baby for?

His squeaks are turning into those wah-wah-wahs that make my head ache. They're why Dad left. I'm sure of it, whatever Mum says. I remember the way he used to push his cigarettes into his pocket and walk out into the garden soon as he started up. I reach out and curl my hand around the black bit on the handle. It feels squidgy under my palm. I rock it gently, like I've seen Mum do. Sometimes it makes him shut up. I like the way the pram bounces and sways as I jiggle my hand. The wind's stinging my face and my hair's licking into my eyes. I turn so that it blows out behind me and forces my eyelids shut. I keep jiggling and rocking the pram. The wind's loud in my ears, but not loud enough to cover his wah-wahs. I hate that noise. I jiggle a bit harder.

"Max! Max – stop it!"

I freeze. It's Mum's voice.

"What on earth do you think you're doing?"

The crying's very loud. I hadn't realised how loud it was till now. I'm shoved roughly aside – so hard that I almost stumble. It's Mum pushing me out of the way. Mum! Pushing me! I'm so shocked I gulp. My face is burning. The wind's stopped and suddenly everything seems quite still. Peter's not crying any more. Mum's picked him up out of his pram. She's cuddling him to her, away from me, her head's bent down so that I can see the back of her neck, and I think of the talcum powder smell of it. The bow of her apron's come undone and the two white ends hang down by the backs of her knees. I want to touch her. Perhaps if I tie up her apron strings she won't be so angry. I stretch out my hand, but before it reaches the string, the wind whips it away from me. It's as if it's done it on purpose. And then Mum swings around to face me.

"What were you doing Max?"

I don't like it when she calls me Max. It's not like when Dad used to call me Max. When Mum says it, it sounds different. Her voice is all hard and sharp. I stare at the flowers on her apron.

"Look at me Max."

I raise my eyes. She's watching me. He's waving his fists about, banging them into her neck. She takes hold of one of them in her hand without looking down at him. She's still looking straight at me.

"I was trying to make him stop crying."

My voice sounds like a whisper.

"Trying to make him stop?"

"He was crying," I say, trying to squeeze it in while her eyes aren't quite so fierce.

"You looked as if you were trying to throw him out of the pram, not make him stop crying," she says. Her voice is half way between hard and soft. "I know it's difficult Maxi – and I know that you miss your dad – I do too – but Peter's only a baby and you have to look after him. You have to be mummy's little man." She takes a step towards me. "D'you think you can do that for me?" Her voice is all soft now. But it's not soft like it used to be before *he* came, before Dad went. It's not buttercup soft. It's because she wants me to say yes. I stand up very straight and ball my hands into fists. I don't want to say yes because I want things to be the same as they were before. And yet I know Mum wants me to say yes, and I want Mum to be happy. "Maxi?" She's bending forward slightly now so that I can see the side of the baby's great big head beside her neck where she's holding him to her. My fingernails are digging into the flesh of my palms.

"Okay." I can hardly hear myself say it.

"Good boy Maxi!"

Mum steps forward, reaches out one arm and puts it around my shoulders, pulling me towards her. But the baby's in the way. His body's between me and Mum and I can't hug her properly. My face is right up against the baby's face. I can smell him – the smell of that disgusting milk that we have to drink at school. As soon as Mum steps back I run back over to my trapeze – the one that Dad made me – and grab hold of the thin wooden bar. I keep running and then I

113

lift my feet off the ground and launch myself into the air. Wheeee! I'm flying up into the sky and swooping back down again. Backwards and forwards I go, running and kicking my legs out, and when I'm going high enough and fast enough, I flip myself upside down and throw my legs over the bar. The back of my knees fold over it and it's wedged there, just right, the way it always is, and I'm swinging and swinging, backwards and forwards, and the whole world's turned upside down.

***

Eleanor's pregnancy didn't begin to show until the days began to lengthen and the alarm no longer went off in the dark but in a monochrome greyness.

One morning Max woke up to find her sleeping on her back, her arm flung out across the pillow, her head turned away from him. A ray of light pierced the gap in the curtains and slanted across her breasts. The velvet aureole surrounding her nipples had changed from milk chocolate to a much deeper brown, verging on black. He wondered when that had happened and how he hadn't noticed. He pulled back the duvet to expose Eleanor's belly, searching for other changes. She shifted slightly in her sleep and withdrew her arm, tucking it in under her chin. He looked down at the creamy skin just above the small blond triangle of pubic hair. Was that a hint of a swell? He placed his hand on her stomach. How tightly her flesh was drawn. How warm it was under his palm, how smooth. And yes, he'd been right. There was just the faintest trace of a bump. Eleanor stirred again and turned away from him, slipping out from under his hand, pulling the duvet up around her chin and tucking herself into a ball. He wondered if she'd noticed the changes in her own body. She must have surely, yet she'd never said anything.

She was, he realised, almost smiling as he thought of it, very much a closed book – even though she'd opened herself up to him in the most intimate way and was carrying his seed. He still didn't *know* her, not really. He still couldn't read her, understand her. But this would come. Wouldn't it? Even as he thought it, he wasn't sure.

Be that as it may, there was no doubt that gradually, subtly, Eleanor's presence was making itself felt in his apartment as more and more of her belongings appeared, often overnight, as if by magic. A handful of work suits and some shirts now hung, crisp and clean in the wardrobe in the spare room. Slivers of silk lingerie were folded neatly in a drawer, exuding – when Max put his hand in to touch them – her distinctive Vetiver scent. One evening when he came home from work he found her stainless steel liquidiser sitting, solid and expensive on his black granite work surface, looking as if it had always been there – *should* always have been there.

At some point – exactly when Max couldn't pinpoint – Eleanor discarded her weekend jeans for dark leggings (something he remembered her once vowing she'd never be seen dead in) and long, loose tops. When Max saw her naked, he could track the alterations in her body: her stomach jutting neatly as a football, her breasts swelling and developing a map of pale blue veins that she said she hated. They astonished him, these incremental changes that silently appeared as the outward confirmation of all that was happening inside her: the secret language of her pregnancy. She still wore her suits to work but he noticed she chose shirts that hung outside her trousers and jackets that hid her expanding waistline.

One evening when he went to hang up his suit he found a glossy carrier bag lying on the bed. Eleanor explained, over supper, that she'd had to buy some maternity clothes.

"I can't put it off any longer – I can't even get into my skirts – they won't fit over the bump." She sighed as if admitting defeat.

But it's wonderful isn't it? Max thought, but didn't say. She was beginning to look different. Not so much Eleanor with a football for a tummy, but a new, rounded version of her old self. Her face was fuller, less structured and even her ankles were no longer as slim, though he'd never tell her that. Her wrists were as fine and the soft skin behind her ear still as white, the swallow as delicate – the hidden signs of who she was. He wondered how much she'd change after the birth, and then stopped himself. He didn't want – couldn't, wouldn't – think beyond the baby's delivery. *Don't want to jinx it now, do we?* Mum's voice whispered in his ear.

He and Eleanor chatted for a while – she told him when the foetus might be expected to move inside her (pretty soon now, she said) and when she was thinking of giving up work (the last minute possible) – and then she put down her knife and fork and looked up.

"I was wondering –" she fixed her pale grey eyes on his – "if I should rent out my flat?"

He was ready for this. She'd laid enough clues and he was able to tell her, quite truthfully, that he thought it made complete sense in both practical and financial terms. But his sangfroid was short-lived. Eleanor's rhetorical question was merely the prelude to a bombshell, for which he was entirely unprepared: that they should buy a house together, complete with a garden for their unborn child.

Caught off guard, all he could think about was how much he loved his flat and how very much he didn't want to sell it. Eleanor rehearsed her arguments: the inconvenience of living on the second floor with a baby and all its paraphernalia – "I'll be constantly lugging the pram up and down the stairs – and the need for a garden, not to mention more space and another spare room. Max batted away her reasons as best he could, conscious throughout that his efforts were fruitless: she was set on moving. Her final argument, her pièce de résistance delivered with a flourish, was that their home should be near a good school.

"School? But the baby's still in utero for God's sake!"

"And in less than five months it'll be here. It'll take at least that long to find somewhere – and it'll almost certainly need some work done before we move in."

Max knew there was no way that they could afford what Eleanor wanted on their two salaries and realised that she was counting on using her inheritance. Out-manoeuvred, unprepared, the best he could do was to buy time. Reaching over to top up his glass, he said he'd need to think about it.

"No problem Max, but don't take too long – the baby will be here before you know it." As if to emphasise her point she pushed her chair back and stood up, folding her hands over the ever-growing dome of her stomach.

Over the next few weeks things gradually began to improve for Max at work. The milky bar kid brought in by Britannic to look over his shoulder seemed to have disappeared over the horizon and slowly but surely he was working his way through the clauses of the Gazprov agreement. And then, one day in late spring Bill summoned Max up to his office. As the lift glided to the top floor Max ran through all his recent sign-offs. There was nothing, surely, on which he could have made a mistake? The glass doors slid silently open and he walked across the grey expanse of tiles, the soles of his shoes squeaking as he did so. Bill's assistant ushered Max into his office.

Bill wanted Max to do a favour for an old pal of his from Cambridge. He called it a "pro bono" project, designed to extricate his friend from a classic Russian tax bind.

"I know you're busy with Britannic Max, but nobody's got your eye for detail or your knowledge of the way Moscow operates."

Max's relief that nothing was wrong quickly turned to irritation. The pro-bono work wouldn't add any weight to his partnership chances; it was pay-back time for Bill having saved his skin. There was nothing that Max could do but nod and smile in all the right places. When the sly old fox had finished skewering him, he glanced at his watch and said he'd come down in the lift with Max as he had a lunch to attend. Standing beside him, Max couldn't help but think of the similarities between Bill and his niece.

As if reading his mind, Bill said casually, "Eleanor tells me you're thinking of moving."

"Oh well, I don't know. It's early days yet Bill." Inwardly, Max cursed Eleanor.

Bill tipped back his head, contemplating the glass ceiling and the hydraulic cable. The lift swished to a halt and as Max stepped through the door he heard Bill's gravelly voice behind him.

"Take a look at the one off Wandsworth common – it's got a spectacular garden."

As Eleanor grew ever larger, the south of England sweltered through an unusually protracted heat wave. The sun bounced off dusty pavements, the squares around Max's office grew brown and parched, and a motionless smog descended on the City's high rise blocks. When Eleanor's blood pressure started to rise the doctor instructed her, against her wishes, to give up work earlier than she'd intended. Her initial annoyance soon gave way to resignation, and the enforced rest gave her more time for her plans. Within a couple of months she'd sold her flat privately to an old friend. Max knew what was coming next and sure enough a week or so later she announced that she'd put in an offer for a five-bed Victorian villa in Wandsworth. Its asking price, she admitted, was a "little over our budget." It was £2.5 million. Max could scarcely believe it, but she brushed aside his concerns. She said the sale of both their properties would raise at least £2 million.

"And the extra five hundred thousand?"

"I'm sure I can bring them down," she'd replied, as if she was buying a bunch of flowers in Portobello Market.

"And if we can't sell our flats?"

"We will Max, we will."

"But not straight away." He felt like the suburban grammar school boy that he was and knew, without having to be told, that Eleanor had Bill – his Northern vowels belying his own inherited wealth – standing by her shoulder ready to bail them out.

Throughout those long, hot summer days, Max hardly visited his mum. Norah was popping in every day and phoning with regular updates; while Eleanor, who'd been adamant about visiting his mum in the early months of her pregnancy, was now so focussed on moving that, to his relief, she let the subject drop.

He started swimming again more regularly. It was often late by the time he got to the gym and the pool was usually empty, the water spreading out before him, clear and still and cool, without so much as a ripple to disturb its mirror-like surface. As Eleanor's body expanded, his tightened up. He hadn't been in such good shape since his trainee stint in Moscow all those years ago. His abs and pecs were taut and he could feel his biceps straining against the fine white cotton of his shirts.

***

You could have knocked him over with a feather when Elizabeth broke the news. She'd phoned him up first, said she was calling in for a coffee because she had something she wanted to talk about – which wasn't strictly true of course, she had something to tell him. It was a fait accompli. His darling Dora would have seen this coming. Whereas he, an ex-detective, Dick thought ruefully after his daughter had left, had completely missed the clues.

Turned out Elizabeth and Simon were moving to Canada. She hadn't put it quite as baldly as that.

"Simon's been offered a job in Toronto," she'd said, just as Dick was dunking his gingernut into his mug. His hand froze, his soggy biscuit disintegrating into the steaming coffee. He'd felt a jolt of annoyance at this and then castigated himself on his pettiness. Elizabeth was telling him something huge. She could be going forever, shifting continents, moving out of his life for God's sake.

Still, he took his time, eating what remained of his biscuit, before saying, "Is he taking it?"

His daughter stared at her plump hands lying on the table, their red nails shining. She was embarrassed, unsure what to say. And Dick thought again of Dora and how she'd have known what words to use to make things less awkward.

Elizabeth locked her hands together in a determined way. "Yes he is Dad." She looked up and caught his eye and he immediately looked down before his expression gave him away.

He was breathing heavily as if he'd been walking too fast. He felt old, he realised. Well he *was* old. Too old for surprises. His hands, curled around the coffee mug, gripped it tighter. Was Elizabeth going too? He presumed she was. Why didn't she help him out and just say it?

"And you're going with him?" He said it without looking up, cursing her for making him ask the feeble-sounding question.

When she still didn't answer, he was forced to raise his head. Her face was a mask. It was hard as bloody flint. How could she be Dora's daughter? Though Dora was there now that he looked more carefully; he couldn't pinpoint where – not in the eyes or the mouth or the chin, but lurking, hidden behind Elizabeth's shoulder. And she – Elizabeth – the only bit of Dora he had left – far from wanting to mother him as he'd thought, was leaving him to go to Canada.

"I can't really stay here can I, Dad?"

It was a rhetorical question and he didn't answer. He was struggling with the unexpected hurt he felt at his daughter's announcement. They didn't have a proper conversation after that. Elizabeth told him various facts: the date they were going, the apartment they'd be living in, the importance of Simon's job. And the only thing he could think of saying was, "What are you going to do?" which didn't seem right. It sounded churlish when he thought of it so he left the question in his head, where it kept ricocheting around without an answer.

Finally, having first rinsed out their two mugs and placed them upside down on the draining board as if to emphasise that he wasn't even up to doing that, Elizabeth left. Funny how he kept thinking of her as Elizabeth now, not Lizzie. Lizzie seemed too intimate for the cold, middle-aged woman who'd sat across the kitchen table from him. When he'd seen her out, he'd walked slowly back down the hall. So that was it. He'd lowered himself carefully onto the kitchen chair, mindful of his back which had been playing him up recently, and sat staring ahead. It was just him now. And the crushing weight of Dora's absence – the finality of her death and the fact that she would never again be there beside him with her comforting words, her apposite phrases, her gentle eyes and her soft skin – piled down on him so heavily that it knocked the breath from him and he let out an involuntary gasp.

***

Dad used to call the strange wooden thing on top of the coal bunker a horse. I don't know why. It doesn't look like a horse. He used it when he was sawing wood. I'd stand and watch him. He'd balance the piece of wood across the top of the horse, lift up his leg and put one of his great big boots on it to hold it still. Then he'd rest the saw's blade just where he'd made a pencil mark. He kept the pencil tucked behind his ear, buried in amongst his thick black hair. When he pulled it out it was almost like a trick because you could never really see the pencil even when you knew it was there. It was always the same one – a short, stubby navy blue one with a rubber on the end. I tried it once – sticking my crayon on top of my ear but it kept falling off.

Right now Peter and me are sitting on top of the horse. From up here on top of the coal bunker we can see over the fence, through the leaves of a tree, into the neighbour's garden. The lawn, the path that leads to the shed, the red and white bike propped up against the wall. We can see it all.

We're cowboys riding the horse. I've brought the long red belt from my Ladybird dressing gown. I've looped it around the two bits of wood that stick up at the front of the horse and I'm holding onto the two ends. The belt's my harness, and Peter is sitting in front of me inside the harness. The hairs at the back of his head come together on his neck in a golden paintbrush tip. The sun's catching them and making them glint. When he looks down I can see the nobbly bone at the top of his spine. That bit of his neck – right at the back, under his hair – is called the nape. Nape. I learnt that last week, off Norah, when we were looking at her nature book with the special pictures. Nape. It's a soft-hard word. Like Treets – the soft, flat chocolates with the crispy shell. I like it.

It took him ages to get up on the bunker. In the end I bent down so that he could stand on my back and it really hurt when he pushed himself off. The heel of his shoe dug right into my shoulder. He's clutching Charlie Rabbit. He's a child and I'm a hero. I'm rescuing him. We're galloping across the desert past the big rocks where the Indians lurk. Another good word. Lurk.

"What does *that* mean?" Peter said when I told him.

"It means they're waiting for us."

"What for?"

"To kill us."

"Really?"

"Yep."

He believes everything I tell him, Peter. We go on adventures. Today we're stopping at the OK Corral. I'm not sure what the OK Corral is but Ian's told me that it's the fastest fight in the Wild West. Peter's gun's sticking out of the back of his shorts. He's got the small grey and white one. I think it's for girls but I'm not telling him that. I've got the proper brown cowboy one that Dad gave me for my birthday. When you push the button it splits in two ready to be loaded and when you pull the trigger it makes a bang. Peter's doesn't make any noise. It came out of a Christmas cracker.

"Whhhooooah!" I shout it out loudly and pull back on my dressing gown belt. I make a clicking sound with my tongue to calm the horse. "Whhooah there Vespa."

I throw my leg over the horse and jump down off the coal bunker.

"Come on Peter – we're going to have our shoot out."

Peter's trying to get his leg up over the horse but he can't quite manage it, his sandal's stuck – and now it's fallen off and toppled down into the gap between the bunker and the fence.

"Oh no." I roll my eyes. "Now look what you've done!"

"It wasn't my fault." He stares down at me.

"Well whose fault was it then?"

I drop down onto my knees and stick my arm into the thin black gap but it won't reach. I twist sideways and stretch until my shoulder hurts. I can touch something that I think's his sandal with the tip of my finger but when I try to pull it towards me I push it away. "Damn!"

"Max! You just said a naughty word. I'm going to tell Mum."

"Don't you dare you little pig!" I look up at him, sitting on top of the horse. He's got snot running out of his nose. "It's all because of you that we're in this mess."

"I want to get down –"

"Tough – I've got to get your sandal back." I scan my eyes around the garden, looking for something long and thin to use. There's a leafy twig lying on the grass underneath the apple tree. I stand up, brush the dirt off my knees and run over.

"Where're you going Max?" Peter's voice is high and frightened. I don't bother to answer. He'll soon see.

I pick up the twig. It's very twisty and it's not very thin. It's got lots of little twigs branching out on either side. I try to pull them off as I walk back over to the coal bunker.

"What's that?"

"What does it look like?" I squat down again and push my arm into the gap, reaching and straining. The twig meets something and I jiggle it up and down. It snaps.

"I want to get down Max."

"Shut up Peter!"

I pull my arm out. I don't know what I'm going to do.

"Boys! Teatime!"

Mum's voice makes me jump.

"Coming Mum!" I shout back as if nothing's wrong.

124

"How am I going to get down Max?"

"Be quiet – I've got to think."

"I want to get down." He sounds as if he's about to cry. I glance up at him. He's clutching Charlie Rabbit tightly in his arms and peering down at the ground. "I'm frightened Max."

I stand up. I hadn't thought about how to get him down.

"Boys!"

Any minute now Mum's going to come down the garden to see where we are.

"Lift your leg over the horse."

Peter stares down at me, his eyes wide. "But won't I fall off?"

"No – course you won't. I'll catch you." I say it in the firm voice that Dad used to use, though I'm not really sure about it. Not sure at all.

Peter's carefully lifting his leg around, over the horse. He's holding Charlie Rabbit by his ear and gripping onto the two bits of wood at the front. I can see his fingers squeezing tight.

"That's it, well done." The heels of both his feet – one in a sandal and one in a sock – are level with my chest, standing on the concrete bunker. "Now turn around slowly." His feet edge around until he's staring down at me. His eyes look very scared. I hold my arms out. "Now, you've just got to jump down into my arms and I promise to catch you."

He bends his knees a little bit, then straightens them again. "I can't Max."

"You've got to Peter – Mum'll be here any minute." The skin on his kneecaps is smeared with dirt. His knees bend again. Come on, I think to myself. Come on Peter. "Good boy." I say it just like Mum does.

"Promise you'll catch me?" His voice is very small and Charlie Rabbit's dangling from one of his hands as he holds them out.

"Course I will."

"Boys!"

And just as I hear Mum's voice, Peter jumps. He knocks right into my chest and almost pushes me over, but it's okay. We're both still upright and his face is smiling up at me.

"I did it Maxi!"

"Come along now boys – your tea's getting stone cold." It's Mum. She's right behind me, in her apron, one hand on her hip, the other shielding her eyes from the sun. And instead of being mad about what she's just seen, she doesn't seem concerned at all. "Where's your other shoe Peter?" She's looking down at his scruffy white sock collapsing around his ankle.

"It's down there."

Stupid boy! He's pointing down towards the gap and I know what's coming next. I'm about to cop it – all because of him.

Mum leans down. "How on earth did it get in there?"

"We were playing cowboys and –" Peter starts, but I butt in quickly.

"It wasn't my fault Mum."

Mum's turning her head from left to right, looking around her. She doesn't seem to be the least bit angry. "Ah – that's what I need." She dips and picks up something from the ground, and then she squats down by the gap. Next thing I know she's got Peter's sandal in her hand. "Come along then boys – in we go. You can carry on with this after tea."

I don't understand it. She isn't cross at all. Soon as she turns, Peter dashes after her. His feet flash brown and white as he runs. One shoe off and one shoe on. *Diddle-diddle-dumpling, my son John.*

126

***

Ben was born two weeks early by caesarean section. Eleanor had been disappointed. She said she wanted to give birth naturally not have her baby handed over to her by a stranger. But the shrewd consultant was adamant that with her raised blood pressure, a natural birth would be too dangerous and Max agreed with him.

"But you're not the one having it Max," Eleanor said as the three of them sat in the plush, blue Harley Street rooms.

"True." Max caught the consultant's eye.

"You can remain conscious throughout if you have an epidural," the bespectacled medic reassured Eleanor.

"Conscious but not in charge," she replied.

"You're hardly in charge during a birth however natural you might think it is," the consultant said drily.

In the end she had to accept. And at precisely 2pm on a crisp, clear Wednesday towards the end of October, Max and Eleanor's son was born.

When the midwife handed him over to Max – not to the woman who'd carried him for nine months – but to him, Max found himself unable to speak. The baby was wrapped in a grey, hospital blanket. He was a bloody, bawling bundle of flesh; he was separate from Max, with his own physical presence, his own weight and his own will. As Max brimmed with intense, bewildering emotion, the baby screwed up his red-raw face, gasped lungfuls of air as though they might be his last and wailed at the top of his voice as if to say "I'm here – get on with it!"

But Max couldn't get on with it, not immediately. He needed to take in the wonder of this baby – to drink him and his weight and his movement and everything, in. He made an incredible noise for such a small thing. His fists flailed;

his black, blood-matted hair, stuck out around his head; his thin legs kicked and jabbed at the blanket as if, having been cooped up in Eleanor's body for so long, released into the world, they couldn't stop moving.

And there was something else in that delivery room. A fleeting memory that came and went like rippling shadows on water. Mum's passing Max another blanketed bundle and cautioning him, *Careful Maxi, support his head.*

"Give him to her." It was the midwife's voice. "Put him on her chest."

Max turned to Eleanor. She was lying on a surgical table under a bright light. Beyond a screen below her waist, the obstetrician and a couple of medics were still working on her. Her eyes were on the baby, and Max could feel her need for her son. He lowered him carefully down, bending his knees until the baby's puckered, screaming face was level with Eleanor's. Her eyes were bright with tears and the moment Max handed him to her, the baby's crying stopped as though he'd caught her love, like a virus.

"He knows his mum," the young midwife said with perfect understatement.

Max watched how Eleanor handled the baby. It was awkward for her lying down, but she cradled his head in the crook of her arm as if she'd been doing it all her life. After a minute or two she looked up at Max and he saw his own euphoria reflected back, and a spark, a connection, jumped between them. It was as if a part of Max, a piece of his flesh, pumping with blood, had been sucked into Eleanor. She dropped her gaze and stroked the baby's face with one of her fingers. Max stood and watched as Eleanor, with the midwife's help, gently pushed her nipple into the hungry, open mouth. The scruffy black head of hair moved rhythmically, almost imperceptibly, as he sucked. And Max knew then, standing there beside the bed, that the tiny creature at Eleanor's breast, that small part of him, had just become the centre of her world.

***

Peter's joined me at school now. He wears my old school uniform. It's far too big for him because, as Mum keeps tutting when she looks at him, *he's such a little shrimp.* She says it with a curl in her voice, though to show him how much she loves him. He *is* small. His hands hardly show beneath the cuffs of my old shirts even though Mum chopped a bit out of the sleeves and then sewed them back up and my blazer swamps him. It really does. He looks like a right jerk. *You're not to say that Maxi!* I can hear Mum telling me off even as I think it. And I remember the way she looked at me after he fell out of the tree – as if it was all my fault. When it wasn't at all. Not AT ALL.

It wasn't my fault that he broke his finger and had to have it all bandaged up with a stick like a lolly stick all taped up around it. He'd only just started school when it happened and she fussed and fussed. To be fair to him, he didn't so much. He used it as an excuse not to tidy up his room or clean his teeth. Which wasn't actually fair because he's right-handed, Peter. He doesn't even need his left one. And anyway, it wasn't a bad break. I overheard Mum telling Norah. *Thank God!* She'd said, when they were sitting in our kitchen having a cup of tea in Mum's best china teacups – *Fine enough to see your fingers through!* Whatever that meant. *Thank God!* I heard her say. *Goodness knows what could have happened. It doesn't bear thinking about. I don't know what Max thought he was doing – letting him climb so high.* I had to pull my lips together then to stop myself from shouting it out. *It wasn't my fault!* It wasn't fair. In the end he only had the bandage on for about two weeks. They went off to the doctor's down the green. Him and Mum. Very important. Him with his arm hanging by his side with that great white blob on his hand. He looked back at me as they walked away. *Why didn't you tell her?* That's what I thought. When they came back the bandage was off. The finger looked just the same as it always had. As if it had never happened.

We get the bus to school. To begin with Mum insisted on walking with us to the bus stop. It was ex-cruc-i-a-ting-ly embarrassing having to walk with her in the morning and see her waiting for us outside the school gate in the afternoons. *Ex-cruc-i-at-ing.* I told her I could look after him, but she looked at me like she had when he'd fallen out of the tree – with all those words piled up behind her eyes. She didn't say any of them. She didn't say. *I can't trust you ... not after what happened ...* But I know that's what she was thinking. But it wasn't true. I'd been looking after Peter. I told him NOT to jump. But after a few weeks she did let us go on our own. *Thank God!* It wasn't as if it was far or anything. It was virtually outside our gate – outside Norah's to be precise. That's what I'd said to Mum. She'd smiled then. A proper buttercup smile. *You do make me laugh Maxi – the things that you say!* And when she was offered more hours at the council place where she works, she said we could go on our own.

As long as you take good care of him Maxi.

Course I will Mum.

And mind you sit next to him on the bus.

No problem.

I don't sit with him of course, even though I said that I would. I know that Peter won't dob me in. I've told him that if he'll sit somewhere else I'll make sure he doesn't come to any harm in the playground. I do, too, though I'm careful not to let anyone know it.

There's a really nasty kid called Richard Marks in the year below me who's got it in for Peter. He probably decided to pick on Peter because he's so small. When I saw what he did I almost gave the game away – almost let everyone else see what I was doing. I was talking to Neil about the offside rule (he'd got it all wrong) when I noticed this great hulking kid in the playground walk up behind Peter and shove him in the back. He punched him right in the shoulder. For no good reason as far as I could see. And Peter still had his bandage on! Great big bully! I stopped in mid-sentence. Couldn't believe what I'd just seen – simply couldn't believe it – and this strange thing happened behind my eyes. Everything went red. My face burnt up as if there were flames under my skin and I took two or three paces towards the thug. He looked up and saw me coming and ran away into the school. I saw the shock in Peter's eyes and the look of relief when he caught sight of me. I stopped in my tracks then, suddenly aware of Neil beside me and how all this would look to him. I felt like a wally. I winked at Peter to show him that it was all right and turned away.

Later, when I caught sight of Richard Marks going into the downstairs cloakroom I nipped in behind him and closed the door. When he saw it was me he looked petrified. Served him right. Even though he's massive for his age I'm still a lot taller than him. And before he had time to react or run away, I pushed him into one of the cubicles, wedged myself in after him and pulled the bolt across the door. I couldn't just see the fear in his coward's eyes, I could hear it in his panting breaths. "You great big shit," I said, my mouth barely an inch from his face, my hands on his shoulders as I pressed him into the thin partition wall. "That was my brother you punched – and if you ever punch him again, or do anything to him that I don't like the look of, I'll make sure you swing." He didn't say anything, just stared right back at me, his eyes popping out of his thick fat skull. I thought about kneeing him in the crotch and pushing his face down into the loo but decided that might be too much. I could see he'd learnt his lesson so I slackened my grip on his shoulders, unlocked the door and tried to squeeze out. It was difficult with the two of us crammed into such a small space but I managed it. The door swung shut behind me with a bang and I strode out of the cloakroom. It was only when I was thinking about it all and feeling pleased about the way that it had gone that I realised I'd no idea what I'd meant by *I'll make sure you swing.* It was just something I'd heard on the telly. Never mind. It sounded good and it had done the trick.

After that I kept a close eye on Richard Marks. He didn't go near Peter again, but I made sure that no one knew why, not even Peter. I don't want to be known as the sort of lily-livered plonker who watches out for his wimpy little brother.

***

When Max went to pick up his mum it was still before six and very dark and dank, with glistening pavements and yellow-haloed street lamps. The roads were virtually empty and he knew he'd make good time. He needed to. He depressed the accelerator to catch the green lights before they turned red and cursed the slight lag of the Audi's engine.

As soon as he'd heard Norah's apologetic voice on the end of the line, he'd known what she was going to say. Even through his thick, sleep-befuddled brain, he'd known.

I'm sorry to phone you at this time Max but it's your mum – she's okay, don't worry, she's absolutely fine, but I think you need to come.

Driving through the tangle of side streets leading onto the A3, Max thought of all the reasons he'd given himself for not visiting her. He was busy … and tired … and he needed to help Eleanor, who was even more tired than he was. She told him that she'd never known tiredness like it. *It's like slamming into a brick wall Max.* He'd return home to find her sitting in her mum's old rocking chair; she seemed to live in it, curled around her baby, her hair falling forward like a curtain. When she looked up, her eyes were almost invisible in the semi-darkness, small beads of black in cavernous sockets, and the planes of her face were sharp and angular; her pregnancy weight had dropped off her like a sloughed skin.

They'd brought the baby home from hospital in the back of Max's new Audi. A few days earlier Eleanor, two days overdue and "fit to burst" as she'd put it, had smiled ruefully as she'd watched Max climb into his Porsche for the last time. He'd acted as though he didn't mind, but it had been almost as big a wrench parting with his car as moving out of his flat. They'd bought the Victorian villa off Wandsworth common. Of course they had. And now every one of its rooms had been redecorated in a different shade of white. Off White. New White. Wall White. Old White. It'll be all white on the night. Max couldn't believe how many there were: he'd left the revamp to Eleanor. He'd neither the time nor the inclination to join in. Given his way they'd still be in Holland Park, inconvenient stairs or not. Eleanor had planned it all like a military operation; marshalling teams of decorators and issuing them with meticulously timetabled instructions. They'd completed bang on schedule, two weeks before Ben was born.

Max liked the name: it had a solid, masculine ring. Choosing it hadn't been easy. Eleanor favoured names like Edward and Charles. Max considered them far too poncy. When Eleanor had suggested Benjamin, he'd curled his lip. "Like Benjamin Braddock in *The Graduate*?" But when a few days later she'd come up with Ben, he hadn't even made the connection. Ben was bold. It was a name that was fit for his son. It wasn't until Eleanor mocked him for his U-turn that he realised what she'd done.

"He's never being called Benjamin, El – let's get that quite clear."

"Whatever you say Max." And she'd smiled her enigmatic smile, like the cat that's got the cream.

But that was in the euphoria of the early days before the tiredness that seemed to eat her up. Eleanor had changed so much. She was determined to breastfeed Ben even though he was perpetually hungry. "Breast is best," she said when Max suggested using formula milk so that he could help with the feeds. *Breast is best.* It had become her mantra. Max had lost count of the number of times he'd heard her say it as Ben wailed for food that his mother clearly couldn't provide. "I'd no idea how hard it was going to be," was another phrase never far from her lips. The fecund confidence she'd shown during pregnancy had vanished as quickly as her extra weight. The slack skin around her waist matching the slow slackness of her movements and the expressionless look that Max sometimes saw in her eyes.

And all this, Max told himself as he braked sharply into a bend, was why he hadn't been to see Mum. Who, Norah had just informed him, had been found by a stranger wandering up and down the road in her nightie.

Luckily Max the woman somehow managed to get your mum back into the house – I think the front door was open which was a bit of a giveaway at 3am – and then she saw the list of emergency numbers that I'd left by the phone and had the sense to ring him.

Mum hadn't met her six-week-old grandson. Was it really because Eleanor was too tired and he didn't have enough time? He was on the A3 now and picking up speed. Pairs of headlights loomed occasionally out of the mist and disappeared past him.

Since Ben's birth, and despite her evident exhaustion, Eleanor had been on at him to visit his mum. She said that proximity to Max's mum had been one of the reasons she'd wanted to move south of the river. Max countered by saying that he doubted his mum would even comprehend that she was now a grandma. Eleanor had looked at him then in her old, pre-Ben way, her eyes narrowing slightly as though she were reading his thoughts. She'd met Mum once, just before Ben was born. Max had given in to Eleanor's persistent pressure and taken her down to Surrey. As they'd pulled up outside the pebble-dashed semi he hadn't had the guts to look at her; he couldn't stomach seeing her reaction or, worse, seeing her trying to disguise it under layers of artificial jollity. Her swollen frame had made Eleanor seem too big for the narrow hall and seeing Mum's Cornish pasties sitting side by side on the doormat had made his heart turn over. He'd never brought anyone to Hillside Close.

Eleanor didn't even seem to notice the funny old shoes. She breezed past them into the living room where the telly was blaring at half-past three in the afternoon.

"Hello Mrs Rivers!"

Mum had carried on watching the screen until Max had walked over, picked up the remote control and switched it off. Then her head turned and her eyes behind their thick brown frames zoomed in on Eleanor, standing in the half-light by the door.

"Who are you?"

"I'm Eleanor, Mrs Rivers." Eleanor was smiling at Mum, her hands placed on the soft woollen tunic draped elegantly over her belly.

The carriage clock ticked on the mantelpiece. Mum had bought it before Max was born with her Greenshield stamps. There was a flash of movement through the window as a bird flew off the apple tree. Max kept his eyes on his mum, on the sprinkling of whiskers on her chin, on the toady, mottled skin of her hands in her lap, on her feet in their sheepskin slippers folded under the coffee table.

"Helena?" Mum turned her face to Max.

"Eleanor Mum," he corrected her. "It's Eleanor, my girlfriend." He motioned to Eleanor to come closer, noticed as she crossed the carpet that her expensive suede loafers matched the caramel swirls.

"It's lovely to meet you Mrs Rivers – I've heard so much about you."

Eleanor's inane niceties slid straight off Mum into the golden pile of discarded sweet wrappers lying beside her. She returned her gaze to the blank screen.

"Could you get us all a cup of tea Max?" Eleanor lowered herself onto the sofa.

"I want the telly back on!" Mum spat out the words like a spoilt child, her eyes still fixed on the silent TV.

"Why don't you put the kettle on Max and your mum and I can sit here together and watch TV." Eleanor eased herself out of her jacket and folded it over the sofa's threadbare arm.

"And then she put her coat on and left – can you believe it? I mean!" A woman's cockney voice shrieked at us from the TV.

"I can't stand that one," said Mum. "She's always moaning – gets on my wick."

Max stared in disbelief. Mum never swore.

"Off you go Max – go on." Eleanor, sensing his shock, motioned towards the door. "We'll be fine in here."

He'd left them to it. It was more than he could bear to see Eleanor – beautiful, pregnant Eleanor – sitting on the sagging old sofa with its floral stripes next to someone he hardly seemed to know. He'd realised then that Mum was right on the edge, that very soon she'd need more looking after than Norah was able to give. As he'd walked into the kitchen with its old Formica-topped table, its chipped, laminated cupboards and worn lino floor, he'd told himself that once the baby was born, he'd deal with all this.

Had he? Had he hell. Now he was roaring down the A3 at half-past six in the morning, forced into action he'd been too much of a coward to take. And because he hadn't planned for this, hadn't faced up to his responsibilities when he should have, he'd have to bring Mum back up to London with him. Like it or not there was nothing else for it; he hadn't got time to make other arrangements and he couldn't leave this to Norah. *Salt of the earth that one.* He'd leant on her too much as it was.

When he saw a queue of red tail lights ahead, he eased his foot off the accelerator. There were road works by the nursery where he'd sometimes used to buy his mum plants for the garden; azaleas and tulip bulbs, or hyacinths. Hoardings covered in pictures proclaimed that luxury four-bed executive homes would soon be replacing the flower beds and greenhouses.

Max had been steeling himself for seeing his mum after so long, but nothing could have prepared him for how she was. At first he thought it was going to be fine. He followed Norah into the kitchen to find Mum sitting at the table, fully dressed, a cardigan slung around her shoulders. Her hair was a bit of a mess, the normally tight curls were limp and dull, and he had to admit her face was thinner and pale, but other than that she looked okay. When he said hello she glanced up at him and beamed. It was a shocking, toothless grin that knocked him sideways: she hadn't got her dentures in.

He was aware of a dampness under his armpits and the clammy feel of his shirt on his back. He took a few deep breaths to steady himself as his mum continued to stare at him obviously unaware of who he was. *Well – you've hardly been here have you?* He could hear her moaning voice in his head, and now he longed to hear her saying it. He should have come before. Of course he should. Well it was too late for recriminations now. He swallowed hard. *Keep going Maxi. Just keep going.*

"How are you doing Mum?"

She just kept smiling cheerfully, unknowing, all the while revealing her terrible, naked gums. He felt as if something inside him had died. She was aware enough to know that he was someone close, a friend perhaps, but the quivering, fearful look in her eyes reminded him of a trapped animal. How long was it since he'd been down? He realised with a prick of shame that he couldn't remember.

Norah hovered like an anxious parent willing her wilful child to behave. "This is Maxi pet, he's come to take you up to London."

Mum's smile vanished as she eyed him suspiciously. "London? Never liked it. Don't want to go."

"It's where I live Mum – me and Eleanor … and …" His voice shook and he paused, unsure whether he should mention Ben.

"Don't want to go."

"Don't you want to see your grandson pet?"

Mum studied Norah with something like contempt and pulled her lips tightly together over her gums.

"She sometimes gets like this Max, when she's confused, but don't worry, she'll be fine in a minute or two."

Max exhaled slowly. He felt winded, as if he'd been punched in the gut. All he could think about was escaping into the fresh air. But it was several minutes before Norah was able to coax Mum onto her feet. For Max, watching the two of them was like viewing some sort of grotesque sitcom. Only he wasn't simply observing it, he was part of it. He looked on with distaste, laced with pity and guilt as Norah helped Mum insert her dentures and listened as she listed the items she'd packed inside Mum's overnight case. He didn't want to hear that Mum now slept in incontinence pads. "But don't worry Max – she knows what to do." To Norah this was all, quite obviously, par for the course. Max thought of changing Ben on his plastic blue mat, holding both his feet in one of his hands, lifting up his backside, slipping in a nappy, bending to kiss him, breathing in his caramel smell. And despite himself – despite all the sickening guilt – he longed to be out of this house and back in his clean, bright London home.

Mum, walking ahead of him, holding onto Norah's arm and slowly progressing towards the kitchen door, stopped suddenly, looked up and said, apropos nothing at all,

"We used to walk to school."

"What's that love?" Norah turned to look at Mum. Their eyes were almost level. Max remembered how Mum used to tower over her stocky little neighbour.

"We used to go down the lane behind Fred Broxham's bakery and past the old pump," Mum said, the back of her head bobbing slightly. "Maxi loved the rock cakes. He picked all the currants out and ate them one by one."

Max realised that she was absolutely right: he'd used to pretend that the currants were ants. Now, as he picked up Mum's overnight case, he could almost taste the explosion of sweetness inside his mouth.

Outside, the sky was a dull yellow and the cul-de-sac was waking up. Lights had appeared in most of the front windows and somewhere a car door slammed. In the distance Max could hear the hum of traffic on the main road. Holding Mum's arm, he took her weight as she lowered herself gingerly into his car and was caught off guard by a faint whiff of the sweet, old-fashioned perfume that she'd used to wear. He shook his head as if shaking off the years, the decades, that were pulling him back. He needed to keep going. *To just keep going.*

"Bye-bye then love." Norah leaned in through Mum's open door.

Of course, thought Max, Norah must have sprayed it on Mum. Good old Norah. *Salt of the earth, that one.*

"Aren't you coming?" Mum frowned, confused again.

"I'm here Mum."

Mum didn't hear, she was turned towards Norah.

"No love, I'm not."

Max could see tears in Norah's eyes.

"You're with Maxi now, you're in safe hands." Norah looked at him over Mum's head. "Promise you'll let me know if there's anything I can do."

Max nodded, but he knew that Norah had done all that she could. He let out the clutch and depressed the accelerator. As his new Audi eased away from the kerb, he sensed again the unfamiliar lag of its engine.

Mum fell asleep almost as soon as they set off from Hillside Close. When Max glanced around at her curled beside him, her head lolling against the window, she looked not much than a bundle of bones. And strangely enough, for all the pain that he knew lay ahead, he was relieved to have her here next to him; it was where she belonged. Where she should have been months ago. She slept all the way and woke up, just as Ben always did, when the engine stopped. She wriggled around until she was sitting up straight and remained like that for several minutes, blinking and turning her head first one way, then the other.

"Where are we?"

"We're at my house." Max looked at his mum's powdery skin and her filmy eyes behind their thick lenses.

She didn't respond and the pair of them continued to sit in silence, staring through the windscreen at the rows of Victorian villas stretching down the road. It was relatively quiet, the early morning dash to the City long over, only a couple of stray yummy-mummies wheeling their buggies around the puddles. Max glanced at his watch: it was almost nine. He needed to get a move on: he had a conference call at 10.15.

As he and Mum shuffled, painfully slowly, like some sort of strange four-legged beast, through the wrought iron gate and up the short path, the front door opened. Eleanor stood there in her dressing gown, tangled hair falling over her face and Ben, swaddled in a pale blue blanket, clasped in her arms. Behind them stretched the newly painted hall, gleaming under its halogen spots.

"I'm sorry El, I got a call from Norah."

"Yes, yes – I saw your note when I got up to feed him." The skin around Eleanor's eyes was puffy and her voice was flat and tired, but she managed a smile. "Come on, in you come."

When his mum didn't move Max tried nudging her forward. But she remained planted to the spot, her head bent as if studying the pattern of terracotta tiles on the step.

"Go on Mum."

"Where's the doormat?" She said it without budging an inch.

"What's that Kate?" Eleanor stepped closer, pulling the blanket closer around Ben.

"The doormat." Mum looked up. "Every house has to have a doormat."

"Come on Mum, in we go."

"The floors get filthy otherwise – all that mud."

"You're absolutely right," said Eleanor. "We've been meaning to get one ever since we moved in, haven't we Max?"

Max pushed his mum over the threshold and followed her in.

"Where am I?" Mum turned to him, frowning.

"At my house Mum, remember I told you."

Max swung around to close the door but before he could get to it, a gust of wind slammed it shut. There was a moment's silence. Eleanor shifted the bundle in her arms. The blast of freezing air that had just been whipped into the hall quivered in anticipation. Max knew what was coming next. Mum was looking from side to side, confusion skimming her features. Eleanor muttered something into the blanket. But it was unstoppable and when it came Ben's wail ripped through the silence. There was a pause as he gathered his breath and then an outburst of sobs and a flurry of movement in Eleanor's arms as he kicked away his blanket.

Max edged his mum forward. "Come on Mum."

She didn't hear. She was watching Ben, her head cocked to one side. When he flailed his arm, she stretched out a hand and caught it in an instinctive movement. Quick, light, deft. And with a shocked, hiccupping gasp, Ben stopped crying and gazed at her with his huge, brimming eyes.

"There – no need to make all that fuss is there his little one." The lilting cadence of Mum's voice sent Max's head spinning. "That's better." Ben was laughing and pumping her hand in his as though he was pleased to meet her. "Horrible isn't it?" Mum said. "When you're woken up – you feel all discombobulated." Max leant against the wall as the long-forgotten word slithered and bumped and rattled out of Mum's mouth like a runaway train. "And that was such a big bang," she said. "Enough to make the bones jangle inside your skin." She stretched out her other hand and Ben lunged towards her. "He wants to come to me don't you?"

"Are you sure?" Eleanor sounded nervous.

"Of course I'm sure." Mum smiled at her grandson.

"Okay then," Eleanor said, "but remember to hold his head."

"I know that," Mum said sharply.

Eleanor clasped Ben to her. "What d'you think?" She looked at Max anxiously.

Unable to speak, he nodded mutely. He could see Mum's eyes shining.

As she took him in her arms, she said quite clearly, "There we are Peter."

Max's heart missed a beat.

"Peter ...?" Eleanor looked at him, frowning. "Who's Peter?"

Mum shifted the blanket around Ben's face. "Who's mummy's best boy?"

"Max – who's Peter? Is he a neighbour's child or something?" Eleanor laughed awkwardly.

"No, no ..." Mum paused and then, in a gesture that tilted Max's world, she chucked Ben under his chin. "He's Maxi's little brother, aren't you my darling."

"I can't believe you didn't tell me Max."

"There's nothing to tell."

"Nothing to tell? You've got a baby brother you haven't told me about and you say there's nothing to tell." Eleanor's voice was a mixture of incredulity and confusion. She was watching Max in the large oval mirror as he tied his tie, her head just behind his; from along the corridor Max could hear Ben's gurgling laugh and the low murmur of Mum's voice as she watched over him in his cot.

"Really El – leave it – I've got to get to work and I'm late as it is."

"But what did your mum mean?"

"Nothing – she didn't mean anything. She's a confused old woman, you know that." The silk slipped through his fingers. "Shit!"

"But she must have meant something."

143

Max fixed his gaze on the reflection of his dark blue tie, aware that Eleanor was watching him for the slightest twitch of a muscle.

"She must have Max."

"Just leave it El."

"What on earth's the matter? Why won't you tell me? Have you got a baby brother or not? Just tell me Max."

His eyes flicked to hers. "He went missing." The word hissed in his head and he pulled his tie apart and started again.

"Missing?"

"Leave it Eleanor, please."

"I'm not leaving it Max; it's important." She shifted slightly, edging closer to him so that he could smell her Vetiver scent and, just beneath it, that new faint sourness that she seemed to carry with her even when she wasn't holding Ben.

"It was a long time ago, ages ago. Now I've got to get on El – I'm late as it is."

"When? When did he go missing?"

"A long time ago."

"How long ago?"

"I was ten."

"Ten?" She turned and Max could feel the intensity of her eyes burning into his cheek. "My God Max, you were just a child."

"Old enough."

"But you were just a child," she repeated.

"Leave it." He'd been on the cusp. The very quivering cusp.

Without meaning to, Max met his own gaze in the mirror. A pair of frightened, haunted schoolboy's eyes stared back at him.

"But what happened? I mean … was …?" She trailed off. "I can't believe you haven't told me about this before. I just can't believe it."

"I haven't told anyone."

"No one?" Her voice was incredulous.

"No one," he said firmly, yanking his tie straight and pulling it tight.

"My God Max, that's extraordinary."

"Well it's true." As he said it he remembered as if it were yesterday, the moment he'd slid his hand in his pocket and found that the piece of folded white paper had gone.

"But he was your –"

"Shut up!" He swung around to face her; she gasped and took a step back. His hands were balled into fists at his side.

"I never talk about this El – never. And I never want you to bring it up again – or ask me about it. Do you understand?" He could see the shock in her eyes. "It's all in the past now. It's gone and I never want to talk about it. Do you understand Eleanor?"

He willed her to let it go – to let *him* go – and, after a few interminable seconds, she gave a slight, almost imperceptible nod, and he picked up his jacket and walked out of the room.

***

Around the back of the tree, next to the fence, is my secret place. I have to breathe in to squeeze around there. The boards of the fence rub against my clothes and I know that if I'm not careful, Mum will tell me off because I'll have rusty brown marks all over the back of my jumper. But if I bend my knees, just a bit, not too much, and inch around and then stretch my arm out at about shoulder height and feel with my fingers, careful not to get a splinter under my nail, then I can just about curl my fingertips into the secret place. There it is. It's a hole in the tree stump. The edge of it is thicker and smoother than the rest of the bark, like the lips around an open mouth. I inch along a bit more and reach into the hole until I can feel its mossy floor and waggle my fingers until they find what they're searching for and clasp themselves around it. I pull my arm back down to my side, inch out from behind the trunk until I'm back round on the lawn and I can see the flower bed that me and Dad dug. It's like a jungle now – all overgrown with giant stinging nettles. You can't see the cliff edge that me and Dad made with his spade; the cliff's fallen into the soil. I sink down onto the hard ground and cross my legs so that my knees stick out like a cricket's.

I found the hole last winter when my football disappeared behind the tree stump and I was scrabbling about in the earth trying to find it. I crawled in as far as I could go and then slithered on my tummy like a lizard, using my elbows to pull myself along. It was dark and damp behind there and thick with old leaves from the neighbour's tree. I must have been smaller then because once I'd squirmed in and found my ball behind the stump, I could stand up fairly easily. The front of my anorak was filthy from all the black, wet gunky stuff on the ground – but still, it didn't matter because level with my eyes, inches away from my face, was a hole in the trunk. It was such a surprise. And then, even more of a surprise, even better, inside it was this. My heart flutters as I uncurl my fingers and stare at my brightly coloured china gnome.

He isn't dirty at all, or chipped, and his painted-on colours are shiny and clean as new. It's the colours that make him so fantastic. Between the back of the trunk and the fence, under the neighbour's tree, it's very dark and gloomy. But the gnome's not gloomy at all. He's wearing a bright crimson jacket with black buttons, blue trousers and fancy black shoes, and he has a long, curling white beard. He's sitting cross-legged, just like I am now, only he's on a red toadstool with three white spots. As soon as I found him the questions started to race around in my head. How had he got there? Who had put him there? And when? And why? I'm still no closer to any answers, and that makes him even better.

I look at him now, and then I glance up quickly to make sure Peter's not coming out of the back door. I know he'll be coming soon. Mum's making him clean his teeth again because he didn't do it properly after breakfast. I haven't told Peter about my gnome. I don't want anyone else to know about him. But lately I've been thinking that it's not much fun with no one else knowing and no one else to talk to about him. Peter would be a good person to tell because he'll be so excited. I know exactly how he'll look if I tell him. His eyes will open wide and his eyebrows will disappear up under his fringe. He won't believe that I found him inside the tree stump. I know though that once I tell him, that's it. I can't untell him. So I need to think about this.

There he is – Peter – he's just come out of the house and he's standing on the back step. I can see him looking for me, his head turning from side to side. He doesn't spot me at first because I'm sitting under the branches of the neighbour's tree. And then he starts to run over; he's seen me. He's wearing my old blue duffel coat. Mum makes him wear it even though it's still far too big for him. It comes down below his knees so all I can see sticking out from beneath the blue are his socks and shoes. He looks like an animal with short, thin legs. An anteater – or an aardvark. I saw its picture in Norah's nature book and she told me. Aardvark. It's a brilliant word.

Peter's nearly here now and I decide, just as I begin to hear his short, fast breaths, that I *will* tell him.

"What's that Maxi?"

He's already seen that I'm holding something. I wish he hadn't asked me first. I wanted to be the one to mention it. I wanted to say, *"now then Peter, I've got something very important that I want to show you."* I wanted to see his blue eyes grow bigger. And then I'd say, *It's very important and it's a secret – do you understand that Peter? A secret.* I close my fingers tighter around the smooth china body of my gnome.

"Can I see?" He's closer now, peering down at my hands in my lap. "What is it? Show me."

I want to show him, but he's spoilt it by asking. "It's my secret."

"What is it?"

He crouches down so that my old blue duffel coat scrapes on the ground around him like a skirt.

"Let me see." He holds out his hand and, with one of his stubby fingers, he tries to pull my fingers off my gnome.

"Stop it!" I jump up and my knee catches him and he topples over.

"Ow!" He starts to cry. He lies on his side and pulls his knees up. I can see that he hasn't really hurt himself. He's pretending to cry – sniffing and coughing – because he wants to see what I've got. I can see his eyes darting across to my hand even while he's pretending to rub them with the back of his fist.

"Don't be such a cry baby."

He sits up. "I'm not a cry baby!"

"Yes you are. *Cry baby bunting, daddy's gone a hunting.*" I sing the words as I look down at him.

He's almost crying properly now. He's revved himself up, as Dad used to say. *All revved up with nowhere to go.* There's snot running out of his nose. This isn't how it was meant to be. Peter's spoilt it all as usual. I start walking away from him towards Dad's old shed. Weeds with small purple flowers have grown up tall around it. I can tell that Peter's got up and is following me. I can hear him sniffing behind me – and I like him following me, it makes me feel more important. I turn my head. He's stopped crying – he wasn't ever really crying – and he's having to walk very fast to keep up with me. His legs are moving quickly beneath his coat.

"You look like an aardvark!" I shout back at him.

"What's an aardvark?"

That's more like it. "It's a strange, mystical creature from long, long ago." I'm pleased with myself for remembering those words from the book that Miss Dodson's been reading to us at school.

Peter's caught up with me now. He looks up at my face and then down at my right hand. I stuff my gnome into my pocket.

"Can I see what you've got?"

"No."

"Please Max."

His snot's left a white snail track under his nose and his eyes are still shiny from where he's been crying.

"I might," I say, tipping my head in that way that Dad used to do when he was talking to me.

"Pleeeease." He steps closer. His eyes are fixed on my pocket as I shove my hand in and fold it round my gnome.

"Remember you're not to tell anyone," I say.

He nods, glancing up at me. "I won't, promise."

"Cross your heart?"

"Cross my heart." He makes the sign in front of his chest that I've taught him.

I suddenly remember something that Ian told me at school. "You can only see it if you do a forfeit."

"What's a forfeit?"

149

"It's something you have to do if you want to see my secret."

"Like what?" He's frowning now and looking a bit nervous, which is just how I want him to look.

"Like –" I pause, trying to think. I spot my trapeze hanging from its branch at the top of the garden. "Like swinging upside down from my trapeze."

His eyes twitch over to it and back to me. "But I can't reach it."

It's true. Even though he's four now he still can't even reach it. Which, of course, I knew.

"I'll lift you up."

He bites his lip.

"It's easy – go on Peter – you want to know my secret don't you?"

"Ye-es."

He's still looking very unsure.

"And you don't want to be a baby do you?"

He shakes his head.

"Well then." I start walking up the lawn and stop by the trapeze. It's almost too small for me now. Mum's shortened the ropes several times and I have to be careful when I swing myself round so that I don't bash my head on the hard ground where I've worn all the grass away with my feet.

I turn round. Peter's still quite a way away.

"Come on." I say. He doesn't move for a moment. "Come on – come and stand in front of me and I'll lift you up."

He walks towards me on his short Aardvark legs and stops in front of me.

"That's it." I grasp him under his armpits and haul him a couple of inches off the ground. He's much heavier than I expected and it's very difficult. His face is in my face, his mouth is open and he's stretching his arms up above his head, but he still can't reach the wooden bar. I make an enormous effort and raise him another inch. His fingers curl around the bar. I can see that they're hardly closing around it but he's too heavy in my arms and I have to let go. As soon as I do, he drops like a stone and falls to the ground. I hold my breath sure that he's going to wail and Mum will come rushing out of the back door and tell me off. But Peter doesn't cry – even though there was a loud thud as he hit the ground. He's rolled over and scrabbled back up onto his feet.

"Can I try again? I almost did it." He's frowning and his two front teeth sit on his lower lip.

"Okay." I hold out my arms and he walks over and stands in front of me again. "Try facing away from me this time."

He does as I've told him and I thrust my hands under his armpits and lift him up. His fingers close around the bar.

"Good boy," I say without thinking. I take my arms away. He hangs for a second. The skin of his knuckles is white. The back of his coat is pulled right up over his neck. "Now – swing back a bit and then swing forward and pull yourself up."

He doesn't reply and I know that it's taking every breath in his body for him to cling on and I'm willing him to do it. I stretch my hand out and pull his duffel coat very gently towards me to help him. It's too much. The wooden bar slips through his fingers and he loses his grip and falls back into me sending us both crashing onto the ground. It's very hard and cold and he lands on top of me, all sticking-out elbows and feet. His head bashes me under my chin. I roll out from under him and stand up. He's got to his feet and he's looking up at me.

"Are you okay Max?"

"Yeh – yeh – I'm fine." I'm still thinking about the way his fingers clung onto the bar and I'm amazed that he's asked me if I'm okay. "You tried really hard Peter." A warm glow is spreading through my chest and melting all the aches and pains away.

"Sorry I fell on top of you." He's watching me closely. He's really worried that he's hurt me. I can see that.

"Doesn't matter." He hasn't done his forfeit but I decide to show him my secret anyway. My hand goes to my pocket and it's only then that I discover that my precious gnome's been smashed to pieces.

Obliterated, I think, as I blink back my tears. O-blit-er-ated. It's a horrible, horrible word.

***

For the first few days after Max's outburst, Eleanor trod warily. He caught her glancing at him once or twice when she thought he wasn't looking, but in that quiet, canny way of hers she seemed to know not to push it, not to say any more, for which he offered silent thanks.

He immersed himself in his work, leaving home early and arriving back when he knew that his mum would be in bed. It helped that the Britannic-Gazprov negotiations were at a critical point; he had a readymade excuse to be out of the house. Even when he'd finished work he didn't go straight home; he went to the gym and swam a hundred lengths in the echoing, empty place. When his rhythmic breaths and the repetitive pumping of his legs failed to stop his whirring thoughts, he swam some more, then hauled himself up the metal steps.

At the weekend, when he had nowhere to escape to, when he saw Mum with Ben and watched how she was with him, it was like undergoing an exquisite form of torture. Max stood on the landing outside Ben's room and listened to Mum singing to him in her quavery voice. The sound traced long forgotten grooves in his mind, like a needle on vinyl. The bright red 45' vinyl of his first ever record. It was *Three Blind Mice*. Peter played it after Max had grown out of it; he sang it in his high-pitched voice, getting faster and faster until eventually the words tangled into laughter that tumbled out of his mouth. Max listened until he couldn't bear it any longer and then retreated to his study, where he sat, staring out of the window at the branches of the neighbour's weeping willow skimming the grass, his papers scattered unread on his desk. Along the corridor came the faint, lilting cadences of Mum's voice. Ripples of sound, rocking gently, like pebbles shifting on the bed of a stream.

Almost a year after it happened, Mum signed Max up for a course of counselling. He went every Thursday after school. He walked up the high street, past Woolworths and the cream building next to Sainsbury's. He turned left into the cobbled passageway and up to the end to the thin, crooked house with its white walls and thick black beams. There was a gold button next to the door and a smart black and gold name plaque that said: *Dr Patricia Mills*. Mum always met him there, but she didn't come in with him; she sat in the waiting room with its table covered in old magazines. Max refused to speak to Dr Mills. He looked down at his ink-stained fingers and smelt the scent of the blossoms outside the open window and tasted the dry sourness of his mouth.

"Think of your memories of your brother like pebbles on a shelf," Dr Mills urged. "You can take them down and roll them around in your hand and your head, then put them back away again. You mustn't be afraid of them."

Max couldn't remember anything else she said, though she must have said quite a bit because he didn't say a word. He went for a few weeks until Mum said she thought it was time to call it a day. The drooping white blossoms had turned brown and dropped off the branches but Max never forgot their sickly sweet smell. As the two of them walked away from the last visit, he asked his mum what the tree was at the back of the building.

"It's a lilac love." She'd turned to look at him, her eyes shattered and bleak behind the NHS glasses she'd started to wear. "Are you sure you're okay Maxi?"

He nodded, his gaze fixed on his scuffed black school shoes, fighting back the tears that had sprung from nowhere. He heard his mum give a massive sigh that seemed to come from somewhere deep down inside her.

"We've just got to keep going Maxi – you and I – for each other now. Just keep going." She sounded so very, very tired.

And Max realised that from then on it would just be the two of them. Him and Mum. Each with silent demons that they couldn't speak, in a world that kept revolving when they wanted it to stop.

Max knew what he had to do – he'd known even before he'd received Norah's early morning call – but he couldn't find the strength to do it. So he buried himself in his work and tried to soldier on.

One night he arrived home late as usual, to find the house wrapped in darkness. He shut the front door carefully and trod softly up the unlit hall, switching on the light when he reached the kitchen, then opening the cupboard and pulling out a half-full bottle of whisky. He drank it neat, sitting at the table, staring into space, feeling its warmth steal through him. He couldn't betray Mum with a call – even an anonymous call – to Social Services. Finding the name of a nursing home, or asking Janis to, was treachery. Somewhere outside a dog barked. A loud, rough noise that shattered the peace. And then, like a faint, nagging itch, Max became aware of something else. Not even a noise, but something different about the shifts and creaks of the sleeping house. Someone was moving about. He pushed his chair back and walked out into the dark hall. Above him, on the shadowy landing, a figure was bending over and peering around. After a second or two, as his eyes adjusted, he realised it was Mum, her long white nightie rustling as she moved. He strode up the stairs quickly, quietly, two at a time.

"Mum," he whispered, "what on earth are you doing?"

"Charlie Rabbit – I know we had him out here. I know we did."

Whisky rose queasily in Max's throat. Charlie Rabbit. He could see him now, dangling from Peter's hand by an ear held on with no more than a thread. He'd been like a part of him. He went everywhere with him. He smelt of him. When the police took the rabbit away for forensic tests it was as if they'd taken Peter's shadow with them. Now, as Max stood and watched Mum looking about her, her glasses glinting in the darkness, she seemed more awake, more alive, than he'd seen her in months.

"Come on now." He took her arm and she reluctantly let him steer her along the landing. The boards creaked under their feet.

"He can't sleep without him, you know he can't Maxi."

Max stopped, his hand clasping her thin wrist through the cotton of her sleeve. *Don't do this to me Mum.*

"Now don't make a fuss Maxi." Mum turned and looked at him, just as she'd always done, that hint of reproach in her voice. "There's a good boy."

"Don't call me that!"

"Maxi …" Her eyes widened in shock. And there, just behind the shock, he saw the quiver of confusion.

"Sorry Mum – sorry."

As firmly as he could, he inched her into the guest bedroom. Combined with the oily, freshly painted smell was the sweet, old-fashioned scent of Mum's talc and her Pond's cold cream. When she sat on the side of the bed her body

155

sagged like a ragdoll's and she slumped forward, the glow from the bedside lamp catching her white curls of hair. She didn't move; she seemed to be waiting for something. When she looked up Max realised she was waiting for him. He crouched down in front of her.

"Are you okay Mum? Would you like me to help you get into bed?"

"Rounds of tomato sandwiches, d'you remember Maxi?" Her watery eyes stared straight through him.

"What's that Mum?"

"He loved them … it was our little joke. I'd cut the bread into circles and he nibbled them like a hamster. He used his two hands like paws and watched what was going on over the top."

My God. Max took a deep breath. Mum's words wobbled and rocked in his head. That was exactly how he'd eaten his sandwiches. Max saw small pink fingers curled around soft circles of bread, a blond head bent over. His gut tightened.

"Mum –"

Her eyes were still locked onto his. Max sat perfectly still as she continued to speak.

"He'd been ill; flu or some sort of virus that doctor said. And he was still very pale. So pale he was, with that white hair of his – white and soft as blossom – and I almost kept him out of school that day."

Her irises flickered and Max reached out and covered her hand with his, rocking slightly on the balls of his feet, trying to take in what she was saying.

"I almost kept him home," she repeated slowly. "We were in the kitchen, having breakfast and I was saying something – I can't remember what – but I can see his face. All drained and colourless it was and I thought that perhaps he should stay home another day. But I'd already arranged to go into work and I knew Norah was busy …" Her voice was straining, becoming tauter. "Can you believe that Maxi?" Her eyes screwed shut and when she opened them again, they glistened moistly. "Can you believe that?" she repeated.

"Oh Mum …" His words came out in a hoarse croak. He hadn't known. She'd cradled her knowledge to her like a baby. "Mum …" He mouthed the word. Her head dipped onto her chest. He carried on holding her hand until he realised that she'd fallen asleep, her jaw slackening, her bottom lip hanging open in a silent cry.

Max stood up, stiff from crouching, and hoisted up his mum's bony legs, feeling the dry, scaly skin beneath his fingers and then pulling up the duvet. Tucking her in. He wasn't aware of how long he stood over her, watching her sleep, letting his thoughts slide back to that day, remembering the shapes of their shadows on the pavement as he and Peter waited at the bus stop in the early morning heat. He could see the small, brown scab on his brother's nose where he'd toppled over the week before, his head of thick blond hair bobbing about a few rows in front as the two of them sat on the bus, and his knuckles curled around the metal rail as he swung himself off.

When, finally, Max tiptoed out of his mum's room, he closed her door behind him and leant back on it, his whole body trembling at the thought of losing her, the whisky warmth of his tears stealing down his cheeks.

Janis put Eleanor's call through late morning when Max was immersed in some complicated clauses, his eyes fixed on his PC screen.

Her high-pitched babble was barely recognisable. "Max – it's Ben – he's gone – when I went to look at him sleeping in the hall he'd gone –"

"Slow down Eleanor." Max tried to keep his voice even as a tight fist closed around his chest.

"He'd been for his nap – you know – like he sometimes does when he's in his pram. I'd had a letter to post – and then I was going to give him a feed – and so –"

"Stop – wait – you're making no sense. Why was he in his pram?"

I heard an intake of breath, imagined her standing by the window in the kitchen, trying to gather herself.

"I'd taken him for a walk with me down to the letter box – and he fell asleep – so I left him in his pram and went up to bed for a nap. He was quite safe, Max, in the hall." Her voice had slowed, but it was still shaky.

"But the front door was shut. No one could have got in?"

"Oh – no – no Max – your mum's taken him – she's gone – and so's the pram. She's taken him."

"Mum?" Cold fingers ran up his spine.

"Yes – yes – your mum's taken him. I don't know where – I don't know when she went. And he's sure to need a feed."

All Max could see was the blind, haunted look in Mum's eyes as she told him about Peter.

"But his cot's still warm Max – I can still smell him in his cot. Still see where his little body was – oh my God Max – what should I do? I don't know what to do." Eleanor's voice rose to a crescendo.

"Let's think Eleanor. She won't have gone far, will she? Not if the cot's still warm. When did you go for your nap?"

"Half an hour ago, forty minutes maybe."

"And have you looked outside the gate, to see if they're somewhere in the street?"

"Of course I have – there's no sign of them. I didn't know whether to get dressed and go out, but then they might come back."

Max thought of Mum pushing Ben along; he smelt the diesel and petrol fumes, heard the cars hurtling past, rocking the pram as Mum's foot stepped off the pavement. He fixed his eyes on the flashing black cursor on his PC screen.

"Stay calm Eleanor – it'll be fine. She'll just have taken him for a walk." He hoped that Eleanor couldn't hear the quiver in his voice.

"D'you think I should call the police Max?"

"The police? No – no."

That first golden hour is crucial. He could still hear DI Gould's voice, see the way his moustache moved above his lip as he spoke. But they weren't talking about the golden hour. This wasn't like then.

"But she's so confused. Oh my God, my little boy. I wish you were here Max."

Through her fear he could feel the soft touch of her need. "Don't worry El."

"Wait!"

He heard a clatter, feet running, the door bell ringing, the rattle and click of the door.

"Ben!" Eleanor's voice. Hers again, as warm and smooth as honey.

Max let out a sigh of relief. The cursor flashed in front of him. Pulsing. Beating. Life going on. In his ear he could hear Eleanor sobbing with joy. He pictured her scooping Ben out of the pram, breathing in his buttery smell, letting his weight settle against her. He wanted to be there. Then faint and in the background but oh so clear came the sound of Mum's voice. The familiar rhythms, the rise and fall, the ripples of mindless chatter.

Max replaced the receiver and sat, watching through the glass wall of his office as Janis tapped away on her computer, her fingers moving quickly over the keys. His heart was slowing now, his breathing returning to normal. He hadn't expected that.

He watched Janis stretch her arms above her head, stand up, smooth down her skirt and walk over to the water cooler. That afternoon he asked her to find him the three best nursing homes in Surrey and leave a briefing note on his desk by the end of the day: fees, numbers, locations, inspection reports. She didn't bat an eyelid. And her piece of A4 was ready for him three hours later.

That night, Eleanor reached out an invisible hand in the darkness of their moon-white room and stroked his cheek. And her touch, that renewed sense of her need for him, moved him and aroused him because for the first time since she'd given birth she wanted him. He was frightened of hurting her, wary of her newly opened body and her hard, swollen breasts, but she whispered to him not to be frightened, or wary, or gentle. When he entered her, she gave a small, involuntary gasp and he stopped still, hardly daring to breathe.

"Go on –" Her voice whispered in his ear and he felt her fingers digging into his back. As they moved together he could feel the soft new folds of her flesh and when she sucked in her breath to try and hide them from him, he kissed her mouth with a smile on his lips and told her he loved her.

***

The irony wasn't lost on Dick. That, having vowed not to move when Elizabeth had seemed to be wanting it, with her gone (or on her way, at least) he was now preparing to do so. The truth was that after being so unexpectedly ambushed by his grief for Dora, he realised that their daughter had been right all along. The onrush of emotion had been cathartic; he knew now that he needed to move on. His darling Dora would want him to. He could imagine her letting him know in her clever, subtle, womanly way – a way that Elizabeth would never have. She'd make sure that she found some positive options before casually mentioning them. No pressure mind. No suggestion that she might be thinking of selling the bungalow. Just a well-placed word here, an estate agent's brochure left lying in a not too conspicuous but highly strategic position where he'd be bound to see it. She'd have made sure, in her wifely fashion, that Dick came up with the suggestion himself. "What a good idea love," she'd have said, and only the infinitesimal twitch of her eyebrows would have given her away. Even then you'd have to have known her for close on fifty years to be able to read the signs.

So, even in death, Dora managed to tell him what to do. She'd spoken to him, obliquely, through the daughter Dick was more convinced than ever he hardly knew. The strangeness of life; the interwoven links of it. He mused on this as he Googled 'small flats in and around Ringwood'. Two bedrooms were all he needed. There was no rush. He had all the time in the world to find what he wanted; looking for somewhere convenient, suitable and safe to live out his final chapter was much healthier than dwelling in the past. When the weather brightened up and the buds began to unfurl in the garden, when the old place was looking its best, he'd put it on the market. He'd turf out the piles of yellowing newsprint that were taking him round and round in circles, leading – if he was to be brutally honest – absolutely nowhere. He could imagine Dora smiling down on him as he loaded up the car and took them all down to the local tip for recycling. It was definitely the right thing to do.

But then, as Dick's work had shown him again and again, life was never that straightforward. Just as you thought that you'd got it all mapped out, fate intervened and sent you swerving off course. It had a knack of doing that. He used to talk about it with Dora. Long before she was diagnosed with cancer, he'd come home from a grim day's work dealing with the dregs of society, the mindless thug who pulled a knife because someone looked at him the wrong way or said the wrong thing, and marvel at how humans could be brought so low. Dora, her back towards him at the sink, would pause for a moment and tip her head – he could see her now, her bobbed hair brushing her shoulders – and tell him of her theory about The Book in which was written everyone's life. Good or bad, young or old, we were all treading a well-laid path.

Dick had never been so sure. He took a Blakeian view of the world. Humans had free will. And with free will came choice: the choice to do wrong or right, to work hard or scrounge off the state, to sin or not to sin, to steal or not to steal, to murder or not to murder. Only when the final diagnosis came through, when the consultant looked up into Dora's eyes and held them for a second or two before saying, remarkably calmly despite his young age – and Dick had been grateful to him for that small mercy – "I'm afraid the news isn't very good Mrs Gould." Only then, or in the next few days as the meaning of the consultant's words truly hit home, did Dick really start to believe in The Book. Knowing that there was nothing that he or Dora or any of the medics or their stockpile of chemical weapons could do to save his wife's life, Dick was forced to concede that she might have a point. Some things were written. Inevitable. Terminal. The rigour of the words took away choice; the only option left to them both was how to react. Dora, bless her, showed him the way. She humbled and inspired him in equal measure. She never moaned, not even quietly into her pillow. She never raged against the dying of the light, the unfairness of it all, as he did, inwardly, every day.

And now here it was again – the moving hand of fate writing the script, beyond his control. The phone rang just as his internet search led him to something quite hopeful on the outskirts of Burley. His eyes took in the well-positioned first floor apartment in its 'sought after retirement complex' – the phrase made him shudder – as he stretched out his hand to pick up the receiver. It was Elizabeth. It seemed they weren't, after all, jetting away to Canada. Something to do with Simon's share options; Elizabeth didn't sound entirely sure and Dick wasn't even that interested. All he knew was that things had changed, yet again. Or had they? He pondered this as he replaced the handset and stared at the first floor apartment laid out before him on his computer screen. Even the carefully positioned, wide-angled lens of the agent's photographer couldn't hide its pokiness. And was he really ready to give up his garden? Had he been stirred into action because he'd been worried – frightened even – of remaining in the bungalow with little Lizzie gone?

***

"I've got another forfeit for you Peter."

His blue eyes watch me gravely. He nods.

"You've got to crawl behind the old tree stump and find the secret message that I've left in the special hiding place. The message –" I stop for a moment or two and Peter's mouth opens a crack as he watches me – "is written in code."

"Code?" His eyes widen. "What sort of a code?"

"Well, you'll have to see won't you – when you find it. If you find it," I correct myself.

Before I can say anything else he drops his rabbit, turns and runs across the lawn to the stump by the fence. The sky stretches above him like a high grey ceiling. He's still got his school shorts on and I know he's going to get them filthy and Mum will go mad. I'm about to shout out after him but then I stop. He's not a baby any more. He knows not to get his school shorts dirty. Instead I walk after him, my hands in my pockets, just like our music teacher Mr Jenks. I try to whistle through my teeth like Mr Jenks does but no sound comes out.

163

By the time I get to the stump Peter's disappeared behind it. I can hear him breathing heavily and the rustling sounds as he crawls into the gap.

"Have you found the special place yet?"

No answer. Over on the other side of the lawn, by Dad's and my flower bed where giant green weeds look over the fence to the neighbour's garden, a robin's landed on a patch of grass. He's got a worm. I can see it dangling from his beak, wriggling about. The robin tips back his head and it's gone. Gone! Juzlikethat! I remember how Dad used to say it and stick his hands out in front of him. *Juzlikethat!*

"Found it!"

Peter's voice is high and it quivers with excitement. Quivers. What a good word. It does just what it says.

"And the piece of paper!"

"Don't look at it yet!"

"Okay."

I know he won't dare to stay behind the stump for too long. He gets scared around there in that dark, damp, smelly place. That's why it was such a good dare. He doesn't want to go there but he wants to do my forfeit. He can't NOT do my forfeit. It's brilliant. He's caught between wanting and not wanting.

There are more rustling noises and then Peter appears from behind the trunk. First the muddy soles of his shoes, then his short white socks, his freckled legs – which are the *exact* colour of the eggs that Mum keeps in the larder – his backside in his grey shorts, his white shirt, his mussed up hair. He stands up and turns around. His white shirt is covered in gunky mud, and so are his school shorts. Mum's going to go ballistic.

"Look!" He holds out the piece of paper I stuffed into the hole yesterday. His eyes are shining.

"Open it then."

His short fingers fumble with the sheet. It seems to take forever and then he unfolds it once, and then again, and stares at it.

"But there's nothing on it." He looks so confused when he lifts his eyes from the paper that I almost laugh.

"Oh yes there is. Remember what I said – it's in code."

He turns the paper over and stares at the other side. He's frowning so hard that his eyebrows meet at the top of his nose in a perfect V. "But there's nothing on it!"

"It's written in invisible ink."

"What?"

And now he looks so astonished that I do laugh. I laugh out loud and bend over, holding my stomach as if I've just been told the funniest joke. "Hah-hah-hah! You should see your face!"

He frowns again and holds the paper away from him, sticking his arm out and twisting his head, trying to see.

"You can't read it like that you dope – you've got to heat it."

"Heat it?" His eyes widen.

"Yep."

This is going exactly to plan. Last week there was a whole page in my *Look and Learn* comic about invisible writing – how to make it (which I already knew) AND how to make it reappear. Soon as I saw it I ran into my bedroom and pulled my box of football cards out from under my bed. I tipped them all onto the carpet. For a moment I thought that the feather wasn't there, but it was. It was clinging to the cardboard. My precious, precious quill.

"But how can I do that?"

"We're going to iron it," I say, slotting my thumbs through my belt and swaying back on my heels.

Peter's eyes widen again. "Really?"

"Yup."

"But what will Mum say?"

"Mum won't know."

He stares at me, his eyes are full of hundreds of questions. So many he doesn't know where to start.

"But when?" he says finally.

"Tomorrow morning when she's in the bathroom."

He's still looking at me and still holding the piece of paper in both his hands as if it's something very special.

"Give me the paper," I say, and he hands it over straight away. I know I've got him right where I want him.

"Boys!" It's Mum, calling us in from the kitchen door. "Teatime!"

I hold my finger up to my lips. "Not a word to anyone, remember Peter."

He nods seriously. As his head moves up and down his thick blond hair seems to stay still, like a wig.

Next morning, when Mum's in the bathroom, singing *Who's Afraid of the Drunken Sailor*, I take the iron and the ironing board from the cupboard under the stairs and plug the iron in the socket on the kitchen wall. It takes me several minutes to work out how to put the board up and I almost begin to panic; I know Mum never takes long about anything in the mornings. Peter's watching me anxiously, bobbing about from foot to foot. The board's heavier than I expected with far more parts to it than could ever seem possible. Eventually, just as I think I might have to give up, it snaps into place.

I take the paper from my pocket and give it to Peter. "Here you go!"

"Am I going to do it?" He can't believe it. His whole face seems to have jumped up in surprise. His eyes and his eyebrows, his fringe, his ears, and now the corners of his mouth as he takes in what it means. "Really?"

"Yep – course you are. I know what it says already stupid."

I pick up the iron and spit on it like I've seen Mum do. My spit sizzles even though I've turned the button to low. For one, quick moment I wonder if this is such a good idea. Then I remember what my *Look and Learn* said.

I grab the tea towel from the oven rail and place it over the blank piece of paper that Peter's laid out on the ironing board. "There you go." Peter steps forward. His head is only just about level with the faded stripes of the ironing board cover. I drag over a chair. "Stand on that."

He looks at me and then at the white painted chair with its bright blue seat, and then he carefully climbs up onto it, holding onto its curved wooden back, and turns around to face the ironing board. I take a step forward and, without him seeing, place my hand on the back of the chair to steady it.

I'm dying to iron the paper but I know that I've got to let him do it. That's the whole point. To see him do it.

"Go on."

He starts to turn to look at me but then wobbles and stops and turns back away again. The skin on the backs of his knees is very white.

"Go on." I repeat. "Pick up the iron and iron the tea-towel."

His hand reaches out towards the iron. It's almost too small to clasp the handle but he manages it, just, and picks it up and moves backwards and forwards over Mum's flowery Co-op tea towel. I'm listening out for the sound of the bathroom door opening. I reckon we've only got a minute or two left.

"That should be enough," I say. I take the iron out of his hand and place it on its end on the metal tray. "Now lift up the tea towel."

Peter shifts his feet on the chair. I can sense his excitement. And there's a knot in my stomach. I will it to work. He slowly pulls back the tea towel.

"Wow!"

We both stare at the paper and at the words that I wrote there yesterday. They don't look how I imagined them. They're not straight and perfect as I thought they'd be. They're wobbly and they slant away down the page. But they're there and that's what counts.

TRESURE HUNT

FIRST CLUE

NORAHS FISHY FREIND'S

"What do they say?" His voice is as shaky as the letters. I'm just about to tell him when I hear the flush of the loo chain upstairs.

"Mum's coming!" I reach over and unplug the iron and put it on the kitchen counter. "Get off the chair – quickly Peter –" He jumps down. "Get out the way –" I push him aside and shove the tea-towel and the piece of paper at him. "Here – take this." I try to make the ironing board collapse. I can't. It's stuck. I don't know how to do it. I can hear Mum's feet coming down the stairs. "Put the paper in your pocket Peter." It's only then that I look at him properly and actually see him. In that moment I know that no matter what punishment Mum gives me for using the iron it will have been worth it. Peter's eyes are fixed on me. I can see that he thinks I've just performed a magic trick. *That I'm magic.* With his eyes still glued to me he pushes the paper into his pocket just as Mum walks through the door.

"What on earth's been going on here?" She looks from me to the ironing board, then to the iron, upright on the counter, and then to Peter and back to me. "Max – what have you been doing?"

"I thought I'd iron your tea towel Mum."

"I beg your pardon."

She's screwing up her eyes and watching me closely.

"I thought I'd iron your tea towel," I say again, and I see her eyes dart quickly up to the clock on the wall. I know she's in a hurry. We've got to get to school and she's off to work.

"We'll talk about this tonight," she says. She walks over and snaps shut the ironing board. *Juzlikethat!* She makes it look so easy.

"Honestly Mum," I say, "I was only trying to help."

She looks at me sideways and I know she doesn't believe me for a minute. Not for one i-o-t-a. But right then, I just don't care.

***

Mrs Minns, plump, middle-aged, with heavy, rimmed glasses and over-lipsticked lips, waved her arm proudly in front of her.

"And this is the day room."

Max followed her gaze. A dozen or so old people were sitting in a horseshoe staring at a TV whose volume was turned down low, most of them slouched drunkenly in their upright armchairs. He noticed there was only one man among them, who kept calling out for a nurse.

Mrs Minns shouted across. "I'll be with you in a moment Jack – just showing someone round."

The old man barely paused before crying out again in a high, cracked voice, "Nuuuu-uu-rse –!"

It was hot and stuffy and Max kept his breaths shallow, not wanting to inhale the sweet smell of room freshener mixed with something else that he couldn't identify. He couldn't think of a single, appropriate thing to say. Not one word.

"What a lovely room." Eleanor smiled at Mrs Minns over the top of Ben's head as he squirmed in her arms. "So cosy – and tell me, what other activities are there?"

A warm wave of gratitude flooded over Max. He could never have done this without Eleanor.

Holly Lodge had been the first of the names on Janis's list. It was a square red-brick building at the foot of the South Downs, with small, thin windows tucked under its eaves like watchful eyes. Max had learned, from Janis's comprehensive briefing note, that its residents were served food cooked on the premises, it had four qualified nurses and eight carers, a large garden and 24 rooms, 12 shared and 12 single, two of which were available. It had never even crossed his mind that residents might have to share rooms. Mum, of course, would never, ever do that. But his conscience nagged at him. What had it come to when a single room of her own was the best Mum could hope for? He thought of her left behind in Wandsworth, blissfully unaware of what was to come, being 'babysat' by Aneta the Polish cleaner. Mrs Minns was droning on about flower arranging, keep-fit and sing-a-longs, none of which, Max knew, his mum would ever take part in. If, that was, she ever came to live here. Sweat prickled at the back of his neck.

"And we have a carol service the week before Christmas." Mrs Minns swung around. He could see her crimson lipstick bleeding into the fine lines around her mouth. He resisted the temptation to tell her that his mum hated Christmas.

"That sounds wonderful." Eleanor kissed the top of Ben's head absentmindedly as she nodded. The overhead light glanced off her cheek and Max thought how incongruous she looked among the slumped and misshapen bodies. He remembered the shock in her eyes when he'd told her that he'd arranged this visit. *Are you sure Max – so soon I mean?* Oh yes, he'd been sure. He'd been forced – pushed – propelled – into taking action by Mum disappearing with Ben. Now, confronted with the hard reality of it, he wasn't so sure.

"Shall we go and look at a room?" Beads of perspiration glistened on Mrs Minns' downy upper lip.

Eleanor nodded. "That would be great – you lead the way and we'll follow." She glanced towards Max, who pulled his mobile out of his pocket and pretended to study it.

"I just have to make a quick call." He looked up. "You go on – I'll join you in a minute."

Max could feel Eleanor's eyes on him as he walked past her and Mrs Minns, his footsteps crackling on the nylon carpet. The narrow hall with its rows of cheap prints and gaudy photographs smelt of boiled cabbage and furniture polish. A stale, nostalgic mixture that whisked him back to school. He quickened his pace, crossed the cramped lobby and pulled on the brass handle of the front door. It rattled but wouldn't budge. A tingle ran up his spine: they were locked in.

"Can I help you?" A small Asian girl in a white nurse's uniform appeared from one of the rooms.

"I just need to get out."

She punched a code into a pad beside the door.

"Thank you."

"You're welcome." She smiled shyly. Discoloured teeth marred an otherwise pretty face. The name badge on her lapel said 'Sumi'. Max tried to imagine this diminutive girl helping his mum up from her chair, tucking her arm solicitously under Mum's as she helped her along. He turned quickly away.

Outside it was still misty and refreshingly cold. His feet crunched across the gravel and out of the black, wrought-iron gates. He had no idea where he was going. A tall, dense holly hedge soon hid the home from view and the phrase, 'Out of sight, out of mind' sprang into his head. Drizzle started to moisten his face, fine raindrops catching on his eyelashes. He blinked them away and licked his lips. It was tempting to keep walking, on and on up the narrow lane, beyond the distant bend, letting the rhythm of his strides carry him along, but he knew he couldn't be gone for too long so after a few minutes he stopped, rested his hands on a wooden gate and looked out over a large ploughed field. On its far side was a coppice of oaks and rising beyond it were the bare wintry slopes of the Surrey Downs. There wasn't another house in sight. Rooks wheeled and cawed, their sound primitive, scratchy and raw.

Standing still, he grew very cold. Max's fingers, clasped around the top strut of the gate, were pink and swollen, and what he craved, more than anything, was a cigarette. He imagined it – conjured it up as he stood, his breath steaming like smoke. Freezing air cut the back of his throat.

Mum wasn't Mum anymore; he knew that. The kernel of her was still there, visible in rare glimpses – the way she buttered her toast in that particular way, right up to the corners, the way she tilted her head, the way she held the palm of her hand to her prim rows of curls. But the movements were no more than traces of Mum, a shadowy, elusive version of her that came and went, just within reach, never quite there. A woman behind a veil that twists and blows in the wind, revealing a smile here, a look, a touch. He saw again, clear as crystal, her quick, instinctive movement as they all crowded together in the hall. Ben flailing his arm and Mum moving to catch it; the breeze blowing and lifting the veil, his heart turning over.

He gripped the gate until his knuckles ached. There was the real danger. The damp, sticky fear in his armpits. The unspoken reason Mum couldn't stay. Yes, she was old, and untidy, and slowly – and not so slowly – becoming more and more unpredictable. She dropped things and burnt things. She waltzed off with Ben without so much as a by-your-leave and worried them sick. But she brought him back safely. She would never hurt her best boy; Max knew that better than anyone. He remembered the terrible, unfathomable guilt in Mum's stagnant eyes when she told him that she'd wanted to keep Peter at home on that fateful day. *Can you believe that Maxi?* Of course he could. He knew all about those terrible, black-winged 'what-ifs' that flew straight into you when you weren't looking. And now, coward that he was, he was letting Eleanor believe that she, and her fear for Ben, lay behind his sudden decision to put Mum in a nursing home. *To betray Mum.* Max felt sick to the pit of his stomach. He wrenched his hands from the gate and clenched and unclenched them; they were almost too stiff to move. His shoulder blades were locked into a painful knot. He had a sense, too, that somehow Eleanor knew what he was doing, and because of who she was – and how strong she still was in so many ways – she was helping him to do it. Right now, up there in Gormenghast Castle, she was doing what he wasn't brave enough to do.

Somewhere far off, a toy tractor crawled over another field, the low rumble of its engine carrying clearly on the still air. Max remembered the words of what had once been Mum's favourite carol. *In the bleak midwinter, frosty wind made moan, Earth stood hard as iron, water like a stone.* He remembered her warm, solid body between her two boys as they stood in the church on Christmas Eve. He wasn't holding her hand, but he was pretty sure that Peter was. *Great big baby!* But because it was Christmas and because, though he'd never admit it, he was bursting with excitement, he peered around the dark blue wool of Mum's coat and allowed himself an uncool grin, brother to brother. Blue eyes laughed back at him from under a thick, blond fringe.

Peter. The boy too precious for words. Too longed for to remember.

Max eased his shoulders, rolling them in their sockets and circling his head, then turned and walked back to Holly Lodge. As his shoes crunched on the gravel he looked up and spotted, at a first floor window, the solid shape of Mrs Minns and, beside her, Eleanor's slim silhouette. As his eyes focused he could just make out, curled on Eleanor's shoulder, the small, sleeping bundle of Ben.

Max could feel Eleanor looking at him. She didn't speak, but he could hear the questions clamouring in her head as, hands locked on the steering wheel, he steered the car through the winding lanes back to the A3. Half an hour earlier, he'd told Mrs Minns that he'd like his mum to move in as soon as possible. When that turned out to be the following week, despite the extortionate fees which he knew he could only cover by using his Power of Attorney to sell Mum's house and (and he knew it was a matter of 'and' not 'or') becoming a partner at Baker Warnes – he'd signed up then and there.

He pulled out to overtake a truck, hesitated when he saw a bend in the distance, made his decision and accelerated past. Eleanor's legs tensed.

"Careful Max." He swung the car back in front of the truck. "I can't believe that you're putting your mum in the first place we've seen." It seemed his daredevil driving had unlocked her tongue.

"We both know it's got to be done Ei, so we might as well get on with it." He noticed how he'd said "we" to pull her into his decision.

"But this is your mum Max."

"I know, but we've got to do something. She can't stay with us forever – and she can't stay at Hillside Close on her own. What else can we do?"

174

"Well – we could have at least looked at the other two homes on Janis's list."

"Why bother? You said the room was fine. They cook the food on the premises, the place is clean, the staff-to-resident ratio's good, they've just had a very good inspection report. What more could we want?" He was aware of Eleanor continuing to watch him, unconvinced, doubtful of his motives, wondering if she'd pushed him into it.

"I don't mind going to look at the other two next week Max."

"But you'd have to take Ben with you – you don't want to go dragging him around nursing homes."

"I could leave him with Aneta."

Max didn't reply; they both knew that this was very unlikely.

"At the very least," Eleanor said, after a few minutes, "why don't you let your mum stay until Christmas?" Christmas. That word again. Once, long ago, he and Mum had loved it. "It's only a few weeks away now, and it'll be Ben's first. We've got to make it special for him."

"Special? He won't even know that it is Christmas."

"That's not the point Max. You can't let your mum have Christmas Day on her own in a strange place."

He gripped the steering wheel tighter, forcing himself to concentrate on the number plate of the car in front.

"She won't be on her own will she, not in Holly Lodge?"

"Max –" Eleanor turned towards him.

He kept his eyes on the road ahead. "Well, it's true. Besides, she wasn't with us last year."

"It was different last year – we were in the Caribbean for a start."

She was right. As soon as Max had made enough money to escape it, he'd run away from Christmas to hot, foreign beaches where carols and tinsel were in short supply. They drove on in heavy silence. Ploughed fields gave way to rows of suburban houses. The traffic slowed to a crawl as they approached some new, temporary lights by the old Shell garage.

Eventually Eleanor said, "Well, there's no need to rush it on my account; you know that don't you Max?"

"I'm not doing it because of you Eleanor, although I know how difficult it's been for you – of course it has – you're the one at home with Ben."

She remained silent, watching him. Max heard Ben stir in the back of the car, heard a bell tinkle as his favourite stuffed elephant fell to the floor. He looked in the rear-view mirror but it had grown too murky to make him out. He imagined him instead: his warm, milky skin, his biscuit smell, his knowing, curious, navy blue eyes. The queue edged forward. Keeping his eyes on the two red tail lights ahead of them, Max took his hand off the steering wheel and placed it on Eleanor's thigh. Her dress was silky under his touch.

"I'll go and visit her every week," he said. "I'll probably end up seeing her more often. And she'll have more stimulation in there, more people to talk to …" His voice trailed off as he thought of the school dinner smells, the spiteful little windows.

Eleanor turned her face away to look out of the window. "You just need to be sure why you're doing it Max."

He slid his eyes over; she was still staring away from him. He thought again of Mum, left behind in London, waiting for them as darkness fell.

***

The postman handed Dick the letter as he was turning his key in the lock. He knew what it was about even before he'd opened the front door. The envelope was stamped with the familiar logo, once so ingrained in his consciousness he'd hardly even noticed it. Now it hit him between the eyes. He closed the door behind him and leant on it for a minute or two, holding the light, white oblong in his fingers and gathering his thoughts.

There could only, surely, be one reason for the letter. And if so, what an irony. Once he'd learnt that Elizabeth and Simon weren't going anywhere after all he'd been tempted to let his life return to normal, to dust himself down after a false alarm and simply take up where he'd left off. But the interruption, the jolt in his otherwise routine life, had stirred things up and made him think. Elizabeth, he now knew, was capable of making plans of her own. The knowledge, which had come as somewhat of a surprise, was also a relief. And although he was surer now than he'd ever been that he scarcely knew his only daughter, he was grateful to her for prompting him to take a look at himself, at his own, singular, life without Dora. Though Dick, in his naturally cautious way, had decided to postpone moving into somewhere smaller for a few more years, he'd concluded that it was time to let the other thing go – to "draw a line under it and move on", to use Elizabeth's awful phrase.

Not wanting to strain his back, he'd distributed the stacks of old newspapers between no fewer than twenty sacks before carrying each one out of the house and hauling it into the boot of his car. The process took him the best part of an afternoon. When it was complete, he drove to the municipal tip and dumped the contents of each bag into the recycling skip.

Now he carried the letter into the kitchen, took a knife from the drawer and slid it under the flap, slitting open the envelope and pulling out a piece of paper folded in three. The few scant lines provided him with a solution that had eluded him for more than quarter of a century. The knowledge, the answer, which he'd guessed at but never known for sure, proffered little relief. The final sentence – the acknowledgement of his role in the unfinished business and the offer, should he wish to accept it, for him to complete it – came as quite a shock. He'd been retired for so long now it seemed a strange request. But once he'd got over his initial surprise, he realised that it might indeed be a good thing to do, and there was no doubt in his mind that he would.

***

The treasure hunt game's great. Peter loves it, and so do I. I've finally found something that we both like. Football doesn't work very well. He's not good enough. He thinks he is – and I suppose for a five-year-old he tries quite hard – but he's not. Take last week for example. We were all playing in the road after tea. Me, Clive, Alan and Michael J, Graham and Christopher. And Peter of course. We'd stuck him in goal. I was on Clive's side, with Alan, and we were winning 5-2. It's always good to be on Alan Geary's team. He hogs the ball but he can't half score. Anyway, this time, he passed it to me – just as we were coming up to Graham's goal. He looked around – Alan that is – and with a quick one-two, tapped the ball up and headed it over. It was an ace move and I controlled it well and dribbled on, getting ready to strike. The ball caught the toe of my boot and arced into the air – far too high away over the top of Graham's head. Goal kick. When I turned to run back I almost bumped into Peter. I shouted at him to get back into goal but he wouldn't listen. Christopher got the ball, next thing we knew he'd raced away up the road and scored. He couldn't not. It was an open goal. He thumped it in straight between the two rolled-up jumpers.

But the treasure hunt's fantastic. I like thinking up the clues. After NORAHS FISHY FREIND'S I did one near

Dad's old shed that said LOOK OUT FOR THE STINGERS (because of the stinging nettles that grow in front of it) and then a clever one about being cornered in the desert which was actually *in* the sandpit. It took him ages to find that one because he couldn't work out exactly where it was buried. Answer: in the top left hand corner. It directed him to the coal bunker, but I haven't hidden the coal bunker clue yet because I can't decide what to put on it. I want to make it easier because I got bored watching Peter going completely wrong in the sand pit. I'll make it easier but riskier. I might hide it in Mum's bedroom. We're not allowed in there by ourselves so he'll have to sneak in when she's not around and I know that that will freak him out. But he'll want to do it. He'll *have* to do it. It's great seeing him not knowing what to do. Risk being called a baby or risk being caught. He bites his bottom lip when he's trying to think and looks just like a chipmunk. In the end though, he'll do it. He always does.

We're getting quite good at ironing the paper too. At least, I am. And it takes me no time at all to put up the ironing board. Which is just as well because Mum would go berserk if she knew what we were doing. Ab-so-bloody-lute-ly berserk. I wait until she's sitting in front of the telly watching *Terry and June* and then I creep into the kitchen and get it out the cupboard. Peter watches out for me through a crack in the living room door and then, when everything's ready, I tap him on the shoulder and he comes through into the kitchen with me and I pull out the chair for him to stand on and let him iron the clue. It's a fantastic moment when the words appear. My eyes dart between the paper and Peter's face. It's magic. He concentrates so hard that his mouth hangs open. And when the words start swimming up out of the paper, his eyes grow wider and wider. Once I had to snatch the iron from him because he'd left it turned down on the ironing board cover. Silly boy! He almost burnt a hole in the stripy sheet. There was a burning smell and when I whipped the iron up it had left a mark. A faint brown outline in the shape of the iron. I made sure that I was out of the house when Mum next did her ironing in case she asked me about it. But she never said anything. I pretended to Peter that she had – and that I'd got him out of it. Clever me.

The only thing I've got to work out now is what to write on Mum's bedroom clue – where to lead him next. I have to be so many jumps ahead in this game – I have to sort of look into the future and work my way back. I've got one idea – it's a brilliant place. It could have been made for hiding clues. But I'm worried it's just a bit *too* risky for Peter. Or maybe not. I can't make my mind up.

***

Once Max had made the decision he couldn't see any point in delaying it. He drove his mum down to Holly Lodge the week after he and Eleanor had been to see it. It was a crisp, autumnal morning under a cut-glass azure sky and when they arrived, Mrs Minns was waiting for them on the front step, her arms folded across her chest. Before he'd even switched off the engine she was opening Mum's door and poking in her powdered face.

"Hello Kathleen – how lovely to meet you."

No one ever called Mum Kathleen. She was Kay or Kate, but never Kathleen. Max felt slightly nauseous. Mum was staring ahead of her, out of the window; she didn't seem to have registered Mrs Minns' words, and because Max didn't want to rock the boat before she was even out of the car, he said nothing.

Inside Holly Lodge, the stuffy, over-heated lobby seemed even smaller than he remembered it. Old-fashioned paper chains looped lopsidedly around the walls and in one corner multi-coloured lights flickered through the plastic needles of a Christmas tree. Max followed behind as Mrs Minns – her large, navy-blue bulk dwarfing his mum's stooping figure – made her way through double doors. Eleanor had bought his mum the camel coat she was wearing. *It's for your special trip Kate.* It swamped her; the back of Mum's head seemed to disappear under its collar as Mrs Minns led her down the tinselled corridor.

His mum thought she was coming to stay for a few nights in a charming, country house hotel nestled at the foot of the Surrey Downs. "We find it's sometimes best," Mrs Minns had said when he was signing the papers, "especially with those of our newcomers who are a little confused about life." *A little confused about life?* He was betraying the one person he'd always vowed never to betray, leaving her in the ghastly care of Mrs Minns. He could still hear the ludicrous euphemism rolling from her fleshy lips. Mum's life had been one long waiting game, one slowly unravelling ball of never-ending torture. Now that she'd finally found some sort of peace in the form of her confusion, he'd snatched it away from her and brought her here.

"Here we are," Mrs Minns had stopped at a doorway. "This is your room Kathleen." It was only then, as Mrs Minns ushered them into Mum's room, that it hit him that he'd never even seen it.

It was small and painted an insipid green. Pushed against the wall was a mean-looking single bed. On a low table beside it was a pink hyacinth in a white pot decorated with roses. It was Mum's pot, with Mum's favourite winter flower in it, and the sight of it in this strange cold room made him want to wrap her in his arms and turn and run. Instead he stood and thought of good old Norah – *salt of the earth that one* – bringing the pot from Hillside Close, just as he'd asked her to. "It helps to settle them if they're surrounded with the things they know and love," Mrs Minns had said. *Them.* She seemed to be pushing Mum out of her own life by constantly using new words to describe her. His eyes went to the flimsy-looking wardrobe standing in the corner. It was full of Mum's clothes, as was the chest of drawers; and there, on top of it, Mum's little white embroidered cloth, her lacquered jewellery box, her wooden-handled mirror and – his heart turned over as he spotted it – her china pillbox with its red rosebud lid. Even as he stood, his feet firmly planted on the cheap nylon carpet of Mum's new room, he could feel the smooth painted porcelain under his fingers.

He's hiding Peter's latest clue. It's here, in his hand, the slip of blank paper with its lemony smell. HUNT AROUND THE SCHOOL BUS STOP. Max knows it's risky and dangerous and exciting but he just can't resist it. He folds the piece of paper into a very small square and lifts off the lid. He's about to squash it down under the rosebud when he hears Mum coming up the stairs. He shoves the clue into his pocket, drops down onto his knees and crawls under her bed. The dust tickles his nose and he wants to sneeze. He squeezes his lips together and just about manages to stifle it.

"Mr Rivers …? Mr Rivers …? Are you all right?" Flashes of silver tinsel reflected off Mrs Minns' glasses.

"Yes – yes." He could hear the tremble in his voice and he ran his fingers through his hair in an effort to steady himself. "Of course – I'm fine."

"I was just telling your mother that this is one of our best rooms, possibly *the* best – with a double aspect as you can see – and on the ground floor with a good view of the gardens." Mrs Minns stood by the window, her gaze swinging from Mum to him.

"Isn't that lovely Maxi?" Mum was smiling up at him. Surely she couldn't think that this place really was a hotel?

"Now –" Mrs Minns continued – "shall we go and have some lunch Kathleen before they start clearing away?"

She's not Kathleen! Max wanted to shout, but his mum was nodding eagerly.

"What is it?" she said, turning towards Mrs Minns.

"Ah now, let me think." Mrs Minns bent down to Mum as if she were talking to a child. "It's Tuesday – so it must be shepherd's pie."

"Oh Maxi," Mum looked up at him. "It's your favourite."

My stomach curdled.

"Would you like to stay Mr Rivers?" Mrs Minns straightened up.

"Well –"

"Go on Maxi –"

"I'd love to Mum, but I'm afraid I can't – I got a call from work on the way down in the car – while you were asleep – and I need to dash back up to London." He said it quickly, staring a fraction to the right of Mum's eyes, just as he'd used to when he'd done something wrong.

"Well, that's a shame Maxi, but never mind." Mum spoke in her old, no-nonsense voice, and then she looked him in the eye and held his gaze. He took a deep breath, felt the room rocking. She knew.

"That *is* a shame Mr Rivers but never mind – we'll take good care of her."

He swung around to Mrs Minns. She too looked him in the eye; then she said, "Off you go – we've got Kathleen's case." She motioned at Mum's overnight bag.

Max couldn't speak, or look at his mum. For what seemed like an eternity the words wouldn't come. The room was full of the hyacinth's sickly scent.

When he finally found his voice, it was strange and gruff. "Okay then – I'll be off."

Cowardy, cowardy, custard!

It was as if he'd crept up behind me and shoved me in the back, his voice clear and high as a bell. Max made himself look at his mum, but as he did so, she turned away

183

and all he could see was her camel-coated back. Then he heard her words. They were no longer clear or firm, but weak and old and barely audible.

"Off you go then Maxi – there's a good boy."

After the fourth whisky Max realised that he'd made a mistake; he should have found a pub in Wandsworth, somewhere local, so that he could stagger back home from it. It was too late now. He'd stopped off at the first one he'd come to and phoned Janis to say that he'd been taken ill with a stomach bug. It was quite clear that she knew this wasn't true, but it didn't matter; she'd put in all the necessary calls and express just the right amount of regret. Right now, he didn't even know exactly where he was or what the pub was called. It was low and dark and festooned with Christmas decorations, shimmering with tinsel like the stuff in Holly Lodge. It was filling up for lunch. The noise level around him was rising, a tide of clinking, babbling, high-pitched chat. He'd plonked himself in the corner, out of the way, and started to drink.

It was almost working; the sharpness of his guilt was wearing off, the images were blurring. He couldn't erase everything though. He could remember opening the car door and sitting behind the steering wheel and seeing, where her small, curled shape had been, nothingness and air. That was what had tipped him over the edge. The void, the space, her not being there. All he could think of was her smile when she'd told him it was shepherd's pie, all he could hear was her voice as she'd said it. It was so much her.

When he finally staggered out of the pub into the lane, the coldness hit him. The sun had all but disappeared and it was growing dark. He had to concentrate hard to read the number that the barmen had given him and then punch it into his mobile with fingers that had somehow detached themselves from his hands. But when at last the taxi arrived and he climbed in, vaguely aware of the driver's watchful eyes in his rear-view mirror, it hit him that he'd got what he'd wanted all along: a ride home without an empty passenger seat where Mum should have been. He slumped into the back seat and watched the shapes spinning away from him beyond the window as they purred through Surrey lanes. Before he knew it they were on the A3, crawling past the building site by the old garage and gathering speed as they grew closer to London; bright, white headlights flashing past them in the gloom.

Eleanor was waiting up for him when he got home. She was sitting in the living room reading a magazine by the light of a side lamp. As she slid it onto the low glass table he saw it was called *Parenting*. Parenting? He needed an instruction manual on how to be a proper son.

"Thank God that's over."

Eleanor looked up at him from the sofa. "I wish you'd let me come – you didn't have to go through that on your own you know."

"No – I did – it was my mum and I had to do it." His alcohol furred tongue was too big for his mouth and his voice reverberated in his head.

"It's a good home Max; you did the right thing."

"She knew – that was the thing El – the thing that killed me. Mum knew what I was doing." He paced backwards and forwards in front of the sofa. "There was this awful moment when she looked at me and I could see that she knew exactly where we were. It was as if the fog of confusion had suddenly lifted and she could see quite clearly exactly what I was doing."

"You couldn't do anything else Max." Eleanor's voice was no more than a whisper.

"D'you know that when my dad was dying I went to see him. I hadn't seen him for over 15 years. He'd vanished – puff – in a cloud of his own filthy tobacco smoke –

185

juzlikethat – *juzlikethat!* He stopped his pacing and repeated the phrase, throwing his arms forward in a Tommy Cooper gesture. "I never knew why. No one ever told me. I never spoke to him – he just left. He never came back … even … even when …" His voice faltered.

"Even when what Max?" Eleanor's eyes were two black pools in the darkness.

"He never came back," Max said firmly, beginning to pace again. "Every year he sent me a birthday card in an envelope with blue airmail stickers from Canada. Canada! It might as well have been the moon. I used to bin the cards. It was like some weird rite – Mum would give me the envelope and I'd walk over to the waste paper bin in the corner and throw it in. She'd just stand there watching me. At Christmas he sent brown paper parcels with rows and rows of different coloured stamps. I never opened them either. Imagine – a 12-year-old boy who didn't want a Christmas parcel. But to me Dad simply didn't exist anymore. It was easier that way."

"And then, one day, when I was at uni in Southampton I got a call from a woman who said that he was dying in a hospice in Suffolk. I remember feeling numb. I couldn't believe that Dad had finally returned into my life – and now he was dying. Turned out he'd come back to the UK several years earlier. The woman said he'd asked to see me. She was a nurse; all she was doing was passing on the message. I had no reason in the world to do what he wanted, to grant him his last wish. No reason to see him. Who was this man? I didn't even know him. He'd walked out on me and Mum 15 years before. He was no longer part of my life. And yet I went – I went to see this stranger as he lay dying. I mean, why? Why did I do that? I don't know – I still don't know – to this day I don't know if Mum even knows that he's dead."

He was staring at the glassy blackness of the window. Behind him he heard Eleanor say softly, "I'm sure she does."

He waited for a couple of seconds and then said, "Perhaps, but that's not the point – I didn't even think about that. I didn't know why I was doing it, I just knew that I wanted to see him before he died. I took a train to Ipswich and then got a taxi to the hospice. It was beside the sea, with long lawns that sloped down to the beach. I remember thinking how much he'd love the gardens because he'd always loved gardening – and I hated myself for thinking that because even the thought – the memory of Dad – was a betrayal of Mum. I almost turned around and walked away again, but then I'd come now, so why not? Mum need never know. And d'you know –" Max paused; he was still facing away from Eleanor, gazing at the opaque window pane. "D'you know when I walked into his room I didn't recognise him. He really was a stranger. He was propped up in bed and his pyjamas swamped him. He was emaciated. It was terrible – he was so weak and frail. His head was tipped to one side; his eyes were closed. There was no sign of Dad – not an inkling of him – not one iota –" The word caught in his throat. "He'd gone. He'd lost his hair, or almost all of it; what was left of it looked like cobwebs. And the skin of his head was pulled so tight that I could see the bones of his skull protruding from beneath the surface." Max stopped, aware that he was shaking.

"You went because he was your father Max," Eleanor said. "Whatever had happened, whatever he'd done, he was still your father."

Max turned, walked over to an armchair and sat down heavily, tipping his head back and closing his eyes. A pulse was thumping at his temple. He remembered the sweet, cloying scent that had pervaded Mum's room at Holly Lodge.

"He ran away," he said. His eyes remained closed. "He left Mum to deal with all the shit in our lives – and yet I went to see him when he was dying. He deserted her, and now I'm doing exactly the same as he did."

187

"No you're not."

He heard the sofa creaking as Eleanor stood up, a fan of air as she crouched down beside him. He opened his eyes. Her face was close to his, her eyes shining in the half-light.

"I am."

"You know you're not Max, if you'll only stop to think straight. One of the things that I liked about you when I first met you was the way you looked out for your mum."

"I didn't do anything; I neglected her."

"You were always phoning her, making sure she was okay."

"I could've visited her more – I should've –"

"Sssh," She placed a finger on his lips. "Don't do this to yourself Max, please."

He rested his head on the back of his chair again and closed his eyes again. It was as if he'd been running and had finally stopped. He felt the soft touch of Eleanor's hand on his cheek. There was so much more that he wanted to tell her, but he was too tired, his thoughts slowing; he visualised them revolving like a cup of tea stirred by a finger of Kit-Kat, the liquid going around and around and around, and then gradually slowing until at last it was still.

He woke with a start to find himself alone, his mouth parched and his neck stiff from where it had been twisted. He massaged his shoulders, tilting his head from side to side and then wincing as a dull ache shot through it. He hauled himself up from his chair, pausing for a second or two once he was upright, blinking to adjust his focus and then walking slowly into the kitchen. It was grey and shadowy. The second hand of the oversized clock on the wall ticked around and around, click-click-click-click. The time was just after eleven. Through the window above the sink, the trees and shrubs in the garden, underlit by spotlights, stirred and rustled like long-limbed ghosts. He filled a tumbler with water from the tap and made his way out into the hall. He tried to go carefully in the darkness but stumbled halfway up the stairs, his shoe clattering on wood, his head spinning and dizzy. He stopped, waited and listened, but it was okay. Nothing stirred. Not a creature, not even a mouse. He had a sudden, vivid memory of creeping down the stairs at Hillside Close to put out Santa's letter on Christmas Eve. Peter was behind him. He could hear his quick, excited breaths. He turned, nudged his brother's arm, saw an arc of inky blue-blackness loop into the air as the pot flew out of his hand. *What did you bring that for? Mum's going to kill us!* She didn't; she barely even told Peter off. Whereas if it had been him … Max took a deep breath, placed his foot carefully on the next step, and then the next. He was nearly at the top now and he could make out the glow from Ben's nightlight. He thought of his warm, sleeping body. He could see his shape through the slatted sides of his cot and the rise and fall of his chest. He tiptoed over. Ben was lying on his back, his legs tucked up like a frog's, his arms stretched above his head in what Max thought of as the 'I surrender' position. A mixture of toffee and baby shampoo mingled with the smoky taste of whisky in his mouth. He bent closer and stumbled slightly, clutching the rails of the cot to steady himself.

"Shit –!" The word rang out in the silent air.

Ben shifted slightly and heaved a long sigh, his chest rising like a drum and then deflating, as if he had all the cares of the world on his white towelling shoulders. His head was turned to one side on the sheet and a single lock of dark hair swirled over his high forehead. *He's Maxi's little brother, aren't you my darling?* The voice whispered in his head and Mum was beside him, stooped over, her eyes shining. He could hear her rattling breaths, smell her clean, Pond's smell. She'd never go back to Hillside Close, or her splash of hope, or the ink stain of Africa on the curl of the stairs. He'd wrenched her away from all of that. Max remembered the thin spiteful windows of Holly Lodge watching him accusingly as he spun the car on the gravel and drove away.

Ben twitched and opened his eyes. They stared straight at him, glazed and unfocussed, then fluttered closed. Max knew he should leave before he woke up his son but he couldn't bring himself to. Ben's hands were curled into fists above his head. When Max reached out and touched one, it unfurled like a bracken bud. His fingernails were tiny. They were pale pink crescents, with Max's distinctive long nail beds. They were his mum's fingers, so small and perfect he wanted to weep.

***

DI Gould's face is very close to mine, so close I can smell Imperial Leather soap. It's the same one as we have at home in the green bathroom. I can see the black, wiry hairs of his thick moustache and the ones curling up inside his nostrils.

"No one's going to tell you off Max, we just have to try and work out what might have happened, so it's very important that you tell me everything you know." His grey-brown-green eyes are looking straight into mine so that I can't look away. "Everything."

The way that he repeats that word reminds me of when I underline the title of my stories to make them stand out. Everything.

We're in Mrs Maishman's room. Just being in here makes me frightened because I've only been in here once before – when I didn't feel very well. It's painted pale blue and there are paintings that we've all done over her walls. Mine's up there. It's a boot with real shoelaces that I poked through the holes. It's very hot. Over in the corner a white fan makes a whirring noise but I can't feel a breeze. DI Gould's sitting on the opposite side of Mrs Maishman's table, leaning in very close to me. Beside him, a little bit behind him, is a woman policeman with short red hair. Mum left a few moments ago. *So now it's just the three of us.* That's what DI Gould said after the door to Mrs Maishman's room clicked shut.

I bite my bottom lip harder and harder until it hurts.

"There's no need to be frightened lad – I'm not going to tell you off. I just need to know exactly what happened this afternoon."

For the thousandth time my hand goes to my pocket. It's the right hand pocket of my shorts. I feel around with my fingers, right into the corners of the lining, but there's nothing there, nothing. Nothing. It's not in there.

"What d'you keep feeling in your pocket for?" DI Gould says it gently, as if it's an easy question, but I know that he knows it's not.

"Nothing," I whisper. When I shift in my seat my school shirt clings to the sticky skin of my back.

"Now – you know that it's very important that we find your little brother as quickly as we can?" He dips his chin and raises his eyebrows at me.

"Yes."

"And to do that we need to have all the information that we possibly can – as quickly as we can. So if there's anything – *anything* – that you're not telling me that might be useful, that might help us to find Peter, then it's very important that you tell me. Do you understand that Max?"

I nod. I keep remembering the way Mum's voice shook as she shouted at me when Peter fell out of the tree and broke his finger. It's all very well DI Gould telling me that I won't get told off. He doesn't know Mum when she's in a rage, especially when it's to do with Peter – Peter and me. *You stupid, stupid boy Max! Peter's only five – he's not much more than a baby.* Her face doesn't look like Mum's. Her mouth is all thin and there's a blob of spit on her bottom lip, and her neck's bright red. I'm shaking so much I think I might fall down.

"Come on Max – there's no need to be frightened, I promise you." DI Gould moves his hands further across the table. He's got a gold ring – a wedding ring – on his finger. How odd it looks with the thin, black hairs of his knuckles sticking out from under it. I wonder if he's still got a wife or if she suddenly disappeared, like Dad did. "In fact, if you tell me what it is that you're not telling me, I'll think you're very brave."

My eyes dart up to his. He nods encouragingly.

"But –" I say it so quietly I can hardly hear it.

"Go on." DI Gould nods again. His eyes are serious, but kind too.

"Well – the thing is –" I stop. I'm remembering how Mum told me about Dad going away. The way her words kept stopping and starting as we sat on the gold, stripy settee. My fingers work away at the lining of my pocket. "The thing is," I say again, "I had a clue in my pocket."

"A clue?"

I can see that he needs me to explain. "We're playing a treasure hunt, with clues – me and Peter."

He doesn't say anything. He doesn't move his face and his eyes are still watching me, but out of the corner of my eye I can see the policewoman shift in her seat. I know this is important. I, too, shift in my chair and it creaks loudly.

"I had one in my pocket – but the thing is, I'd decided not to use it because I thought it was too difficult – too –" I swallow, suddenly aware of what I'm about to say.

"Yes?" DI Gould's looking at me. His eyes are not so kind now; they're harder. He's frowning ever so slightly.

"I thought it was too dangerous for him," I say.

"What did it say?" DI Gould speaks very quickly, like Mum does when she's angry. "Remember," he says, in his gentler voice, "that you're not going to get into trouble for this Max."

I take a deep breath. I'm not sure if I can believe him. "Are you going to tell Mum?"

Beside him, the woman policeman moves, just a little bit. I'm concentrating on DI Gould and I think she's looking at him too.

"Would you rather that I didn't Max?"

I nod slowly.

"Okay – well – why don't you tell me and Margaret?" He dips his head to the woman. She doesn't seem to move.

"There's a tree," I say, "It's just along the road a bit from the bus stop outside school where we wait in the afternoons, it's –" I stop; I can feel a pulse at the base of my throat.

"Yes?"

"It's in someone's front garden – right at the front though, by the gate, not too far in."

"That's okay lad – go on."

"Well –" I take another deep breath. One of the worst bits is over and DI Gould doesn't seem angry. "It's a brilliant tree because at the bottom of its trunk, where the roots start to come out, there's a big hole." I can see it now. The light brown and dark brown ridges in the bark and the black, yawning gap. I found it a week or two ago when the bus was late and I was hanging around at the bus stop. It's even better than the hole in the stump at home because you can see right into it. It's like a miniature cave. It's the perfect place for hiding a clue.

"Go on –" DI Gould's watching me.

"What I thought was, that I'd hide the next clue in there you see. So the clue that I was going to hide in Mum's bedroom said, HUNT AROUND THE SCHOOL BUS

193

STOP. But I decided that I'd better not use it, after all. It was in my pocket – I'd decided not to give it to him –"

"Guv –?" There's a loud scraping noise. The policewoman's pushing her chair back.

"Wait –" DI Gould lifts up his hand, and my heart's beating fast. "Which house was the tree in Max? D'you know the number?" His voice is quick again. I try to think. I can see the house; it's one of those big fancy ones beside the school fields, with a brown and white front and a black front door.

"Sixty-two," I say. I can see it on the front door. Gold figures on the shiny black paint.

"Tape it off … ten houses either side … search … interview … occupants … you know what to do…" DI Gould shouts, he rattles off words too fast for me to hear and before I know it, the policewoman's gone and the door's clicked shut behind her. He turns back to me. My heart's thumping so hard I think my chest's about to burst.

"Well done lad." His voice is quieter. Well done? I don't understand. I'm very confused. But the main thing is, he's not telling me off. As long as he keeps his word about not telling Mum I should be all right. "Now then Max, tell me about these clues." He leans forward. "You say that you had this one in your pocket and it said, *Hunt around the school bus stop.*"

"Yes, but –" I pause. My heart's slowing down now.

"You think that Peter might have somehow got hold of it, is that it?"

"Sort of – but –"

"Go on Max –" DI Gould's eyes are watching me very closely.

"The thing is – you couldn't see the words –" Now I can see that he's the one who's confused. He's frowning. "You couldn't see them," I explain, "because they were written in invisible ink."

***

There was no denying that it was easier without Mum in the house. Eleanor visibly relaxed and on Saturday morning she announced that she was leaving Ben with Max while she went to do some Christmas shopping. When Max asked her how long she'd be she said she didn't know.

"But what about his feeds?" Max turned, his hand poised above the coffee machine.

"There are two bottles of formula in the fridge – all you need to do is heat them up in the microwave." She smiled over Ben's head as she held him in her arms. "I thought it was about time that the two males in my life spent some time together – just the two of you, on your own."

"Well, this is a change of heart. I thought breast was best."

"It is – of course it is, but I didn't think he was getting enough and it seems I was right. I gave him some yesterday evening and he wolfed it down."

"And then slept till seven."

"Exactly. I should have done it weeks ago."

Max didn't say anything. It was enough that Eleanor was finally taking his advice; and it was certainly true that Ben had slept uninterrupted for longer than he'd ever done before and they'd all woken the better for it. She showed him how to test the temperature of the milk by squirting a drop of it onto the inside of his wrist and demonstrated how to hold him while he fed.

"It's okay Eleanor – I'm sure we can manage." Max could see her hovering in the kitchen doorway. "Off you go – go on." He virtually had to push her out of the house.

It was only when the time came for Max to feed Ben – when he picked him up and felt his weight settle against his chest, when he brought the warm bottle up to his mouth and Ben grasped it greedily and began to suck, holding Max's eyes with a grave, concentrated look – that Max fully understood the potency of the bond between mother and child. Ben fell asleep in his arms, his eyes rolling like a drunk's before finally closing as his chubby fingers loosened their grip on the bottle. And though Max had work to do, papers to read in his study, half an hour or so elapsed before he laid his son gently in his baby rocker and carried him through.

Things continued to improve for Max at work. At each of his daily briefing calls Gazprov's old woman of a finance director came up with new nit-picking queries that Max was forced to spend valuable time re-explaining and disentangling for him. But the two parties were nevertheless making slow progress. Bill was pleased. The Russians had conceded two important points in the management oversight clauses and Max was close to getting the suite of agreements wrapped up. The deadline, in his head, was Christmas.

Bloody Christmas. He just wanted it to go away, to evaporate into thin air.

Eleanor had bought Ben an Advent Calendar and pinned it onto a cork board in his room. An Advent Calendar for a baby who wasn't even three months old? It was madness, but she insisted that Ben loved it. She held him up in front of it every day and opened each door. One morning, after Eleanor had taken Ben downstairs, Max walked past the baby's empty room on his way to fetch a scarf from their bedroom. The glittery calendar caught his eye and he found himself standing in front of it, running his finger over the shapes and colours of the nativity scene. Mary's blue cloak, the rustic crib, the golden halo over the oddly drawn baby. He prised open a tightly shut door on its folded hinge to reveal a childish picture of a holly leaf. There was nothing to it but coloured paper; so how come the touch of it stopped his heart? Without answering his own question, he turned and walked quickly out of the room.

In her gentle but persistent way Eleanor was pushing Max to bring Mum up for Christmas Day.

"I don't know why you're so against it Max," she said, as they strolled along an avenue of birches running beside the common.

"She's settled into the home now Eleanor; I just don't see the point of disrupting her so soon."

"But she's your mum Max."

A clear blue sky arched above them and Ben lay in his pram, turning his head from side to side, watching the movement of the trees. A jogger panted past and Ben balled his fists, punching the air. A fleeting déjà vu skidded past Max; it was of a curious baby with wide-open eyes, constantly looking.

"Won't it make you feel strange to think of her down in Holly Lodge on Christmas Day, without any of her family around her?" Eleanor, pushing the pram, was trying to keep her tone measured rather than nagging, and only just succeeding.

"She'll be fine down there."

"Well, I don't know Max. It doesn't seem right." Eleanor bent and tucked Ben's arms beneath the blanket.

Max could see Ben didn't like it. "That's too tight El." He leant forward and loosened the covers.

"It would be lovely to be together though, wouldn't it, on Christmas Day?"

Max glanced across at her. The sun was burnishing her hair and her cheeks were flushed from the cold. Now that Ben was sleeping so much better Eleanor was starting to lose her exhausted, haunted look.

"Well, maybe," he relented, "but just for a couple of days mind – no longer."

"Max – that's brilliant! Ben will love it, won't you my darling?" She caught the baby's fist in her hand.

"She's not staying though El." It came out too sharply.

"No, no. I know that Max."

"I mean, it wouldn't be fair on her, or you for that matter."

"I know."

They walked on in silence for several minutes and then Eleanor said, "We must get a tree." When Max didn't reply she said, "Mustn't we? Don't you think?"

Of course they'd have to have a tree now, and baubles and decorations, and a turkey and a Christmas pudding and crackers with silly paper hats. The whole bloody caboodle. And despite the sunshine, Max shivered as someone walked over his grave.

The nursery was blaring out a crackling version of *Once in Royal David's City* and half its car park had been cordoned off for Christmas trees. The shop itself was framed in tinsel and throbbing coloured lights. But it wasn't the tinny carols or the garish lights or even the hordes of overhyped children that got to Max; it was the smell. The sheer number of trees crammed together in one place made it overwhelming, and the evocative spruce scent sent his head spinning back to his childhood as soon as he stepped out of the car into the drizzling rain.

"Ummm – smell that Max – it's the very essence of Christmas isn't it?" Eleanor tipped back her head and breathed it in.

It was, and it was all around him, impossible to escape. They were in Christmasland. It even said so in sparkling red letters across the front of the shop.

"I think we should get a pretty little one, not too tall, but bushy and shapely, and put it in the bay window." Eleanor gazed out across the car park and beyond the shop to the dense green forest of the nursery, her breath steaming in the air. The tip of her nose was pink.

Max pulled Ben's sling out of the car and straightened up. "Why not get a big one?"

"Really?" Eleanor swung around, surprised. "D'you think so?"

"I do," Max said firmly. "Our living room's large enough – why not go for it?" He manoeuvred Ben's kicking feet into the baby sling on his chest. "We need a tall, elegant tree to light up that dark corner beside my Arne Jacobsen chair."

"Wow – you've changed your tune."

"Well – if we have to have a tree, that's definitely where it should go."

"The old cynic's finally coming around Ben. Even he can't resist Christmas." Eleanor pulled Ben's woolly hat onto his head and slipped her arm through Max's. "Come on then you funny, unpredictable man, let's go."

Once they were close to the trees Max realised that he'd forgotten how shiny and plastic-like their needles were. He picked at one with his thumb and it clicked under his nail. He ran his fingers carefully over the smooth green spikes. How sharp they were. He'd forgotten how dense the branches could be where they overlapped. Dark, secret, hiding places up against the hairy trunk. He could see his brother plunging his arm in up to his wrist and pulling out nets of golden coins, holding them up in front of him, glowing with pride. *It's treasure from the sea Maxi – look!* There were thin, red scratches on the milk white flesh of his wrist.

"Max – which one?"

Max was suddenly aware of Eleanor. "Sorry, I was miles away."

"Which one d'you think Max?" She was running her eyes up and down the trees.

"I really don't mind El. You decide."

"Oh, okay." He could sense her disappointment.

"You're much better at this sort of thing." He caught sight of a small playground over by the entrance to the car park. "I'll take Ben over to the swings."

As he turned and started to walk away, he heard her voice behind him. "Don't forget he'll need his feed soon."

He didn't bother to reply. He wove his way through the crowds as *Santa Baby* replaced *Once in Royal David's City* and the smell of hot dogs wafted over from a small, white caravan with a straggling queue. A young girl barged into his knees and looked up, eyes wide, crackling with excitement – "Sorry!" He ploughed on towards the edge of the car park. Beyond a low wooden fence was a see-saw on which a couple of children were playing, a miniature plastic slide and a frame from which three black rubber swings were suspended. He walked through the gate in the fence, clicked it shut behind him and sat down on one of the swings, rocking gently backwards and forwards with his foot. The pom-pom of Ben's hat tickled his chin as he strained around and his legs, poking out from beneath his papoose, pumped up and down on Max's thighs. He could hear his yelps of delight, and he pushed them higher, using his legs, remembering the tipping, giddy, soaring sensation of being on a swing. And a memory, stirred by the movement, the rush of the air, the looping and dipping, the wind whipping past him, dislodges itself from the bottom of his brain where it's lain, buried and hidden, for 24 years, and flies slap bang wallop into his face.

He's swinging on the trapeze in the garden and the apple tree's in blossom. It's a warm afternoon, after school. Peter's cocooned in his own world in that way he sometimes has, even though he's only – what –?

"Four years, six months, two weeks and three days old."

"Not even five!"

"Nearly!"

He's kneeling down, too close to the trapeze – annoyingly, peskily close – scrabbling around in the dusty dirt. The fair, downy hairs on his knees catch in the low sun and shine like gold.

"Get out the way Peter!"

He looks up, his wide face under his thick blond fringe is like a flower turning to the sun. His clear blue eyes stare into Max's.

"Guess what I'm getting for my birthday."

He doesn't say it, he sings it in his irritating, sing-song voice.

"What?" Max is sullen, jealous before Peter's even answered the question he didn't mean to ask.

"A new bike!" Just like that. *Juzlikethat!* So quick and easy. Max had to wait years for mine. It's not fair. He manages not to say the babyish words, but he thinks them. He holds them close to his chest like cold, hard pebbles that he knows he'll throw back in his brother's face one day. And he runs faster and faster, curling his fists around the thin bar of wood, then throwing his legs out and looping them up into the sky.

"Max! Max! For God's sake Max! Stop!"

Max slowed, juddering, scuffing the toe of his shoe on the springy black tarmac and skidding to a halt. Ben was crying, lurching away from his chest, his gulping, frightened wails suddenly so loud under Max's chin that he couldn't believe he hadn't heard them. Ribbons of snot streamed from his nose and clung to the thick nylon padding of his jacket.

"What on earth were you doing?" Eleanor was leaning into him, her eyes shining with fury, her hands scrabbling with the straps of Ben's sling, then plucking him out and hugging him to her. For a few moments she was wrapped up in him, comforting him, then she took a step back, away from Max.

"Sorry Eleanor." Max's voice shook. The youngsters who'd been playing on the see-saw were huddled, heads together, watching from a few feet away.

When Eleanor lifted her head her eyes glittered. "What the hell were you doing Max?"

He stared at her, unable to answer.

"I don't know. I'm sorry Eleanor – is he okay?"

"Yes, he's okay now." Her voice was flat, and her face closed and pinched as she looked at Max, but at least Ben's sobs had quietened and his breathing was slowly returning to normal. He was indeed okay. Untouched. Unharmed.

"I really am sorry Eleanor. I don't know what came over me." Max scooped up Ben's hat from a dirty, black puddle and stretched out a hand to stroke his face. Ben's navy blue eyes gazed back, his tears already dried. He was wary though, watching Max and shrinking back into Eleanor. For a moment Max thought she might start a row right here, with the youngsters looking on, but she didn't. She bent and kissed Ben. As her lips brushed his soft, sooty hair, Max saw how it swirled like a question mark from the crown of his head.

When they were safely in the privacy of the car, en route to London, with Ben asleep in his babyseat behind them, Eleanor turned to face him.

"You need to talk to me Max – you can't go on bottling this up, whatever it is." Her voice was calm and controlled and he knew she'd been thinking about what she was going to say, and how to say it. "I know that I agreed not to ask you about your brother and what happened to him, but this is ridiculous. You're not acting rationally and it affects us all." She paused. "*All of us,* not just you. I think you owe it to me to explain what's going on, why you were in such a rush to get your mum into a nursing home and why you don't want her to come to us for Christmas when it's obvious how much you love her."

Max's grip tightened around the steering wheel. He'd been shaken by what had happened in the playground and his thoughts were still whirling, whizzing, swooping back in time. He didn't know what to say, how to put what was happening to him into words that she, or he, might understand.

Eventually he said, "I will tell you Eleanor, I promise, but could you give me some time?" He darted her a look; her face remained impassive and he went on, "D'you remember when I drove you home to my flat when you were pregnant and you said that you hadn't told me you were pregnant because you were trying to work out your own reaction to it before you told me?"

"I do, yes," she said.

"Well, that's what I'm trying to do."

"But it's been weeks – months – since Ben was born – months since you found out that I was pregnant. I don't know how you can compare the two."

"Because it's not just the pregnancy El, or even the birth, or becoming a dad – it's not even that."

"Well what is it then Max?" He felt her eyes on him. But he couldn't speak. He couldn't explain – he didn't know how to. Headlights flashed past him in the dark. "Why can't you just tell me – talk to me? I don't understand and after what's just happened I don't think it's fair. We're living together Max. We've got Ben. And yet there's still this huge part of your life that you refuse to talk about."

"I know. And I will tell you Eleanor. I promise, but can you give me some time?"

He thought she was going to keep on, to keep chipping away. It was what anyone else would have done. But after a long pause, as the clock on the dashboard clicked over the seconds, she shifted in her seat and said, "Okay then Max. I do – sort of – understand what you're saying about wanting to work things out in your own mind. It's what I do. And I know that's how you operate, but you'll have to give me a timeframe, a deadline. I don't want to carry on in the dark, not knowing how you're going to react, not knowing what you're feeling or thinking. It's just not possible. It's not right." She paused for a second and then said more quietly, "It's not fair … on any of us."

"I know. I know."

"So, when will you tell me?"

He took a deep breath and, as they slowed to a stop behind a queue of red tail lights, he said, "After Christmas. Just let me get Christmas with Mum out of the way, and then I'll tell you everything, I promise."

They set the tree up in the living room as Max had suggested. It filled the space just as he'd imagined, its thin, hairy tip skimming the stuccoed cream ceiling, its scent spiking the air. With its soaring grace and long, elegant lines, it was – just as he'd hoped – everything that the round little tree that had stood in the bay window at Hillside Close could never be. Its simple elegance suited the style of the house and if he'd had his way they would have left it just as it was in all its unadorned beauty.

When Eleanor came to stand beside him he heard her intake of breath. "It's gorgeous Max."

The warmth of her voice broke the uneasy silence that had existed between the two of them since their fraught conversation in the car, and when she said that she'd have to go and buy some more decorations to fill the expanse of branches, an idea began to form itself in his mind.

"There's no need for that."

"What d'you mean?" She glanced at him warily. Ben, asleep in her arms, stirred slightly.

"Just leave it to me Eleanor."

"But what d'you mean? What are you going to do?"

Max leant forward and kissed Ben's silky hair. "You'll see."

"I wish you'd stop talking in riddles Max."

"Trust me Eleanor, please." He knew he was asking a lot of her – too much after what had just happened – but he wasn't sure enough of his own resolve to say more. Before he could change his mind, he turned and crunched his way across the carpet of needles covering the floor, out into the hall.

"But where are you going?" Eleanor's voice carried after him as the front door banged shut.

The white oblong of wood dropped open with a flurry of dried paint flakes that settled on the swirling green carpet like snow. How many years had it been since anyone had ventured up here? Max took the rod from the lintel above the bedroom door, hooked it around the ladder and pulled it down. As he placed his foot on the first rung, the pattern of its metal grooves matched a pattern in his mind and small shock waves of memory rippled through him. The ladder creaked and sighed as he climbed until, a minute or so later, his head emerged into the cold, whispering eaves of Mum's empty house.

When he'd pushed open her front door it had almost jammed on the pile of junk mail that had collected on the mat. *Everyone has to have a door mat Maxi – place gets filthy otherwise.* He could hear her saying it as his feet slipped and slithered on the cellophane-wrapped brochures and pizza flyers. Hanging on its wrought iron hook was her old blue anorak and there, next to it, Constable's Haywain. He took a deep breath. Soon, he knew, he'd have to put the house on the market.

He held up the torch that he'd brought from the car and clicked it on. Its beam sliced through darkness and his heart missed a beat. High in the rafters was a grey, papery tumour and an image – like the long-forgotten spools of home-made movies that they used to watch – flickered in front of his eyes. A man in white overalls and a protective mask climbs up the ladder and disappears above them. A strange, chemical smell comes from a large box he's carrying in his arms. Bold red letters shriek: CAUTION! CONTAINS TOXIC MATERIAL.

He's a spaceman Maxi! Peter's staring after him, open mouthed.

He's gone into the loft silly.

Max could still hear the sneer in his 10-year-old voice. He swung the torch around the loft. Caught in its light were tea chests marked in Mum's looping black writing. *Clothes. Books. China.* He thought of Peter's clothes, smelling of him, and his thin little body, his freckly, sparrow-like legs, the way the smooth planes of his knee caps caught in the sun as they waited for the bus to come. It had been so very hot.

Max exhaled, and as clearly as if she were beside him, he heard Mum's voice urging him on.

We've just got to keep going Maxi, you and I – just keep going.

But they hadn't, had they, not really. Mum had refused to change anything about the house in case he came home. When days turned to weeks and weeks to months and months to years, she still refused to change the smallest detail. The front door was always repainted the same garish yellow, their bedroom still had its pair of single beds with their red and white Man U duvets, the swirling green carpet was so thin in parts that you could see the floor boards through it.

Max swung his torch around the eaves. A pile of white-painted gates lay pooled in its light. Where did they come from? Cold sweat prickled his top lip. They weren't gates. They were the dismantled pieces of Peter's cot. Mum must have put them up here. He clicked off the torch and stood, leaning against the eaves of the loft, listening to the thumping of his heart.

One day, when he'd been at uni, walking along a crowded corridor next to the union bar, he'd suddenly seen his brother's name next to a picture of someone else. *Peter Rivers. Do you recognise this young man?* It was as if he'd been punched in the chest. He couldn't breathe. He was looking at a teenager with straggly, straw-coloured hair and a long, thin face. All Max could recognise were his eyes. They were laughing at him, on the beach at Climping. Click! Caught in the lens of Mum's Polaroid camera.

Max waited in the darkness of the loft until his breathing slowed and then tilted the torch up and clicked it back on, shining it up into the eaves and bringing its beam warily down, ready for what might spring out at him. He rolled the light over an unmarked cardboard box, a pair of broken kitchen chairs, an empty black holdall. And there it was: a scuffed old leather suitcase, its fastenings black with age, its battered lid plastered with faded stickers.

Balancing gingerly on the loft's wooden struts, he edged towards it. Dust gritted his tongue. The torch beam picked out the worn bone handle and he reached out and cautiously ran his hand over it as if touching it might conjure up the past. All he felt was cool smoothness. His eyes travelled over the torn stickers stuck randomly over the cracked old leather. Nepal … Geneva … Hong Kong … Bombay. Of course they hadn't ever been there, they didn't even know where half the places were. Mum had found the case at a jumble sale and thought it might be useful. Peter loved the word Bombay. He kept repeating it – *Bom – be-bom – be-bom – be-bay* – until he got on Max's nerves and he shouted at him to shut up. And there, on the side of the lid, curling at the sides, is the label for New York. Tall, thin letters on mottled paper. A skyscraper of a name. And suddenly Max's legs were shaking, his knees buckling, as he looked out over the view, way beyond the Hudson and all the other buildings laid out on their grid and called out to Eleanor.

The first Christmas after Peter disappeared, Mum brought the case down from the loft and the two of them started to decorate their squat little tree. Even then Max knew what she was trying to do, that she wanted to keep going. *To just keep going.* He tried hard. But as they struggled to pretend that everything was all right, as they painstakingly, heartbreakingly, hung their painted decorations among the needles, a silver bauble slipped through his trembling fingers, knocked the side of a box and shattered in a thousand pieces that rocked and flashed on the floor. His eyes shot to Mum, terrified that she'd tell him off. Her arm was stretched towards the tree, her hand curled around a strand of tinsel, her gaze fixed on the shimmering shards of glass. As Max watched, heart in his mouth, Mum's face paled and her whole body seemed to crumple. As if the rod that had been keeping her upright had been taken away. She sank to the floor, still clutching the tinsel, and he saw the life drain out of her. He saw it happen. Watched Mum's life seep away into the green swirling carpet.

He undid all the baubles and decorations that he and Mum had attached to the tree – the red and gold cardboard boxes, Peter's favourite owl, his strange, wonky, brown and cream pipe-cleaner man – and placed them back inside their boxes, tucking them carefully into each individual tissue-lined partition as if they were the most precious things on earth. He couldn't untie some of the knots, his fingers shook and his nails caught at the cotton, so he went into the kitchen, fetched Mum's red-handled scissors, snipped off the tips of the branches and put everything – bauble, twig and all – into each small compartment. He pulled the rope of lights off the tree and curled it in its plastic box and then he packed all the boxes of baubles and painted decorations and fairy lights into the old leather suitcase and carried it into the hall. He took the dustpan and brush from under the sink and swept up the scattered shards of the broken silver bauble. They made a soft tinkling sound as they rolled across the plastic tray.

When the tree was finally bare and Max had cleared away every last trace of Christmas, he glanced across at Mum. Her face had regained some of its colour, and she looked more like her old self, though he could see she must have been silently crying because there were black smudges under her eyes where her mascara had run. After a moment or two she nodded as if to say, it's all right, and then she said, "Thank you Maxi – thank you for that." Max took those words and the way that she said them and the nod of her head and the look in her eyes and tucked them up in tissue and bundled them away inside himself. He never took them out again for fear of hurting her, and they never celebrated Christmas again.

Max eased himself onto his feet, ducking his head under the eaves. His thighs were stiff from crouching and his left foot prickled with pins and needles. He shook it out as best he could and bent to pick up the leather case; its lightness caught him by surprise. It shouldn't have; all it contained was tinsel and glass, and the small, desiccated tips of Mum's shattered heart. He carried it back across the struts, stooping awkwardly, lighting the way with his torch. He twisted himself through the trapdoor until his foot connected with the top rung then started to climb down. When his head was level with the joists, he snapped off the torch, shoved it in his pocket and pulled the suitcase towards him, before lowering it carefully through the hatch and descending the ladder.

***

DI Gould's come over to our house. Me and Mum are sitting on the gold stripy settee and he's on a chair by the window. I can see the apple tree outside, a few small, green apples are half hidden in clusters of leaves. The trapeze hangs still, as if it's pinned to the grass by invisible strings, and the whole garden seems to shimmer in the bright sun. Mum's hand is placed over mine as DI Gould asks me more questions. Some of them he's already asked me, only in a different way, and I wonder if this big policeman who I thought was my friend is actually trying to catch me out.

"Would Peter ever get into a stranger's car?"

"No."

"Even if they offered him something he really wanted?"

I have to think about that. "I don't think so."

Mum nods. "He wouldn't – not my Peter –" And then she makes that funny sound in her throat and puts the scrap of tissue that's always in her hand now up to her mouth.

"What does Peter really like?" DI Gould's bending forward to me now, as if he's asking me a secret. "What's his favourite thing?"

Easy. "Football."

210

"So if someone said that they had football tickets for a Manchester United game, do you think he might be tempted to get into their car? Or if they said he could meet Gary Bailey?"

I can hardly think to answer straight. My hands start shaking. I know Mum won't want to hear what I'm about to say but DI Gould leans forward even further. I can smell his Imperial Leather.

"Yes," I say. It's barely a whisper. Mum lets go of my hand and I feel her sink back into the settee.

Later that day someone called Audrey comes to stay with us. I don't like her name. It's flat and dull and hopeless and I know she won't bring Peter back. I want DI Gould. When Audrey bends down and says, "Would you like to talk Max?" I shout, "No!" I run upstairs as fast as I can but when I see the ink stain, I sink down on the swirling green carpet and put my head in my hands. I screw my palms into my dry eyes and hope like mad for the front door to bang open on its hinges and for Peter to come running in without wiping his feet on the mat and for Mum to shout at him. None of this happens. I can hear low voices in the living room. It's Audrey and Mum. I rise to my feet, shaky at first, and then carry on walking up the stairs and open the door to our bedroom.

It's full of him. There's his bed with its red and white Man U duvet thrown over it. The wardrobe's open and his clothes are hanging on their hangers, his shoes under the window hold the shape of his feet, his glass of water is still beside his bed.

I stay in my room all day. I don't want to talk to Audrey, or Mum, or anyone, except perhaps DI Gould, and I don't know where he's gone. I pull the tattered old Children's Encyclopaedia out from under my bed but it seems too heavy on my knees and the thin pages slip between my fingers. The words are too close together and too long, too com-pli-cated – I stretch out the word in my head as if I'm saying it to Peter. I reach up to my bookshelf and take down his Faraway Tree. It used to be mine. Some of the pages have splashes of gravy on them where I used to read it while I was eating my tea. I love this book. I love the thick black print and the coloured-in drawings of Moonface and the elves, and I love the way the words curl and wind their way around the pictures. Sometimes, he'd lie on his back on his bed, looking up at the ceiling and, if I was in a good mood, I'd read it out loud to him, running my finger along the bottom of the words so as not to lose my place.

But today I keep losing my place. I'm thinking about the conversation I had with DI Gould in Mrs Maishman's room.

"Could the hot sun have made the letters appear – say if he left it by the window in his classroom – on the window sill –?"

DI Gould had scratched his chin in just the way that Dad had used to do. I could hear it – scratch-scratch-scratch – and I was praying for him to say that there was no way that Peter could have read the invisible writing.

"I suppose it's possible –" It was as if he'd squeezed my chest so all the breath came out of it. But then he said – "but not very likely though."

When my heart stopped thumping I said, "That's why you sent Margaret up to the house isn't it – to number 62?"

DI Gould nodded.

"Did she find anything?"

"No lad, she didn't – and we've no reason to believe, have we, that he even found it. No reason at all."

I'd lowered my eyes then and bitten my lip very hard to stop myself from crying in front of him. And that's when he'd told me about The Book. He reached his arm across Mrs Maishman's table and put his big hand over mine so that it covered it completely. He asked me to look at him. I couldn't move my head for a second or two, but then I lifted it up – it felt incredibly heavy – and I looked straight into his brown eyes and somehow I knew that he was my friend. I think it was because I knew that whenever I'd asked him a question he'd always done his best to tell me the truth.

Downstairs I can hear noises. Something's happening. Audrey and Mum must be moving about, now the front door's opening and clunking shut. Then there's a tap on my door.

"Maxi –" It's Mum. She opens the door a bit and puts her head around. She's wearing her new glasses and this makes her look strict, and her face is thinner and paler than it ought to be. "I've got to go out, just for an hour or so love, I won't be long, but Audrey will be downstairs if you need her."

"Okay," I say, and she closes the door quietly, as if she doesn't want to disturb me.

I get up off the bed and walk over to the window. I let my eyes travel around the garden. Past the apple tree and down along the snaking path to the thick grey stump. It looks almost white in the glare from the sun and a thick dark shadow, like a stain, spreads out across the grass from it. My eyes carry on past Mum's new vegetable patch and her dirty old greenhouse and stop at the sandpit in the corner. There's a small blob of red in it that I know is Peter's bucket; laid out all around it are his pebbles and shells. As I stand looking, they seem to flash and glint at me as though they're signalling or trying to tell me something, but I don't know what it is. I can feel warm tears sliding down my cheeks. I walk back to my bed and flop down onto it and stare up at the ceiling just like he used to do when I read him those stories. When I lick my lips, I taste salt.

I think I must have fallen asleep because the next thing I know I can hear voices – tinny, TV voices – wafting up through the red carpet. I lie, listening – and then I sit up straight. One of them is DI Gould's. I'm sure of it, I recognise the firmness of it and the way he raises his voice at the end of his sentences. I swing my legs onto the floor, tiptoe over to my door and open it, careful not to make a noise. It's definitely him. I edge my way along the hall and ever so slowly down the stairs. I take each step at a time, pausing and listening, until I can see into the living room through the open door. I crouch down on the swirling green carpet and peer through the banister. Audrey's sitting on the yellow settee watching the TV, and there, on the screen, is Mum. She's sitting next to DI Gould and she looks very small and frightened. DI Gould's asking anyone who might have seen anything – "anything, no matter how small and insignificant it might seem –" to come forward to Surrey CID and ask for him. I don't know what in-sig-ni-fi-cant means but I can guess. He looks very serious as he says all this. He stares straight ahead of him and says a number, which appears at the bottom of the TV screen and then – suddenly – Peter's looking straight at me out of the TV and the sweet taste of vanilla ice cream rises into my mouth. It makes me feel sick. It's a photo of Peter – the one that Mum took at the seaside the other week. And now DI Gould's turning towards Mum, sitting so small beside him on the TV, and she starts to speak very quietly.

"If somebody's got my son, could they please give him back to me ... or at least ... please ... contact me to let me know that he's okay ..."

She keeps stopping and starting, as if she might grind to a halt at any moment, and she's so polite. As I sit watching her from the stairs I think of how puffy her eyes are in real life and how no one else can see that, and I think that she's hiding her fears behind her glasses. When she falters over a word I see DI Gould reach out his hand and put it over hers. Then he says that that's all they have to say for now. He hasn't mentioned the clue or the invisible writing. He's kept to his word. I stand up and I'm just about to turn and go back upstairs when a voice shouts out of the TV – "DI Gould, do you think Peter Rivers is still alive?"

***

Three golden spotlights pooled into the window, jewels danced and dazzled and finely cut clusters of breathtaking beauty twinkled alluringly as fierce tides of last-minute Christmas shoppers circled Max in the darkness.

Earlier that afternoon, Bill had summoned him up to his office and offered him a glass of whisky. His Northern vowels had purred compliments about Max's leadership, his focus, his attention to detail. With just four days to go before Max's self-imposed deadline of Christmas, they'd signed off the management clauses, and now his head was spinning with the all-conquering elation of professional success and a couple of large, cut-glass tumblers of Bill's 15-year-old single malt. He rang the bell at the side of the jeweller's door, heard a discreet buzz and saw the blonde behind the glass counter look up, take in his black cashmere coat and decide that he could be allowed to enter.

The idea had been forming in his head for weeks. A slow building up, a layering, an accretion of images and thoughts that had all led inexorably to this moment. He wasn't sure when it had first started, this process. As he'd sat beside Eleanor's hospital bed and struggled to assimilate the news that she was pregnant? When the midwife passed him the bawling scrap of life that was his son? When he'd watched Eleanor talking to Mrs Minns in Holly Lodge and realised just how far they'd come? Or was it at that heart-stopping moment when Mum stepped into their home and everything collided, when what should have been obvious for weeks and months finally sunk in: that he and Eleanor were bound together, their futures governed by the child that she was holding in her arms?

Once inside the shop, up close to the blonde, he saw that she had an unusual, pared-down beauty. There was a simplicity to her, and she – or perhaps the shop itself – exuded a spicy scent reminiscent of dark mahogany and fine cigars. It was Eleanor's sort of shop.

"Can I help you?"

"I hope so; I want to buy a ring." Max paused for a fraction of a second. "An engagement ring."

"Ah – how lovely." The blonde's beautiful face was wonderfully impassive. "And have you anything in mind … a diamond … a solitaire perhaps … or something else …?"

As her large, hazel eyes looked at him enquiringly, Max realised that he'd no idea. He hadn't thought further than buying a ring.

"Why don't I look at something else first, then work my way back to a solitaire?"

"We have some lovely Burmese rubies." The blonde reached down, unlocked and pulled out a tray, and placed it on the counter. Rich reds glinted up at them like jellied sweets.

"How very delicious –"

"They're exquisite, aren't they?" She picked one out of its velvet bed and passed it to him.

He turned it in his hand. It was flame coloured. A bright, pillar-box, traffic-stopping gem set in thick gold claws.

"It's extraordinary," he said, trying to imagine Eleanor wearing it. "Like looking into a roaring fire."

"It's a pigeon blood ruby."

He looked up. The woman's irises were flecked with splinters of emerald, and he thought of the almost conspiratorial way that Bill had spoken to him, his implicit suggestion that his partnership was all but in the bag.

"It contains hardly any iron," the woman continued. "And in the light it phosphoresces to produce that deep intensity of colour."

After she'd replaced it in its slot, the two of them stood, heads bowed, looking at all the rings. Max could smell her perfume now, a citrus tang that cut through the sweet, moneyed scent of the shop and mixed with the peaty aftertaste of whisky lingering in his mouth.

"D'you know," he said, after a few seconds, "beautiful as these undoubtedly are, I don't think she's a ruby person."

"Is she a diamond person?" The woman straightened up, slipping the ruby tray under the counter and turning the key. Her fingers were ringless. Very slim, very elegant, but ringless, with unpainted nails.

"Yes, I think she is." He thought of Eleanor's pale face. "In fact, I think that's just what she is."

"Classic, understated?"

"Exactly – yes that's exactly what she is."

"One moment." The blonde disappeared through a mirrored door behind the counter and Max was left facing his own reflection.

His face was flushed; he looked gaunt and, he realised with a sickening shock, middle-aged. And – and now he felt the floor spin slightly under his feet – for the first time in his life, he could see Dad in him. In his high, receding forehead of dark hair, in the new flecks of silver at his temples, in the furrows beginning to crease his cheeks.

"I've brought some classic solitaires for you to look at sir." The woman had returned and was watching him over the top of a shallow tray. "They're all white diamonds; the most perfect diamonds you can buy."

The most perfect diamonds you can buy. He silently repeated the phrase.

"They sound just right for Eleanor."

The mention of Eleanor's name seemed to bring her into the shop. He could almost sense her beside him, her head tipped to one side as she considered the rings.

The blonde placed the tray on the counter. It held four massive solitaires.

"This one –" she held it up and studied it through a jeweller's loupe – "is just about flawless, three and a half carat; it's what's called a cushion cut."

It was a gobstopper of a diamond sitting deep inside tall platinum shoulders.

"It's far too ostentatious," Max said at once, as if pre-empting Eleanor's disapproval. "She'd hate wearing it."

"No girl in her right mind would *hate* wearing it," the blonde said, replacing the ring in the tray. "But I know what you mean. These are statement rings. They're not for everyone. Perhaps you want – or should I say, she'd want – something more like this." She stepped out from behind the counter. She was wearing dark, tailored trousers and a cream top; the sort of clothes, Max realised as he followed her across the room, that Eleanor used to wear to work. And he imagined the look on Eleanor's face when he presented her with the ring. The blonde opened the glass lid of a cabinet and took out a small box. "This is 18 carat white gold, which suits the flowing lines, and although there's almost three carats' worth of diamond here, it's not too obvious." She handed him the open box. The ring was a swirl of soft silver enclosing a large, circular diamond; the overall effect was of a cresting wave.

He let out a sigh. "Now that is beautiful."

The woman didn't say anything, merely stood watching him as he took the ring from its box.

"Could you put it on so that I can see how it looks on your finger?"

"Of course."

As soon as she slipped it on he realised why she didn't wear jewellery. She was a blank canvas waiting to be painted. She held out her hand and they both stared at the strong, rippling shape. She moved her hand, holding it up with her fingers fanned out and then dropping it down to her side.

"It feels lovely too," she said. "Different rings suit different hands of course. But this is soft and smooth – any woman would love wearing it."

"Actually, I think Eleanor's hands are very like yours."

The woman moved away a little, reached under the counter. "And then there's this … in a year, five years … fifty years … when you have your first child … whenever … you can add the eternity ring." She slipped on another ring and held out her hand. "See –"

The cresting wave had become an oval. The second, diamond-studded band had completed the loop of the wave, closing the circle and encasing the diamond in its white gold setting.

"Now it's just another diamond engagement ring," Max said. It was true: somehow, completing the jewelled circle of the setting had extinguished the magic.

The blonde took off the eternity ring. The curved flourish returned. Its boldness changed the look, the style, the personality, of not just the jewellery, but the woman herself.

Who said, "Yes. Often the best pieces are those that aren't quite perfect, that have something fractionally out of line, or a tiny bit missing." She paused and looked at Max with eyes that had softened to smoky grey. "It's as though looking at perfection is almost too easy. But the trick lies in knowing just what to leave out and what to alter without ruining the beauty." She paused. "Actually, she's my discovery – the designer I mean."

"She's got a lot of talent."

"I think so. She's French, the daughter of a well-known painter. You may have heard of him – Dominic Bellicardi?"

"Bellicardi?"

"Yes – d'you know him?"

"My God –" He thought of Julie's almond-shaped eyes turning towards him as the glitter ball span over them.

"He died a few years ago."

Max heard Julie's voice in his ear. *I'm so sorry about Peter.* And it seemed as if he'd been directed here, to this place, this shop, and this ring.

"I'll take it," he said. "The single diamond. Julie Bellicardi's ring."

"Well, that's wonderful sir; I'm delighted."

He slid his wallet from his inside pocket and then, for some inexplicable reason, found myself saying, "A long time ago a person I admire very much told me something that I've never forgotten."

"Really?"

"Yes." He held out his credit card, only then realising that he hadn't even asked the price. "He told me that there's a book in which is written all our lives, and nothing that we say or do can change the final outcome. Until now, I've never believed him."

"And now?" The woman said, raising her perfectly shaped eyebrows and taking his credit card.

"And now –" Max sighed. "Now I don't know what to think."

***

We're waiting at the bus stop, talking about Man U. It's very hot – *blistering* Mum called it – even though it's not yet eight o'clock. I think about the pavement getting blisters, the tarmac on the road bubbling up. It's a very strange thought.

Peter's going on and on about Joe Jordan. He calls him "Toothless Joe" and every time he mentions his name he pulls his top lip down with his finger and jiggles about from one foot to the other. He's been off school for two days. He seemed okay to me but Mum said he was poorly and had to stay in bed. She took two days off work to stay at home with him. *I had ice cream!* That's what he said as soon as I came home from school, in that pesky sing-song voice of his, and I thought of him, propped up in his bed with two cushions behind him, eating delicious vanilla ice cream with those wafers like peacock tails. Whenever he stays off school it always makes him even more annoying than he already was. It makes him more *bumptious.* That was one of Dad's words. It's what he called my friend Ian once. *A bumptious little so and so.*

What does bumptious mean Dad?

It means he's full of himself.

But isn't that what we all are?

Dad had laughed then. He'd laughed so loudly that I joined in too. When he finally stopped, he told me that being bumptious meant you were uppity and pleased with yourself – *too* pleased with yourself. Today Peter's pleased with himself. He's bumptious. Bumpppp-tious. It's because he's been at home, eating ice cream with Mum, and she's made me promise to take extra special care of him today and make doubly sure to sit next to him on the bus because he's been poorly. And the way she looks at me makes me think that she knows that I don't always sit next to him. She ALWAYS seems to know EVERYTHING, Mum. I don't know how but she does. I crossed my heart and promised to look after him. And now Peter thinks he's special. He thinks he knows it all. He says Joe Jordan's a better player than Gordon McQueen.

Duh? One's a striker and one's a defender. Everyone knows that – everyone except Peter that is.

"Mum likes him –"

He thinks this will get me. "She doesn't know anything about football."

"Yes she does –"

"No she doesn't – she's a girl. Girls don't know anything about football."

"My friend Lucy does."

"She's four!"

"So?" He's kicking Norah's red brick wall with the toe of his shoe, scuffing it. Mum will be mad at him. Or perhaps she won't – because he's been *poorly.* I can hear her saying it. I turn away from him and look up the road, shielding my eyes with my hand. The bus is late today. Still, it doesn't matter, it's the last day of term. My very last day at St Joseph's. In September I'll be off to big school. I've got a place at the Grammar on the other side of town, where all the really clever kids go. When I heard that I'd passed the exam the first person I wanted to tell – after Mum of course – was Dad. The thought that I couldn't was like a kick in the shins. Like when you're running fast up the football pitch, you can see the goal ahead of you, the ball's right there where you want it to be at the tip of your toe, you're about to strike and then someone tackles you. You still get the ball in – you still score the goal and jump up and down and feel on top of the world – but your shin's sore. Mum was brilliant though. She bought me a new football, a proper black and white one like you see on telly. I think of it sitting slap bang in the middle of our sparkling lawn this morning. I remember how Dad used to say that the lawn was *heavy with Jew* and how I could never understand it. I know what it means now: Norah told me. The thought of Dad is like another quick clip around my shin. But knowing that today is the last day of school, knowing that in September I'll be heading off for the clever kids' Grammar *on my own,* without Peter getting in the way all the time and butting in, makes me so happy I turn around to talk to him.

He's gone. The space where he was standing just now – just a second ago – is empty.

"Max –"

I whip my head around. He's in Norah's garden, beside her pond, his hands on his hips.

"Look at me!"

"What are you doing in there?"

"I jumped in, off the wall."

"The bus is going to be here any minute you idiot." I can see mud sticking to his knees where he must have fallen over in Norah's flower bed. Looking down I see where he's crushed all her purple flowers. Their pale green stems are flattened and smashed and the silky soft petals look all limp and sad. Stupid boy. If he doesn't hurry we'll get *a right tongue sandwich* from Norah. I can hear Dad's voice saying it.

"Come on Peter – get out of there!" I flick my eyes up to Norah's windows and pray that she's in her kitchen around the back. In the distance, up the road, shimmering in the sun, is the squat green shape of the 414 bus. "Come on – quick – the bus is coming!"

Peter runs around the pond, across the lawn, onto Norah's driveway and past her red car. But he can't undo her gate. He's shaking it, rattling the catch. The bus is trundling closer. I can see the driver now. I hoik the strap of my satchel higher onto my shoulder and, sticking my arm out, still facing the bus, I lope towards Peter.

"You stupid berk!" His hand's in my way. "Let go!" He springs back, his eyes beneath his thick blond fringe, shoot towards the bus. I get my fingers under the catch and force it up. The gate swings open and Peter dashes through just as the bus hisses to a stop beside the verge.

He hitches his leg up and hauls himself onto the step. The back of his knees are level with my eyes. Up close they're white as snow. How stupid he was just now, I think. He could have got us both into lots of trouble – even though it wouldn't have been my fault at all. It's what always happens. I swing myself up behind him and he stops almost at once beside a pair of empty seats. I know he's wondering whether this is where I want to go. *Not so bumptious now, are you?* I'm just about to nudge him forwards when I hear Ian's shout.

"Come on Max!"

I look up. Ian's got the back row. He's sitting there, his arms stretched out along the back of the seat, legs stuck out in front of him, ankles crossed. Trust him to get the best place today – the one day I know I really, really ought to sit with Peter. But then I think, why not? Why shouldn't I sit with him since Peter thinks he's so grown up he can jump off the wall into Norah's garden.

"Stay here Peter."

He looks up at me with his babyish eyes. "Mum said you had to sit next to me."

"You'll be okay."

And as the bus lurches forward I swagger and sway my way up to the back, my arms outstretched to grab the metal poles, and swing in beside Ian.

"Watcha mate."

"Watcha."

I lean back, stick my legs out in front of me and shove my hands in my pockets. Several rows ahead of me, towards the front of the bus, Peter's blond head turns and his eyes glance back at me. I know I should sit next to him because

I've promised Mum, but I pretend not to see him and start talking to Ian about Gordon Hill.

***

It was raining when Max went to collect his mum from Holly Lodge on Christmas Eve. Not hard, just enough to mist the air so that he was constantly having to turn the windscreen wipers on and off. Ben was asleep in his car seat in the back, his head lolling, one sock hanging from his foot. Eleanor had insisted that Max take him; he hadn't wanted to but she'd said that she had too much left to do to.

"I've still got to make the cranberry sauce, the bread sauce and the stuffing Max. I simply can't get it all done with Ben around."

"Can't you buy them from M&S?"

"No. I make them all from my mum's old recipes." She'd pointed to a folder laid out on the counter, its pages smeared with grease and wrinkled with age.

"I've never seen that before."

"I've never cooked for you at Christmas before."

Touché. What could he say?

"And don't forget to pick up the turkey Max."

Of course, being Eleanor, it wasn't just any old turkey she'd ordered, but an organic Norfolk Bronze, whatever that was. When Max had put it to her that it was ridiculous having a five-star turkey for a woman who hardly ate meat, a breastfeeding baby, his dotty old mum and him, Eleanor had replied that together the four of them were more than the sum of their parts.

"What – like giblets, you mean?"

"No Max, like a family."

As he'd walked past the living room door his eyes had flicked over to the Christmas tree. Perched high on its thin, hairy tip was their old porcelain fairy with her stiff net wings. *She's not wearing any knickers!* Max had forgotten all about her until he'd watched Eleanor carefully unpacking her from her tissue. As soon as he saw her painted eyes he'd heard Peter's words. How old had he been then? Three ... four ...? Scattered among the dense branches of their Christmas tree were the remnants of Max's childhood: faded pieces of coloured-in cardboard, shimmering baubles fragile as eggs, his pipe-cleaner man, arms twined around sharp green needles, clinging on for dear life.

As he drove down to Surrey, Max thought about the journey back. The three of them – he, Mum and Ben – would be trapped in the car. He could already hear his mum prattling on, reciting rhymes, tracing circles on Ben's palm and singing *Round and round the garden*. He thought of the diamond ring glinting in its small, domed box at the back of his sock drawer and told himself to carry on – *to just keep going*. In fact, the trip back up with Mum wasn't nearly as bad as he'd feared. The thin windows of Holly Lodge had squinted at him as spitefully as ever as he'd pulled up outside its yellow door, but Mrs Minns wasn't there, and Mum was waiting for him in the lobby, her hair freshly set in its helmet of curls and her lips painted with pale pink lipstick. He didn't even have to go to her room. Sumi helped him to get Mum out to the car and she slept all the way home, her white head resting on the padded curve of Ben's seat, her arm thrown protectively over his leg. It was only once they arrived back in London that reality kicked in and Max remembered just how difficult the next couple of days were going to be.

"Where are we?" Mum, her face damp from the rain and creased with sleep, gazed in confusion at the tasteful holly wreath fixed to the front door.

"We're at my house Mum."

When the door swung open, Mum stepped back and clipped the side of Ben's car seat slung over Max's arm. "Whoopsie! Sorry little man."

And he remembered with a dizzying sense of déjà vu, the first time that he'd brought her up here.

"Hello Kate." Eleanor was framed in the doorway.

"Who are you?"

"I'm Eleanor, Kate – remember – we met before."

The smell of mince pies drifted out from inside the house and Max was back in the kitchen at Hillside Close, Mum pulling trays out of the oven as he stood and watched.

"In you go." When he nudged her forward she felt as light as balsa wood. "I'm going to take Ben for a walk on the common."

"What on earth are you on about Max?" Eleanor looked at him in disbelief. "It's still raining, and there's loads to do. Have you got the turkey?"

"Shit!"

"Language Maxi!" Mum's voice beside him was sharp as a razor, just like it used to be.

"Don't say you've forgotten the turkey Max."

He had. It was the perfect excuse. "Sorry El. I'll go and get it now. I'll take Ben with me – keep him out of your hair." He stepped back and turned away.

"Well don't be long." Eleanor's voice followed him out of the gate. And in his head, faint and in the distance, that pesky voice again.

Cowardy, cowardy custard!

The queue for the butcher's snaked out into the rain, along the glistening pavement and all the way around the corner. Max pushed Ben's buggy under the awning and ducked in behind it. There were several other men in the queue. Many of them had babies in buggies covered with transparent bubbles and, like Max, most of them seemed quite happy to be there. We're all escapees from Christmas, he thought as he watched the butcher – a man with a barrel of a belly who could have come from central casting – throwing cuts of meat onto the chopping board and cracking them apart with a cleaver. When he'd finally been presented with his award-winning turkey and handed over the fifty quid – it was bloody daylight robbery! – he returned to the car and put it in the boot, then started to push Ben along Northside Road towards the common. He was killing time. He repeated the phrase to himself as he walked along. *Killing time.* It was an odd notion, the idea of wiping out time. Of abolishing the minutes and moments, the hours and weeks and months and years of one's life. O-blit-er-at-ing them. He pushed the buggy up the hill past twinkling fairy lights strung among hedges and bay window after bay window of tastefully decorated Christmas trees.

By the time the two of them arrived at the duck pond, the rain had stopped. Old-fashioned lamps cast pools of light onto its inky surface. Max wheeled the buggie over to a bench set under the shadowy bulk of a tree and hauled Ben out. He gripped him under his armpits and watched as Ben paddled his soft leather shoes on his thighs. He was wearing fawn-coloured cords and a dark brown fleece. Now that Eleanor was starting to put him in clothes, and when his hair was brushed in a certain way, over to one side with a well-defined parting, Max could begin, just begin, to see him as a boy. He had a beautifully proportioned head. As Ben turned and dipped his head to look at the reflections in the water, Max could see the perfect curve of it melting into his fragile neck. The line, the purity, the innocence of his bent little back, touched something inside him and set it reverberating: he was no longer sitting on Wandsworth common but standing on the beach. Looking down at his brother scrabbling about on his hands and knees as the midday sun catches the fine hairs at the nape of his neck. He looks so young, so vulnerable that Max stoops down and puts his arm around him.

What you doing Peter?

I'm collecting these.

Lined up on the wet sand in front of him are three shells. A pearly, grey and white razor shell with a ribbon of inky black seaweed trailing out of one corner, a small, curling froth of a shell that looks like the ice cream in a Mr Whippy and two ribbed, fan-like shells that are hinged together.

That's a clam. Max points. *And that one's a razor. I'm not sure what that one is.*

Can you help me Max?

And because they're at the seaside and Max can feel the sun on his shoulders and see the sea sparkling a few feet away and because Mum's said that they can have another swim before they get the train home – because of all these things, he says yes. The two of them clamber over the smooth piles of rocks that rise like magic out of the sand. They find small puddles of water that the sea has left behind in crevices and dips. When Max stirs the mirror-like surface with his finger, a crab rises up from the sand on thin, crane-like legs and scuttles away sideways. He shows Peter how to drop sand into the waving, velvet fronds of sea anemones and watch them curl tight shut into shining chestnut balls. They find branches of stinking dried seaweed that they use to poke and probe into shady corners where hidden fish lurk and watch them dart away. By the end of the afternoon Peter has over 40 shells for his collection. Mum's so pleased with Max for looking after his brother she buys them both a Mivvie. Max sucks icy sweet strawberry until it melts into creamy vanilla. Bliss.

Look this way boys!

And that's when she takes the picture.

Eleanor and Mum were sitting at the table with a canteen of silver cutlery splayed open in front of them when Max walked into the kitchen. It was very warm after the freezing dampness outside. It smelt of cloves and ham and red cabbage, of Christmas and all its ingredients. He took a deep breath and placed Ben's car seat on the counter, steeling himself for a tirade from Eleanor about how long he'd been gone.

But she merely raised her eyebrows. "You were gone a long time."

"Sorry El. The queues at Swann's were unbelievable, as were the prices." He shrugged off his coat and hung it over the back of a chair.

"Well, you're here now." She half rose to take a look at Ben dozing in his car seat and then sat back down again. "And he's got some fresh air which is good."

Max glanced at his mum. She didn't seem to have noticed his arrival; she hadn't even looked up. She was arranging knives in rows. Picking them out of Eleanor's large, velvet-lined canteen and placing them carefully in front of her, nudging them precisely into position with her crabbed old fingers.

"What on earth's she doing El?"

"She's helping me clean the cutlery for tomorrow." Max could hear the smile in Eleanor's voice. "She's an expert isn't she?"

"As far as I know she's never done it before in her life; we didn't have silver cutlery in our house."

"Well, she must be a natural then."

Now that she'd got all the knives lined up, Mum was dipping her cloth into a tub of polish, picking up a knife, smearing it on and setting it down. Each time she reached the end of a row she picked up the first one, took a clean duster and buffed it to a shine. She had a lovely methodical rhythm and she was completely immersed in her work.

"How's she been?" Max said.

"She's been fine, absolutely fine." Eleanor pushed her chair back and came to stand next to him. "You were running away weren't you?"

So, she'd known all along. The confirmation of what he'd suspected settled inside him. He nodded. "I just couldn't face it."

"I know, and I understand Max, I really do. You don't have to keep hiding it from me."

He slid his arm around her shoulders and brushed the top of her head with his lips. Through the glass doors he could see the Christmas tree lights reflecting off the fragile baubles hovering in space.

"She loved the tree Max."

"How did you know what I was thinking?" He pulled away to look at her.

"Because I knew you were looking at the tree. Because you went back down to Surrey specially to pick up your old decorations." She paused and her face softened. "And because I know what that must have cost you."

"Do you?"

"Well, yes, I think so. When my parents died I went to see the place where their car crashed," Eleanor spoke calmly. "I knew they were dead, there was no purpose to going there but I had to see it. I *had to*. I was compelled to go. I had to see it with my own eyes. My aunt – Bill's wife Valerie – didn't want me to go but she couldn't stop me."

"And ... what was it like?"

"It was a beautiful early autumn day; one of those gorgeous, golden afternoons, with a low, red ball of sun catching the leaves alight and throwing long shadows over the road. Everything looked incredibly peaceful ..." Her

231

voice slowed as she remembered and her eyes looked beyond him. "It was a narrow, country lane in Norfolk near the hotel where they'd been staying for the weekend. The hedges were still thick with leaves, bulging out around the corner, obscuring the view I suppose, contributing to the accident, and yet, on that afternoon, when I saw it, it all looked so innocent ... a bucolic English country scene. I remember hearing a thrush singing and then, in the long grass at the side of the road there was a rustling, a great flapping, and a partridge ran out into the road and rose up into the sky and away, across a ploughed field." She breathed deeply and her eyes seemed to refocus so that she was looking at him again. "And in some strange, subliminal way, seeing that comforted me. I took it as a sign that they were at peace – their souls departed, or whatever a bird in flight is meant to signify, even though I don't even believe in God. It's madness I know, but there we are. It helped and I was glad that I'd been."

Max nodded. At the edge of his vision he was aware of Mum's hand reaching out, picking up another piece of silver and buffing it silently.

You were lucky. That's what he wanted to tell Eleanor – lucky to see the last things that they'd seen, to hear the last sounds that they'd heard. To know. To feel the unbearable weight of the knowledge. But how could he say that? *You were lucky.* What – because the tail end of that particular summer had been so wet that nature had run rampant, a council hadn't clipped back a hedgerow and two cars collided head on? Eleanor was watching him with her steady blue-grey eyes. And Mum's movements – an outstretched arm, the soft scrape of metal on wood as she replaced one item, a flash of silver as she picked up another, the silent backwards and forwards of her duster – were there, right beside him.

After a few moments Eleanor said, "Your mum gazed at the tree for ages Max, she stood in front of it running her eyes over it, and then she did something rather odd ..." She paused.

"Go on."

"She poked her hand right down into the branches and then pulled it out again. I asked her if she was looking for something but she just stared at me blankly. To be honest I think she was a bit confused."

"She was looking for his owl," Max said, turning away so that there was no chance of Mum hearing.

Eleanor frowned. "I don't understand."

"Peter's owl," he said quietly, and his eyes travelled back towards the tree. He felt as if he'd given up part of himself, as if Eleanor had taken something from him. And all the while he was aware of Mum sitting just inches away, polishing the silver.

"Peter's?"

Max nodded. "I'll tell you all about it – all about him – I promise – after Mum's left."

"Okay." Eleanor slipped her hand in his.

Max kept seeing his brother pushing his favourite owl deep into the branches when he thought Max wasn't looking, turning his head to check if he was watching. Of course he was, although Peter never knew it, and Max could still see, in his mind's eye, the blood red traces on the back of Peter's hands where the needles had scratched him.

"Max!" Mum's voice made him jump. "There you are." He dropped Eleanor's hand and looked around, disorientated. Mum was peering up at him, her eyes magnified behind their glasses. "We've been cleaning the – " she broke off – "the what d'you call it – the –" She fixed her eyes on the neat rows of knives and forks.

"The cutlery Kate."

233

"That's it." Mum beamed at Eleanor and repeated it triumphantly. "The cutlery! And Helena's been telling me all about her family's Christmas traditions. Haven't you dear?"

Eleanor nodded. "I have."

"They have clean sheets."

"She's quite right Max."

Mum nodded. "See."

"It was one of our traditions. My mum used to put fresh linen on our beds on Christmas Eve."

"You had walnuts."

"What's that Kate?" Eleanor placed her hand on Mum's shoulder and Max imagined the thin, bony feel of it under her fingers.

"Walnuts – in your stockings – didn't you Maxi?" Mum looked up at him. "And chocolate umbrellas."

Chocolate umbrellas. My God. He'd forgotten about those. He could hear Peter's voice floating through the darkness in the cold early hours of Christmas morning, his hands tugging at his shoulders, the blinding torchlight in his face, the chocolate smudges around his mouth. *Max – Max – are you awake?*

"We had satsumas," Eleanor said.

"No – no – I don't think we had those." Max could see Mum's eyes narrowing behind her lenses as she tried to remember. They'd had clementines. She maintained they tasted better.

"No." Mum shook her head firmly. "Definitely not those." She paused, and then said in a clipped, business-like voice. "And now if you'll excuse me I've got to get on." It was the tone she'd sometimes used to use – her bossy, I'm-more-important-than-you tone when she'd got something to do. He hadn't heard it in years.

Mum took a spoon out of the canteen, dipped her duster into the polish and started smearing it over. She placed it on the table and picked up another, pushing the cotton into the curve of the spoon with her thumb and then turning it over, sliding it through with her fingers. And then, just behind him, Max heard a clicking sound. No more than that; the soft, intermittent, ticking of plastic on granite. Eleanor's eyes darted past him. He knew what it was before she moved. As she went to Ben – as she lifted him up and out of his car seat, as his blanket fell from him and she wrapped her arms around him – the rhythm of Mum's polishing didn't miss a beat. And Max heard her words again, in his head.

Keep going Maxi – just keep going.

***

I'm feeling so good. *So good!* The knowledge that this is my last day at St Joseph's – this lovely golden-wrapped chocolate coin of knowledge – makes me feel taller, older and wiser. I suck it and enjoy it all day as the sun shines through the classroom window, warming my cheek, and I breathe in the summer-green smell of cut grass. I can hear Mr Jakes' mower roaring up and down the playing fields; the noise gets louder and louder as he comes closer and closer and then turns – I can see his hands on the horizontal steering wheel as he rolls it through his fingers – and rumbles away again.

I can't wait to finish this lesson, this very last lesson of all, and run out of the door as fast as my legs can carry me. When the mower suddenly stops, it's as if the world outside the classroom's started up again. I hear the high, faraway hum of a plane and the hoot of a car's horn, the drone of traffic on the main road, the laugh of someone I can't see.

"Okay class – you can put away your books now – the bell's just about to go." The whole room seems to quiver as

Mr Beattie says this. "I want to wish you all the very best of luck in your new schools."

The jangling alarm cuts off his words so that all we can see is his mouth opening and closing. Everyone's up on their feet and crowding out of the door. I'm in a crush of hot, sticky bodies that smell of sweat and then I'm out into the corridor, my shoes clattering on the shiny floor as I run towards the cloakroom. MAX RIVERS. There's my peg. I'm just about to pull my PE kit off when Ian and Micky charge past me, swinging their boots.

"You coming Max?"

"Where're you going?"

"Up onto the playing fields – Beattie says it's okay."

I pause, my hand on my peg. Peter will be waiting for me inside his classroom.

"Come on Max!"

"Okay then!" I grab my boots and sprint after them through the rows of hooks and the smell of dried mud. Peter can wait.

The field's up behind the classrooms, miles away. Other boys are up there already, all from the top two forms, all leaving today. The atmosphere's crazy. The blue sky stretches above us and the sun shines down as I run as fast as I can over the newly mown grass. We don't stop to form teams, we just shoot wildly into the goal. Jimmy Slater's in there, his massive hands in their goalkeeper's gloves hover beside him and fly up to catch the ball. When the ball's passed to me I dribble it – one-two, dodging past Ian out onto the wing – and then I thump it with my boot and it flies past Jimmy so fast he barely seems to see it. I punch the air above my head. Before I know it, the ball's mine again. I take it through Micky and Ian, bash into Robbie and jostle him away, then my foot makes that sweet connection and I ram the ball home again through Jimmy's legs.

"Heh Max! Give us a chance!" Jimmy's standing, his hands on his hips, and all the others are cheering me on as I run back to the centre.

We play on and on. My right foot's charmed. On this golden, gilded day I never seem to miss. When I look at my watch it's four o'clock. I can't believe it. We'll have missed the bus. Mum will kill me. I start running off the pitch.

"Max? Where you going?" It's Ian's voice.

I shout over my shoulder, "I've got to go – I'm taking Peter."

"Spoil sport."

As I run, panting, across the field, I think of Peter sitting in his classroom. He'll be colouring in the shapes on those big white pieces of paper that Miss Sally hands out to them all, his blond head curled over his wooden desk, his tongue sticking out from between his lips as he tries not to go over the edge. Or he might be standing by the window, looking out, wishing he could join the big boys. I barge through the double doors and my boots clatter on the tiled floor as I race up the corridor. If a teacher sees me, it'll be detention. We're not allowed to wear our boots inside. Then I realise it doesn't matter; it's my last day. When I get to his classroom, he's not there. Through the glass window in the door I can see that the room's empty. My chest's heaving. It's hurting. Sweat's sticking my shirt to my back. Where's he gone? Would he have walked up to the bus stop all by himself? Even though I don't think I've got enough breath to move, I start to walk and then run, clattering down the corridor, through the double doors and out into the bright sun. My legs feel like weights as I force myself up the slope of the drive between the rows of frothy white blossom on the trees. I'm at the top now, through the gate. I look left towards the bus stop. There's no one there. I know I've got to go and check at No. 62. I push myself on. It's as though I'm running through treacle my legs are so tired and my head feels as if it's about to burst. Just as I knew it would be the front garden of No. 62 is empty. The tree stands motionless in the sun, its shadow spills out across the concrete towards me like a stain. I bend over, each breath rips at my throat and I think I might be sick. Gradually, my breathing slows. A tuft of grass has pushed its way through a raised crack in the concrete. I think about Mum, and what she'll say – *You stupid, stupid boy Max!* She'll make me stay in my room again. Idiot Peter! Where have you gone?

***

Max lay in bed, waiting. He heard the give of the floorboard outside Ben's room and his door creaking on its hinges as it was pulled to, but not quite shut. There was a momentary pause and he imagined Eleanor in her white silk nightie, lifting her fingers from the handle, careful not to make a noise, her bare feet padding quietly towards their room. The same sounds every night, even on Christmas Eve. The night before Christmas, when all through the house, not a creature was stirring, not even a mouse.

The footsteps outside the door stopped, turned with the soft squeak of skin on wood, and tiptoed back along the landing. This was a change in routine. Max realised she was checking on his mum. Eleanor had been great with her, keeping her occupied all evening with the sort of small, domestic tasks that had once been Mum's life. He'd seen them in the kitchen when he came downstairs for Ben's bottle, tears were rolling down Mum's face as she peeled an onion for the bread sauce. When she brushed the back of her sleeve against her eyes it traced a pattern in his mind. As he changed Ben and gave him his bath he could hear carols on the radio and Mum's quavering voice. By the time they ate their supper, Ben was safely tucked up in his cot, fast asleep, and Mum was tired, not saying much, yawning widely, tapping her hand against her mouth.

Underneath the bed, on his side so she wouldn't see it, was Eleanor's stocking. Max had used an old sock that he'd found kicking around at the back of his drawer and stuffed the engagement ring in its small domed box right into the toe of it. It would be the last thing she'd come to, after the walnut, the saggy-skinned Satsuma, the Jo Malone, the Bacchi chocolates in memory of Venice, the Myla lingerie. Each present was wrapped in thick crimson paper. He imagined Eleanor's trembling hesitation as she opened the box, her face as she saw the ring. He shifted slightly and smelt the fresh, outdoor smell of clean linen.

In a moment, he knew, the door would rattle and a smudge of light would enter the room with Eleanor and remain – he'd just about got used to it now – because she wanted to be able to hear Ben if he woke up. And Max knew exactly what she'd do next. She'd walk over to the mirror, pick up a pot of her expensive cream and slick it onto her finger. He'd smell her scent. She'd dab the cream on her face – dab, dab, dab, forehead, cheeks, chin – then she'd massage it in and stroke it off with cotton wool. She'd loosen her hair, shake it out and run her fingers through it. Turn, switch the light off and come to bed. And he'd reach out for her.

There was a click, a rattle, the room lightened. Max thought of the unseen ring waiting for her; of the new page turning over, the story being told.

"And this is for you Mrs Rivers." Bill leant forwards and held out a slim flat parcel wrapped in silver paper.

Mum studied it carefully. She was sitting on the sofa next to Eleanor and for a moment or two Max didn't think she was going to respond at all, but then she said, quite normally and very politely, "Thank you, thank you very much," and took the package from Bill. She didn't open it though, just left it in her lap and carried on watching Ben, who was sitting on Eleanor's knee fisting her paper napkin into his mouth and grizzling on and off.

Bill's face was flushed and he smelt of cigars. He'd arrived about ten minutes ago, straight from the Dorchester and, Max was relieved to see, fairly pissed. They were all in the living room, Ben's presents in a slithering pile beneath the tree.

"Aren't you going to open it Kate?" Eleanor prompted Mum gently.

When she didn't respond, Bill said, "How are you getting on at your new place?" Mum looked at him blankly. The glassy black window behind her was steaming up. Come on Mum, Max thought. Say something. Bill leant towards her, tilting his glass of Margaux at a dangerous angle, and repeated loudly, "How are you getting on Mrs Rivers?"

"I'm not deaf you know!" Mum said quickly.

Max had offered her a glass of sherry before lunch but she'd hardly touched it – or much of her lunch. She'd been far too interested in Ben.

"She's getting on fine, aren't you?" said Eleanor, pulling the napkin out of Ben's mouth. His grizzles immediately turned to cries and he strained around trying to snatch it back. "No you don't." She pulled it away.

"Why don't you open this?" Mum held out her parcel.

He grabbed it from her and shook it like a tambourine. Eleanor stilled his hand and nudged her forefinger under an edge of the wrapping paper. Her ring flashed.

"My God!" Bill put down his glass and took her hand in his. "Now *that* is what I call a ring." He rubbed his thumb against the diamond. "You should have said something Eleanor."

Bill looked up and Eleanor started to smile. A small, crinkle-lipped smile at first because she was trying to play it

240

cool. Then she caught Max's eye and her expression, her brimming, uncontainable happiness, was the same as it had been this morning – as it had been, on and off, all day.

"It's wonderful isn't it?" she said, holding out her hand, looking down to admire the ring and then glancing quickly up at him again.

"It certainly is." Bill turned her wrist. The diamond winked and glinted. Ben dropped Mum's parcel and thrust his hand towards it.

"No you don't." Eleanor retrieved the present, tore off some paper so that it curled temptingly and handed it back to him to rip open.

"It's beautiful," said Bill. "Did you both choose it?"

"No." Eleanor's eyes shone. "Max chose it. I found it in my stocking this morning."

Her chin was balanced on the top of Ben's head as he tore silver paper into shreds, and Max knew she was remembering. She'd delved her hand into the toe of the sock and pulled out the small black box and he'd known, by the slight quiver of doubt in her eyes, that she wasn't quite sure. That she was telling herself, as her fingers closed around the domed lid, that it could be earrings, a locket, a bracelet. But she thought she knew. He'd pulled the duvet closer around him and watched her face as she opened the box. For what seemed like an eternity she didn't move. The image had sunk into his mind, flavoured with the tang of satsuma. Her bent head, her tousled hair framing her face, the thin white strap of her nightie slipping off her shoulder. Her eyelids hid her eyes, her thoughts, her emotions, as she looked down. Her eyelashes shadowed her cheeks. For one, mad, elongated moment he thought she might not like it – *that she might say no* – and then she'd looked up, into his eyes, and the moment was over.

"We always have walnuts in our stockings don't we Maxi?" Mum's voice, over-loud, cut in.

"What's that Mum?" Max had been remembering the touch of Eleanor's hands on his face, the quick, fierce passion with which she'd kissed him.

"Well that's some walnut!" said Bill.

Ben, tired of tearing up paper, started to whimper. Eleanor jiggled him about on her lap.

"So –" Bill looked from Eleanor to Max. "This is wonderful news." Max returned Bill's gaze. It looked as if he meant it. "Any thoughts on a date?"

Mum turned to Ben. "What's the matter then, my little one?"

"We haven't really thought about that yet," Eleanor said, bending to retrieve the flat blue box that Ben had dropped on the floor.

"A summer wedding's always nice," said Bill. "Mary and I were married on June the first."

"Well, yes, I suppose it is …" Eleanor looked unsure. Ben was waving his arm about trying to snatch the box. Eleanor handed it to Mum.

Mum held the box in front of her. "Let's have a look see what's in here shall we?" Ben lunged for her hands.

Eleanor pulled him back and turned to Bill. Ben immediately started to cry. "Max wants – well we both want – something simple, nothing too grand."

"When you were a little girl you used to dress up in Mary's veil and pretend to be a bride." Bill spoke loudly over Ben's whimpers.

"Did I? I never knew that."

"You were only little."

"Who's going to be a bride?" Mum said, looking up. The box slipped off her lap and Ben, startled by her voice, stopped crying and looked at her.

242

"Eleanor is Mum – remember – we told you, we're getting married."

"About time too if you ask me!"

They all laughed, but Max had spotted the look of terrified confusion in his mum's eyes.

"Well, it's wonderful news," said Bill. "And it goes without saying that I want only the best for Eleanor. Have you thought about where you might have the reception? Personally, I love the Lanesborough."

"We haven't really got that far yet Bill," Max said.

"Well, it's up to you of course, but Eleanor's like a daughter to me you know Max and I'd like to be involved."

"It's a wonderful hotel Max." Eleanor's eyes held mine as she jiggled Ben on her knee.

"I thought we were going to keep it small."

"Nothing to stop it being a small affair at the Lanesborough." Bill winked at Eleanor.

"It would be rather lovely Max." Eleanor was pulling Ben back as he strained towards the box on the floor.

"D'you remember when Mary and I had our silver wedding there?" Bill scooped up the box and handed it to Mum.

Max watched her. She was turning the box over and over.

"I do," Eleanor laughed. "Aunt Jane ended up singing *The Girl from Ipanima* – and trying to dance the conga with one of the waiters."

"And then Mary tripped over."

"Oh my God yes – I'd forgotten that." Eleanor giggled. "I'd never seen her so tipsy."

Mum was still examining the box. Ben was straining out of Eleanor's arms, his arms flailing.

"Let me help you Mum." Max leant across and opened the box to reveal an elegant silk scarf in various shades of blue. He thought of her wearing it, sitting in her wingback chair in her lonely green room. "Thank you Bill, that's most generous of you."

Bill lifted his glass in salute. "Not at all. You're virtually family now, both of you – all three of you," he corrected himself.

Ben's wind-milling arms tipped the box off Mum's lap and he started whining again.

"What is it my darling boy?" Mum leant towards him. "What's the matter then my little man?"

Eleanor, laughing at something that Bill had said, didn't hear. Max picked up the box and got to his feet.

"What about a glass of Champagne to celebrate?"

"Marvellous idea Max," Bill said.

"That would be lovely." Eleanor looked up at Max, her eyes shining. As he brushed past her, she extended her hand to touch him and the Christmas tree lights danced and dazzled off the diamond on her finger.

***

My football boots clatter on the tiles. I'm not meant to wear them inside. I'm not meant to run. The classroom door's open now and there's Miss Sally in her pink dress, reaching up to one of the shelves. As I clatter closer she looks around, her arm still held up above her head.

"Max – have you forgotten something?"

I'm so out of breath. I feel as if I've been running for ever, my heart's pounding and I can't speak. As Miss Sally drops her arm and turns to face me, I can see that she thinks he's with me. When I shake my head, sweat sprays off my hair.

"Well what is it then?" She stares at me. Her eyes are as blue as the sky outside. "What on earth have you been up to Max – you look dreadful. And where's Peter?"

I still can't speak. My chest's heaving.

"You did collect him just now didn't you?"

I take a deep breath and watch the blueness of her eyes flicker and waiver. "No." It hardly comes out.

"What?" She frowns and bends closer. "I thought that you'd collected him."

"I was up on the field."

"Well where is he then?" There's a quiver in her voice. "I've been tidying up in here for the past ten minutes." She walks quickly away from me towards the door, and as I follow her, my heart's still thumping hard. I'm not sure if I should tell her about the bus stop – that he's not there. Her dark hair flicks from side to side as she looks up and down the corridor. "Let's go and check the loos."

She's hurrying now, her black shoes clicking along the tiles in front of me as I try to keep up. And now she's running. Both of us are running when we're not meant to. When Miss Varley steps out of her classroom we almost knock her over.

"Have you seen Peter Rivers?" Miss Sally's face is bright red. "We can't seem to find him."

"No – no I haven't." Miss Varley frowns. "Have you tried the cloakroom?"

"No – you go and check there – we're doing the loos." Miss Sally barks it out and starts running again and I see, as I follow her, a strange, startled look on Miss Varley's face that makes my legs go weak.

Miss Sally barges through the green toilet door and it slams open against the wall. She strides along, pushing each of the cubicle doors. Red-yellow-red-yellow-red-yellow. Bang! Bang! Bang! Bang! Bang! Every loo is empty.

"Follow me." She's walking quickly, striding out so that I have to gallop to keep up with her. We're walking towards Mrs Maishman's room. "What were you doing up on the field? You were meant to collect your brother." She throws the words over her shoulder.

"Mr Beattie said we could play football up on the fields Miss."

She doesn't answer. She walks straight into Mrs Maishman's room. "We can't find Peter Rivers."

My heart jumps up into my throat again.

"What d'you mean, you can't find him?" Mrs Maishman's much older than Miss Sally. She smiles at me from behind her desk. "Hello Max – my you look hot."

"Max was meant to come and collect him from his classroom. I'd been waiting with him for Max to arrive. I had to pop out for two tics to deal with Lily and when I came back, Peter had gone. I thought Max had collected him so I didn't do anything about it."

Mrs Maishman stands up behind her desk. "So how long's he been missing then?"

"That's the thing – it must have been about four when I popped out." Her eyes flick up to the big black and white clock on Mrs Maishman's wall. I glance over and I know Mrs Maishman's looking too. Both hands are pointing down. It's half-past four.

"So he's been missing for almost half an hour then." Mrs Maishman's voice has a nasty, sharp edge to it. And when I look back to her I see that her face has gone all fixed and hard, like Mum's does when she's angry. I inch back behind Miss Sally's legs.

"Who's left on the premises Sally?"

"I'm not sure – most of the teachers I think – no other children – certainly not from my class."

"Right – let's gather the staff in my room and start a proper search."

"I'm so sorry Lynne – I assumed Max had collected him."

"Just go and round up the others Sally."

Miss Sally looks as though she's about to cry and I can sense that warm, liquid feeling starting behind my eyes. *Assumed.* I don't know what the word means, but it hisses like a snake inside my head.

"Max – you'd better sit over there." Mrs Maishman points to the purple settee in the corner that we lie down on when we're not very well. I walk over to it and sit right on the edge, looking down at my white knuckles on my brown knees and wishing Mum was here. Miss Sally's gone and Mrs Maishman's picked up the telephone. "Do you know your number off by heart Max?"

"Yes miss." I say it out to her. I realise that she's phoning Mum.

***

Max thought at first that the noise was all part of his dream – a siren, an alarm blaring out, a car horn going off. Then he heard Eleanor's urgent voice in his ear.

"Max! Max! Wake up!" Hands gripped his shoulders and he registered that the wails – distorted, louder, more insistent than usual – were Ben's.

He staggered to his feet, banging his thigh on the corner of the bed as he saw the pale shape of her back disappear through the bedroom door. When he reached Ben's room she'd already picked the baby up from his cot and was cradling him to her, her head curled over his writhing body.

His cries were deafening and when Eleanor looked up Max could barely recognise her contorted, frightened face.

"What's the matter with him Max?" Her voice was high and shaky.

Ben's forehead shone with sweat, his fists flailed at his ears and Max could smell the rank sweetness of his nappy.

Eleanor brushed her son's cheek with her lips. "He's burning up Max."

"Okay – okay." Max took a deep breath. "Let's get his clothes off." He had to shout to make himself heard even though he was right beside Eleanor, so close he could sense her trembling.

His head filled with Ben's cries as he wrestled with the poppers between his kicking legs. The more Eleanor tried to restrain him, the more he twisted away until, with a fierce tug, Max dropped his damp towelling sleep suit onto the floor. The soft rolls of Ben's thighs were smeared with his milky shit.

"I think we should phone the doctor." Eleanor's panicked eyes stared back at his as he rapped out the order. "Come on El – where's the number?" She was almost crying. "Come on El – think!"

"It's on the board –" she burst out suddenly – "in the kitchen. There's a list of emergency numbers."

All the time, as Max ran along the hall, down the clattering stairs and into the kitchen, scrabbling for the light switches, snatching up the phone, scanning the board and punching in the number, he could hear Ben's cries. There was something very wrong with them. He told himself that babies were always getting ill, that this was nothing, that he'd be fine. When he skidded back into Ben's room Eleanor was standing over him, trying to clean him up as he wriggled on his changing mat.

"We should take his temperature."

She looked up and Max could see her fighting to keep her composure. She swung around, and then back again. "Where's the thermometer?"

"God El – don't you know?" The phone's ring pulsed in his ear as Eleanor pulled out a drawer, then another and another, then yanked at a cupboard door. He realised she was panicking with fear.

"I think it's in the bathroom."

"Is it?" She spun around.

"Give him to me." He held out his arms but she'd already gone. *The Bellevue surgery is now closed. Its hours of opening are ...* The recorded voice in his ear was painfully slow. Eleanor brushed back past him. "Where's a pen?"

"What?" She looked at him blankly.

"A pen."

"In my bag by the bed."

Max ran down the hall and into their bedroom, fumbling for the light switch, scanning the scene for Eleanor's bag and dropping down beside it. His fingers pushed aside her wallet and scrabbled among tissues and lipstick before closing around a pen. When the voice in his ear recited the emergency number he wrote the digits faintly on the back of his hand, the nib pushing into his skin. And in his mind he saw thin red trails on soft white skin where the Christmas tree had scratched the back of Peter's hand. *Please God no!* His finger shook as he punched in the number.

When he ran through Ben's door, Eleanor was standing with her back to him. She was trying to take Ben's temperature, but the more she fought to pin him down, the more he writhed away. When she turned, her weeping face shocked Max again.

"I can't do it Max. He won't let me."

"Give me the thermometer." He thrust the phone at her. As soon as he touched Ben's skin, his clammy body squirmed out of his grip and the thermometer slipped through his fingers onto the floor. He bent to retrieve it.

"What's going on here?" Mum's voice, over his shoulder, made him jump.

"Not now Mum." He looked at Eleanor. "Has anyone answered?"

Eleanor put her finger to her lips and concentrated her gaze on Ben. "Yes ..." she said into the phone. "No ... no ..."

"What a lot of noise you're making my little one." Mum moved in beside Max and held out her hand to Ben.

"Not now Mum." Max resisted the urge to push her aside, to shout at her to go back to bed, to tell her this wasn't Peter but Ben. His boy. His little man. And this time everything was going to be all right.

When Mum touched Ben's cheek he flinched away, took a deep breath and let out another howl.

"He's got an ear infection," she said.

Max swung around. His mum was wearing her faded old dressing gown over her nightie and her face was pale.

"They're very painful." She was calm as a rock.

"How d'you know?" Max said.

"And now look; he's worn himself out with all that crying."

She was right. Without warning, as if his battery had run out, Ben's eyelids were starting to droop, his cries were subsiding to hiccuppy sobs. His tense, screwed-up body was unfolding itself.

"But how d'you know?"

"He was cuffing his ears with his fists," Mum said, laying the back of a claw-like hand against Ben's cheek. "Dead giveaway."

Eleanor clicked off the phone. Into the silence Ben gave a deep, stuttering sigh. His face was already less flushed and his arms were stretched above his head. His eyebrows were two perfect paintbrush strokes and a coal-black comma of hair clung damply to his forehead. His chest rose and fell, revealing the fragile ladder of ribs beneath his skin. Without warning a tear stole down Max's face, soft and warm as a kiss, and then another and another, splashing silently onto the changing mat and forming a salty pool on the plastic.

"What did the doctor say?" Max looked at Eleanor.

She was watching Ben. "That it could be an ear infection, to give him some Calpol, and see how he is in the morning. He might need antibiotics, in which case we can pick up a prescription from the emergency chemist in Northside Road." She stretched out a hand and touched Ben's cheek, then glanced up at Max. "Oh Max ..."

"I know." He could see the sharp pain of her love for their child reflected back at him.

"You used to get lots of ear infections Maxi." Mum's voice cut in.

He turned. "Did I?"

"You certainly did." She grinned and her shocking, dentureless gums were redolent of Ben's. "And you bashed your ears with your fists just like that."

She turned and shuffled off, rational as a ruler – his old mum – leaving the two of them standing over Ben's sleeping shape. After a few minutes Eleanor picked him up, carried him over to his cot and gently laid him down before covering him with a blanket.

They stayed with him for the rest of the night. Max told Eleanor to go to bed and get some sleep, but she refused, so he brought another chair from their room, set it by her rocking chair and they sat, side by side, watching the small, breathing lump. Every now and then, Max's head drooped and he caught his breath and jerked upright, his eyes locked onto the rise and fall of the pale blue blanket. Eventually, as the room began to lighten, Eleanor dozed, her head slumped awkwardly to one side, exposing the tiny butterfly behind her ear. Max settled a cushion under her shoulder and tucked a rug around her. He heard the birds start up, the familiar rattle of bottles, the departing hiss of the milkman's float, the plop of the newspaper on the front step. The new day dawning.

He pulled the frying pan out of the cupboard with a clatter and plonked it on the hob. "How about I make us all some cooked breakfast?"

He felt light-headed with exhaustion and relief. They'd just arrived home from the surgery, where the duty doctor had shone a torch in Bens' ears, confirmed that Mum had been right about his ear infection, and written him out a prescription.

"That sounds delicious." El was pumping bright yellow syrup into Ben's mouth with a plastic syringe. "God –" She stood back and watched him. "You'd never believe he was the same boy would you?"

It was true. Ben was curled in his baby rocker, smacking his lips together.

Max's old Italian espresso pot was just beginning to bubble up, the hot, rich smell of coffee permeating the kitchen.

"They're like balls," Mum said.

"What on earth are you on about Mum?"

"She means they bounce back … children." Eleanor was transformed too. There were dark, violet smudges under her eyes and her hair wasn't as sleekly combed as usual, but the wild-eyed panic of the previous night might never have been.

Max pulled eggs and tomatoes out of the fridge. "Have we got any bacon?"

"Yes. There was some left over from the bacon rolls – and there are some chipolatas."

He foraged around among heaving shelves. "My God El – there's enough to feed an army in here."

"I don't like chipolatas."

"You don't have to have them Mum." He piled everything on the counter beside the sink.

"They're not proper sausages – far too thin. I like proper sausages. Big, fat beef sausages."

There was a tinkle as Ben threw his toy elephant onto the floor.

"Ben –"

Max heard Eleanor's reprimand as she stooped to pick up the elephant and then, after a second or two, another tinkle as Ben pushed it onto the floor again. She pulled a chopping board from under the counter.

"Let me help you." She came to stand beside him and he smelt her scent as she stretched across him for a knife and caught a flash of her ring as she scooped up a handful of tomatoes. There was something touching about the thought of Eleanor, in all her exhaustion, putting on her ring.

"Round and round the garden …" Max could hear his mum's voice as he tugged the chipolatas out of their bag "… one step, two steps, tickle him under there …" and then Ben's squeal of laughter.

When his mobile pinged to announce a text, he pulled it out of his pocket and flicked it open. It showed one missed call. He remembered that it had gone off at the doctor's and he'd silenced it. He tapped into his voicemails. "You have one new message. Message received today at nine thirty-eight." Max heard the click, then an intake of breath before the voice began.

"Mr Rivers, this is Richard Gould, formerly of Surrey CID …"

A finger of Virginia creeper tapped on the window pane. Wind moved among the sparse leaves of the crooked tree halfway down the garden. A fat pigeon heaved itself into flight and skimmed over the grass up into a branch where it sat, oversized and heavy, outlined against a pewter sky.

"Max? Are you okay?" He became aware of Eleanor frowning at him, the skin at the top of her nose bunching into a V of tiny lines. "You're white as a sheet."

"Round and round the garden …" Mum's voice starting up again.

Max's stomach turned over.

"Who was it?"

Ben's loud, chortling laughter.

"It was no one … nothing …"

As he brushed past Ben's high chair something clattered to the floor and Max heard his son crying as he opened the French window, then Eleanor's soothing voice as he closed it behind him, then her muffled call, "Where are you going?"

He walked down to the end of the garden, to the old shed where he'd found the pot for the Christmas tree, wind whipping his face, mud caking his shoes. He turned to look back at the house. He could see Eleanor at the kitchen window. He knew she was watching him. He spotted a gap in the ivy behind the shed and remembered the estate agent saying something about a cut-through, an overgrown snicket she'd called it, that led onto the common. He pushed his way through. Twigs snagged on his jumper, tugged at his trousers and scratched his hands. When he was almost about to give up, he emerged into a small clearing surrounded by bushes and the thick, soaring trunks of horse chestnut trees; beyond those was the open grass of the common and, in the far distance, a scattering of small coloured shapes moving about.

The last time Max had heard from Richard Gould had been about six or seven years ago, by which time he'd long since retired to the New Forest. But Max knew that for many years the former DI had returned to Surrey, to the cold cases unit, to go through the roomfuls and computer-loads of files, the reams of paperwork, the cabinets of meticulously preserved exhibits in the case of the boy who never came home. That's what they'd called it, the newspapers: they'd had to make their story; their narrative they'd call it today. Gould had called to warn Max that the press were going to run a piece about bones being discovered quite close to the school. His voice was deeper and older, but he'd spoken in the clipped, precise phrases of the ex-copper he was and Max had recognised a man trying to maintain his distance. *They're not those of your brother, Mr Rivers. Wrong DNA. We've done the tests. Just wanted you to know. But rest assured your brother's case remains open. In cases such as this, the file is never closed.*

Max watched a leaf twirling, skittering across the scrubby grass. It could be just another such call to keep him informed. *In cases such as this, Mr Rivers, the file is never closed.* Max thought of Peter's bed, flat and red-and-white and empty, waiting for him all these years, in Hillside Close.

He thought of Sam Whiley. Two days after Peter disappeared, the police got Sam to reconstruct his last movements. Sam was six, a year older than Peter, but with the same build and the same white-blond hair. Max had been too old, and anyway the two of them had always looked very different. Peter's face fatter, broader than his. His laugh more open. His eyes more trusting. Max had often imagined what it would have felt like to take part in the reconstruction. To walk in the footsteps that Peter had walked at the exact time of day that he must have walked. To go back and be there with him. To *be* him for a few minutes. He used to see Sam sometimes and he'd search him for signs of Peter. The last time Max had seen Sam he'd been about 13. Tall and lanky, his once chubby face had been as lean as Max's. He'd had the first signs of stubble. Max knew that his mum's eyes had searched in just the same way.

He realised he was shaking. It was freezing out here of course, but it wasn't that. He punched the number Gould had left into his phone, heard it ringing out at the other end and tried to imagine what the burly ex-policeman might look like now. A woman answered. She spoke quickly, almost brusquely, as she asked him his name, and when he told her Max thought she hesitated just for an instant but he might have been mistaken. He wondered who she was and how much she knew. As he waited for Gould his eyes fixed on a curling fern of brown-tinged bracken, its claw-like fronds delicate and perfect as eyelashes.

"Mr Rivers." Gould's voice, though that of a pensioner, was firm and steady, for which Max was grateful.

"You wanted to speak to me."

"Yes … yes I did …" and in that moment's hesitation Max knew. "Mr Rivers, the police have reason to believe that they've found your brother's remains."

The browning curl of bracken shivered in the breeze.

"Do they have reason to believe or do they know?"

Another hesitation, then, "They know. I wanted to be the one to tell you."

Max smelt the earthiness around him. The quick, sharp smell of it. He took in the curve of the stem running down the centre of the bracken, the pairs of leaves branching off on each side, one below the other, their fine serrated edges like small, green, rounded teeth.

"How do they know it's him? How can they be sure?"

"At first they thought the remains were those of someone else, another boy who went missing some years ago. They were able to take DNA from bones that they believed to be his. It wasn't, so they ran it through the DNA database and it turned out to match that taken from your brother's toy rabbit …"

Max didn't hear DI Gould for some time after that. All he could see, in his mind, was Charlie Rabbit, one bald ear hanging from Peter's hand. And Mum searching for him on the landing. Mum. The word, the sound, the thought of her, was like a cold black stone in the depths of him.

"How good a match?" His words were detached from him; someone else's.

"Sorry?"

"How good a DNA match did they get?"

"Nineteen out of 20 numbers."

His foot shifted, crushing the fragile frond of bracken.

"And they also found a hairline fracture on the second phalange of the left little finger."

Peter splayed out on the grass, face down. Mum dashing towards him faster than he'd ever seen her run before. *What on earth were you thinking Max?* For several seconds Max was unable to speak. He kept his eyes focused on the smashed bracken.

"So it's him."

"It's your brother Mr Rivers."

Your brother. The two words wrapped themselves around him.

"Where was he found?"

"About ten miles from the school, just off the A25 between Ashworth and Needham."

"Where they're building the new estate?"

There was a slight pause. "Exactly."

The traffic lights, the queues, the luxury family homes in wide brushstrokes of colour painted on the hoardings.

"They were excavating the foundations and they drained the pond at the old nursery."

Light green and brown fingers of willow brushed its surface, wind rippled over it. Max had forgotten about that pond. He'd used to go there sometimes, with his mum, before she got too frail; they'd sit on the varnished wooden bench under the trees and watch the ducks. They'd feed them with pieces of bread that they'd roll into soft, squidgy balls in their fingers and throw onto the water. Bile rose in his throat.

Gould's words continued. "The pond was put in twenty years ago ... the remains were found ... when they were digging out ..." But Max was no longer taking them in. He was thinking of his little brother under all that weight of water while he and Mum tossed bread onto its green-tinged surface.

"I want to go there." His voice scratched. "To see where he is."

"You can – as soon as they've finished at the site."

"When will that be?"

"In four or five days' time."

"And then I can go there?"

"Yes."

After the call, Max sank down onto the grass. He was very, very cold. He could feel the damp seeping in through his jeans, up through the earth. A weak shaft of sun filtered between branches and glanced off the top of a few meagre blades. He felt its gentle touch on his skin. Smelt the dank green smell of the bracken. Peter's smell.

His brother, his missing limb with its shadowy ache, was back in place. A deep, dark grave of a place, but a place. A known, certain place. And from somewhere inside Max's numb, frozen depths came a sweet, warm trickle. No more than a thread at first. But he could feel it. In the pulse at his throat and the thump of his heart. Blood was flowing through his body, through his veins and arteries. Pumping and moving in a stream of relief.

He sat, perfectly still, as DI Gould's words settled, like slowly sinking pebbles, on the floor of his mind. Peter. The name rocked in its sandy indentation. Back and forth. And settled.

He was found.

Soon as he thought it, Peter was there. Standing right beside him with his tanned summer face, a frown of concentration curling his eyebrows under the thick wedge of blond fringe, the ends of a couple of hairs sticking to his damp forehead like paintbrush tips as they waited for the bus on that bright, scorching day.

"Max –"

Max reached deep into his mind, trying to touch his little brother and feel him and conjure him up.

"Max –"

But the pull was too much. Peter had gone. Evaporated into thin air.

"Max!"

He looked up into Eleanor's face. She was bending down, her hand on his shoulder. "Max – what on earth are you doing? I've been looking for you everywhere. You're frozen stiff."

Max couldn't speak. To speak would undo him. It was all within him, inside his head. The words, the looks, the memories. The most fragile, most precious things in the world. Bundled up, packaged and parcelled in tissue, with no rips in the wrapping paper. No holes. No flashes of daylight. No hopes. Not even a fragment of one thousandth of a hope.

Peter had gone. It was over.

And at last, from somewhere inside his other reconstructed self, Max found a voice. It wasn't as firm as the one he'd used with Gould, but it was a voice.

"I've got something to tell you Eleanor."

The four of them travelled down the A3 in a taxi, its tyres hissing through brown slush. That morning, they'd woken to a changed world. When Max had pulled up the bedroom blind the scene that met his eyes had made him gasp. The road, the cars, the long line of angled roofs opposite were all covered in a blanket of snow. As he watched, a car moved off revealing a dark rectangle of road. It looked like a missing tooth. A gap. And he'd thought of the missing pom-pom in the fringing of Norah's blind. A clump fell softly from a branch. He'd called Eleanor over and they'd stood together, their skins touching, as flakes began to flutter down, silent as death.

Ben, strapped on Eleanor's lap, had fallen asleep almost as soon as they'd set off. As had Mum. Max hadn't been sure she should come.

"Can't we leave her with Aneta? She won't know what's going on; she doesn't even know he's ..." He'd been unable to finish the sentence.

Eleanor had gently insisted. "He's her son Max – her *son* – she has to be there."

He knew Eleanor was right but he couldn't push aside his doubts. Mum's head lolled against the car window and Ben's slumped forward onto his chest. Eleanor placed her hand over Max's to still it. He hadn't realised it until then but he'd been clenching and unclenching his fist. He kept imagining the sound of the first handful of earth hitting the wooden lid of the coffin.

The snow-covered parish church looked like a chocolate box picture. The graveyard sloped up behind it, a dazzling white arc against the cut-glass blue sky. He could see the

260

hearse parked in the road close to the lych-gate and, beyond it, being held at bay by several uniformed policemen, the hungry animals of the press, their long-lensed cameras sniffing the air like snouts, and he remembered how voracious they'd been as they'd prowled around the garden wall at Hillside Close. To begin with they'd been assiduous as lovers in marking the anniversaries. Alongside his brother's beaming seaside picture they'd retell the story again and again.

It's been a week now since five-year-old Peter Rivers set off for school with his brother Max on a bright summer's day ...

Ten days ago ...

It's been a month now ...

But after a while they petered out. Petered out. Even as the phrase entered his head, the truth hit him again.

Peter was gone.

Max felt Eleanor's fingers closing around his. He could hear the bells tolling. Long, low peels that echoed across the valley.

A week ago, on a miserable, sodden afternoon he'd knelt inside a nylon forensics tent and bent his head until it almost touched the soil where Peter had lain for 24 years. He'd smelt the loamy smell of the earth and dug his hands in until he could feel the grit under his nails and the clods pushing at the soft, sweet skin between his fingers. In the early days, the first few years, he'd used to have terrifying nightmares. He became fixated with Peter being buried underground, imagining the soil crushed into his mouth, his fingers scrabbling like a desperate mole. He'd tasted the brown, clumped grittiness of the earth, flinched at the jarring crunch of teeth on flint and stone. And he'd heard searing screams that turned out to be his own as he woke in a tangle of sodden duvet, Mum bending over him. *It's okay my love; it's okay Maxi. Mummy's here.*

She was here now, the driver supporting her as she uncurled herself from the back of the car. At a distance, shutters clicked and flash bulbs popped. She seemed oblivious to the mob of reporters, the big white TV trucks, the people calling her name. Thank God. Max stepped out of the taxi and went to stand with her, tucking his arm through hers and steering her away from the photographers and press. Behind them, the driver was now helping Eleanor with Ben's buggy. Above them the sky soared, cloudless, blue, perfect.

Mum had no idea where they were or what they were there for. She didn't know what Max knew. That Peter hadn't tasted the soil because he'd been strangled with his school tie before his body was buried in a scrubby section of Alleyn's nurseries, metres outside the 10-mile radius of the search. She didn't know how her little boy had somehow remained hidden in a pocket of rock, a chamber – "a sort of tomb" Richard Gould had called it – when the pond had been built all those years ago. A lifetime of waiting that need never have been. When Gould had told him this, Max's heart had twisted at the thought of how Peter had always hidden his things out of harm's way.

Ex-Detective Inspector Gould had commandeered a small, impersonal office from one of his successors. He was indeed an old man now, his thinning moustache peppered with grey; but his dark suit was immaculate and he was trying hard to straighten his stooping back. He wore glasses that glinted in the bright, overhead light and half-hid the eyes that Max remembered. He poured two glasses of water, opened the file and asked if Max would like to read about how his brother had died, or prefer to be told. Died. It was a soft sigh of a word that Max knew the old man had chosen with as much care as he'd picked out his respectfully sober suit that morning.

Max had asked the other man to tell him. Gould had flicked his eyes up to him then, with that same quick look of compassion that he'd used all those years ago in Mrs Maishman's classroom.

"Are you sure Max?"

"Yes – go ahead."

Max wanted the ex-policeman to tell him because he wasn't sure that he could trust himself to focus on the words. The facts of the case. The black lines of letters on the white sheets of paper lying on the table in front of them. When he was a boy he'd loved words; he'd collected them in his head. Cren-all-a-tions. O-blit-er-ate. Lurk. Qui-ver. But he'd grown to distrust the stories and adventures that they could create. All he'd wanted to deal in were hard, concrete facts. Now he couldn't even do that.

Gould's chest rose and fell as he took a deep breath and gathered himself to speak. "Your brother died at the hands of a 44-year-old plumber called Jason Brant. Brant is now an old-age pensioner serving life in the high security wing of Broadhurst prison. When he was questioned, he told us he'd driven his blue Ford Escort down the school drive, parked it in the staff car park and waited –"

"Driven it in?"

"Yes. I know, it seems unbelievable now, but it was a long time ago and security at schools wasn't what it is now."

Max nodded and tipped his eyes down to the peppery grey hairs sprinkling the back of Gould's hands. A knot – a fierce knot that had been tightening in his stomach ever since he'd heard that Peter had been found – eased just a little.

"He drove in and waited," Gould continued. "He knew what he was doing. He sat there quietly, virtually unnoticed, until all the children had been collected, on the off-chance that there might be some stragglers. When Peter walked through the door at the front of the school, he wound down his window and called him over. He told him he was a policeman and that Peter's teacher had asked him to talk to him, and Peter got into the car. It didn't take more than a couple of minutes – and then he drove off. He was clever: he used different cars and vans and different identities in various parts of the British Isles over a period of several years in the '70s and '80s. Peter was the third of his five victims. As well as being a plumber he was a psychopath who saved what he called his 'little golden angels' from the sins of this world."

Gould paused. Heels clicked along the corridor outside the door and Max heard a woman's laughter. Peter had waited and waited for him, and then he'd wandered outside into the hands of a monster called Jason Brant. He'd never gone up to the bus stop. Never looked for an invisible clue that wasn't there.

"Are you okay Max?"

"Yes – carry on – I want to know."

Gould cleared his throat. "He drove the car to a clearing in some hazel woods a mile from the school, covered his mouth with gaffer tape so that he couldn't shout out, and then sexually assaulted him and strangled him with his school tie. He placed his body in the boot in a large, commercial bin bag and then waited until dusk, which wouldn't have fallen for several hours as it was July. Then he drove to Alleyn's nurseries and buried him there."

He paused again, watching from behind his glasses, and Max knew what it must be costing him to tell him all this. He knew how precise and formal the ex-detective was trying to be, but behind his moustache, his deep voice was underpinned with emotion, and Max remembered the nod that he'd given Mum on their old 12" screen, the hand that he'd seen him reach out to cover hers when she'd started to falter.

"Max … Max …" He felt a hand on his arm and turned to see Eleanor's calm grey eyes watching him. "Are you okay?"

His mouth was too dry to speak. He saw that they were almost at the church now, where two figures were standing in the timber-framed porch, one upright, one stooped.

It was Eleanor who'd told him that Bill wanted to come; Max hadn't been sure. *But he'd like to Max, to pay his respects, and I'd like him to.* And he'd conceded.

The second man, Max knew, was Richard Gould. He too had wanted to pay his respects – "Without in any way intruding ... and only of course if you and your mother don't mind ... I'd like to ..." He'd made the clumsy request at the end of the sodden afternoon under the tarpaulin when Max was wrung out of emotion. Numb and emptied as he'd been, Max had been struck by how old and unsteady the other man seemed. As if, now that his difficult duty had been discharged, the weight of his years had borne down on him; and Max had thought once more of what it must have cost him to do all this, and why he'd done it when he was under no obligation to do so. He'd since learnt that Gould's wife had died and wondered if he had anyone – children perhaps – to support him in his old age. As Max drew nearer to the church the ex-detective turned away and disappeared into its shadowy interior.

Bill held out his hand. "Max."

"Bill." Max looked into the other man's inscrutable eyes and wondered if he'd be here if Eleanor wasn't wearing an engagement ring.

"Kate." Bill turned to Mum.

Mum looked from Bill to Max. "I know this man Maxi."

"Yes, yes of course you do Mum. This is Eleanor's uncle." Max realised, watching his mum's clouded eyes searching Bill's face, that they couldn't take the risk: she couldn't come into the church in case she understood.

"Eleanor –" He turned and saw immediately that Eleanor knew too.

She stepped forward. "Why don't we take Ben for a little walk Kate?"

"No!"

Eleanor jumped, startled by the sharpness of Max's voice.

"No," he repeated more gently. "I want you to come with me."

"Why don't *we* go Kate?" Bill leant forward.

"Would you mind Bill?" Max said.

"Of course not. It would be a pleasure. Come on Kate, we'll take Ben for a walk around the village green." He linked his arm through Mum's and carefully, almost tenderly, turned her round as Eleanor steered the buggy towards them. Max saw Ben's face begin to crumble as he realised that Eleanor wasn't coming with him.

"There we are my darling." Mum chucked Ben under his chin, distracting him. His legs kicked under their blanket. "Off we go."

"She'll still be here Max; she's here for him."

Max heard Eleanor's voice. "I know." He took a deep breath as the vicar, his face too young for the voice that Max had heard on the phone, appeared from inside the church and introduced himself. There was a shaving nick on his neck. A small red scratch above his dog collar. A tiny, trivial thing that, even as Max noticed it, knew he'd remember and associate forever with standing in the doorway of the church just before they went in – with being on the brink, the entrance, the beginning of the end. The vicar uttered a few phrases but Max didn't take them in. He took in the firmness of his handshake and his unflinching gaze; realised he was a professional doing his job. As they stood on the doorstep of the church Max had a sense of the other man relieving him of some of his burden and when the vicar turned away his cassock rustled after him – a strangely comforting sound.

Eleanor took Max's hand and he inhaled the smell of ancient polished wood and the damp, mossy past as they entered through the chancel door. A woman was sitting alone in a pew towards the back of the church, head bent so that he couldn't see the face. He knew who she was though. *Salt of the earth, that one.* As he turned to walk up the aisle he dropped his eyes to the smooth stone flags, but not before he'd seen the low shape at the head of the nave. When he reached the front pew he looked up and caught his breath. Felt Eleanor's hand tighten around his. It was the smallness of it. The softly spoken undertaker had warned him about it. "It brings it home," she'd said, "when you see the coffin." Max exhaled slowly. As he stood back to let Eleanor into her seat, he thought of Mum, pushing Ben's buggy, and being guided around the snowy village green by Sir William Stockley.

On top of the pale, oak lid was a posy of winter flowers that Eleanor had helped him to choose. Winter jasmine and hyacinths. And Max knew, even though he couldn't see it from here, that beside the posy a simple brass plaque read,

Peter John Rivers

1975-1980

Somewhere behind them, ex-DI Gould coughed quietly. The bells stopped and the cool church air wrapped itself around Max. He didn't hear the vicar's words, or his prayers, or his short address. He heard the rhythm of them. The calming rhetoric of the age-old phrases. Their soothing rise and fall. And all the time he kept his eyes on the flowers, trembling on top of his brother's coffin, as he conjured up the very last breaths of him.

"Where's it to be today?" It's warm, and Max can feel the sun on his head and knees even though it's so early. Peter's standing by the sandpit, hands on his hips. His navy blue shorts are already covered in sand – Mum's going to kill him. Max can see her dark shape, moving by the window in the kitchen, clearing up the breakfast things. He's sitting on the grass, which he can feel, through his shorts, is wet with dew.

"Let's make a boat and sail away in it, *please*." As Max looks up, the white-washed sky behind Peter's head is a seascape, the light tails and trails of the clouds, the white-tipped foam of the ocean.

"No, no. I've got a much better idea. You'll love this Peter. We're going to make an aeroplane."

"An aeroplane! How can we do that? It'll never fly." To Peter, Max knows, sand and boats go together like a bucket and spade, but a plane made of sand can never leave the pit, never take off. How does he know this? Because he feels exactly the same. But he's older than Peter and it's his choice.

"Of course it will, silly. I'm going to be the pilot. I'll have a joystick."

Max knows his brother won't have a clue what that is. Which is the main reason he says it. But will he ask what it is? He doesn't.

"You, Peter, are my co-pilot." Max says.

"What's a co-pilot?" When he screws up his face, the scab on his nose creases in two.

"He's e-ssen-tial." Max says the word slowly, splitting it up, making it last in his mouth like one of his favourite toffees.

"Really?" Peter's eyes are wide blue circles of wonder and Max know he's hooked.

They dig out the sand, scooping off the light, dry top layer and digging with their hands into the rich, deep moistness underneath. Max pushes his fingers in up to his knuckles and enjoys the sensation of the grains grinding under his nails, filling them up. When they've made the two seats, one behind the other, Max tells his brother that they need to make some wings and he watches as Peter runs over to the sycamore hedge to look for twigs and stones. After a few minutes Max looks around to see what Peter's doing. He's shading his eyes from the sun and scanning the garden, his gaze running over the vegetable patch, where the green, frondy tops of Mum's carrots stir every now and then in the breeze, past the dirty greenhouse and up towards the grey, pebble-dash house, which looks bright and shimmery in the sun.

He sees him walk up to the greenhouse and disappear around the side and he knows that Peter's lost in his imagination. That's what happens to him. He drifts off. Mum's warned Max about it. *You need to keep a tight eye on him Maxi.* And what about their plane? Its wings? He's so annoying. Mum'll be calling them in soon – it'll be time to go. After a few seconds Peter reappears with his hands held out in front of him, looking a bit like Jesus in his 'Illustrated Lord's Prayer'. As he comes closer, Max sees that his hands are full of large white objects – the pebbles and shells! He's remembered the pebbles and shells we found on the beach last year. He starts laying them out and, after a couple of minutes, Max bends to help him. It's a brilliant idea. Soon their plane has two wonderful white wings which catch the sunlight and look for all the world as though they're flying through the sky.

As Max stands up, the pall-bearers walk past him to the front of the church, lift Peter's coffin onto their shoulders and adjust it slightly to make it secure; the care, the respect in the movements of those four tall strangers takes his breath away. A beam of sun slants in through the stained-glass window and sends a kaleidoscope of shifting colours twirling over the flowers. And Max can hear Peter laughing. *Look at that Maxi!*

The men's pinstripe trousers get darker and damper as they pick their way gingerly up the hill, and Max can feel his own feet wet in his black leather shoes. The posy of flowers dances high above their heads, frothing against the cobalt sky. He turns and looks back to the church and the carpet of snow laid out before it on the village green. The TV lorries are still there and the gaggle of press, but there's no sign of Bill and Mum and Ben; they're probably waiting in the warmth of the taxi, or the Royal Oak pub. Max hasn't even spoken to Norah; she'd disappeared by the time they emerged from the church. Richard Gould had shaken his hand, pulled his coat closer around him and walked away. A public servant who'd shown Max a glimpse of the person he kept hidden inside his professional persona; a detail merchant just like him, whose meticulous preservation of the exhibits in the case of the boy who never came home had led them all here today.

And now the young vicar's preparing himself, his black cassock stark against the whiteness behind him, his hands pale against the dark, worn leather of the bible. The pall-bearers let out the ropes and begin to lower the coffin into the ground. The boy into his bed. The rich brown soil of the four cliffs under the snow are like slices of Christmas cake covered in thick, frosted icing. It'll be warm down there, under that blanket. Max remembers all the years that Peter's flat, red-and-white duvet waited for him in their room and his heart twists to breaking at the thought that his brother's never coming back. The vicar's voice saves him; his calming, religious phrases slide over him like silk. And Max watches as he takes a handful of earth from inside his cassock and lets it slip through his fingers. "You gave him life … receive him in your peace …" There's a soft rattle, no more than a gentle shower of rain, as the earth hits the oak.

Beside him he's aware of Eleanor bending and an arc of glittering ice cascading silently into the grave. Max likes the idea of using the snow; he knows that Peter will too. He's just about to bend down when he sees a figure in the distance. It's emerging from behind the Christmas card church. It's Mum. He can't make out her face but he knows it's her.

She's pushing Ben's buggy along the snaking path towards them. She's coming closer. Until he can make out the black and green checked buggy cover, Ben's pale mittened hand on it. His heart races. Why isn't Bill stopping her? He's about to shout out but then, just in time, there's a touch on his arm. It's Eleanor. Of course.

"I'll go." Her voice is low and firm, and he watches as she heads off, picking her way through the dazzling snow with careful high-kneed steps to stop Mum in her tracks.

He scoops up a handful of snow. He squeezes it until it compacts and his palms begin to burn. He mouths his brother's name soundlessly, rolling the two sweet syllables over his lips and releasing them into the shivering air. He watches as a shower of icy diamonds falls through his fingers and dissolves into shimmering, luminous pools on the pale oak lid. He's transfixed, unable to summon up the courage to walk away, to acknowledge that he's gone, when a breath of wind springs from nowhere and ripples the surface of the snow, blowing it into the grave and covering the coffin with a thin white sheet. Max realises that Mum's here, after all. She's with her boy now, tucking him in, making him warm before he falls to sleep. He hears her voice whispering Peter's name, and then the rustle of her skirt as she leaves his bed.